PENGUIN MODERN CLASSICS
Restless Was the Night and Other Stories

Buddhadeva Bose (1908–74) is widely considered to be the successor to Rabindranath Tagore for the versatility and breadth of his literary work. A multifaceted writer and one of the leading lights of modern Bengali literature, Bose combines lyricism with a style of writing uniquely his own to create an unmatched legacy.

Arunava Sinha translates classic, modern and contemporary Bengali fiction and non-fiction from Bangladesh and India into English. He also translates fiction from English into Bengali. Over ninety-five of his translations have been published so far in India, the UK and the USA. He teaches creative writing at Ashoka University, where he is also the co-director of the Ashoka Centre for Translation, and is the books editor at Scroll.in.

BUDDHADEVA BOSE

Restless Was the Night and Other Stories

Translated from the Bengali
by Arunava Sinha

PENGUIN BOOKS

An imprint of Penguin Random House

PENGUIN BOOKS

Penguin Books is an imprint of the Penguin Random House group of companies
whose addresses can be found at global.penguinrandomhouse.com

Published by Penguin Random House India Pvt. Ltd
4th Floor, Capital Tower 1, MG Road,
Gurugram 122 002, Haryana, India

Penguin
Random House
India

First published as *The Love Letter and Other Stories* by Rupa Publications,
New Delhi 2013
This edition published in Penguin Books by Penguin Random House India 2025

10 9 8 7 6 5 4 3 2 1

ISBN 9780143469872

Typeset in Sabon by Manipal Technologies Limited, Manipal
Printed at Gopsons Papers Pvt. Ltd., Noida

www.penguin.co.in

100%
Paper from well-
managed forests
FSC
www.fsc.org   FSC® C191020

Contents

Contents

The Love Letter

~ 1 ~

Walking though the drizzle in a raincoat, he kept stopping every now and then—to fill his lungs with oxygen, to swallow a few mouthfuls of light air. It was lovely—this drizzle, this fresh air which seemed newly awakened, this quiet narrow serpentine lane, which—although a little uneven, paved with stones, a little too clean and desolate—still, it vaguely reminded him of Beltala Road. So . . . I'm going back? Yes, of course; my job, my family, my *Speech* magazine, my linguistics society—all of them are in Calcutta. How will Calcutta survive unless I return? But there are still three days to go.

He chanced upon a street corner, on the right a mansion with Doric columns, in front of it Diana surrounded by her nymphs, a wide avenue bursting with the sound of scooters. This is Rome, I have arrived in Rome, the infinite city of memories and loveliness—I arrived this instant, for the first time . . . and now? The lane after the statue of Diana—wasn't that what the girl at the hotel said? Looks like that street there . . . yes! Another narrow, paved lane, small shops on either side—furniture, silverware, clothes, books—behind the glass the latest books on four languages—I'm tempted to enter, but not now: first, the letter. The rain had almost let up, the sunlight became visible on the last few drops, the enormous square was lit up—crowds of people, taxis coming to a halt, two horse-drawn phaetons awaited the most sophisticated among the tourists—and a flight of steps began where the square ended; steep, wide, venerable, like a concentrated, silent welcome. So this was the Piazza di Spagnia. He didn't stop for a look, he walked on quickly, a wall caught his eye—a deferential notice on a plaque: Keats-Shelley House. That second-floor room—that window, through which a foreign young man would gaze occasionally, an unknown, dying poet, seeing nothing, understanding nothing. I will be in that room in a few minutes, from the same window I will look out on the Hispanic steps—the same I who had till the age of forty-two considered Delhi my western frontier. Excuse me for a few moments, Shelley-Keats: first, the letter.

After a single glance, he tore his eyes away from the fountain before him; American Express was just two buildings away.

It was summer, there was a crowd of American tourists, long queues snaked up to every counter. He was behind nine or ten people. He was looking at the letters arranged in their pigeonholes—envelopes of different colours, red blue yellow green airmail flags, stamps glittering as though they had been crowned—inside them, scores of languages, so much hope, happiness, comfort. Is it that light grey envelope there . . . no, that's been given to someone else. Even after scouring the racks with his eyes, he didn't seem to spot the familiar grey envelope. Was it just an aerogramme then, or perhaps a picture postcard with a couple of paragraphs? Or was it actually possible that not one of those numerous envelopes had his name on it?

Suddenly, he felt warm; taking off his raincoat he folded it over his arm.

Who was this distant friend for whose letter he was so distraught? Sadly, the answer was rather pedestrian. A woman, whom he had met—unexpectedly, unbearably—in a Midwest town in America, because of whom his days had become burdened for several weeks now and his nights tumultuous, whose absence accompanied him everywhere in Europe, from one city to another, from one country to another, continuously. And continuously the letters from this woman, in every country, in every city, while travelling on the train, while eating at the restaurant, on a bench by the river, on the steps before the museum; in the spaces between all he had seen on his travels, all the sights, all the paintings, all the palaces, all the old manuscripts, the letters ebbed and flowed like waves, a secret longing in his middle-aged veins, exciting and pleasurable like the beginning of an illness. Of course he had written back too—staying up nights in his hotel room after the exertions of the day, sometimes the moment he arrived at a new town, sometimes he had constructed sentences in his head while travelling, which he no longer remembered when it was time to write the letter. There were no significant developments to report, no questions that had to be answered, nothing new that needed to be said, but still—he had to write. He had to write in a language that was foreign to both of them; she could at least use her mother tongue German from time to time, but although he could read five European languages he could write only in one, English, which he had once prided himself on knowing very well. But when he tried to write to a special person during a particular state of mind, he discovered that what he had thought of as English was nothing but a tight, ill-fitting dress, which he could use to accommodate his research on linguistics, but in which it was impossible to express what was in his heart. It was a formidable obstacle—but still he had to write. Such a turmoil in his heart—he could not find the words to match it, he condemned his own fate because she did not understand Bengali, and then the very next moment he bowed in gratitude to his destiny, because his life—his humdrum Bengali life on which the shadow of old age had fallen already—had experienced something so astonishing.

Her last letter would reach him here in Rome. Last, for he was going directly to Calcutta from Rome, and to him Calcutta was synonymous with a well-defined, disciplined, clearly articulated circle of life, which included many other people, and which had no room for anything purely personal. He would board the eastbound plane three days from now, and the woman of his desire on the other side of the ocean, living on an unknown longitude on a distant western continent, who had awakened him, who had aroused his sadness, would be lost at once. What had been alive in two chaotic hearts would be converted into a silent point on a lifeless atlas. That was why today's letter was crucial.

From the other side of the counter came a voice: 'Yes, sir?'

'Ray, Birupaksha,' he said, offering his passport; the handsome young clerk, as efficient as a machine, met his expectations at once. A strange sensation spread over him as soon as he saw the envelope, as though all distance had been banished for an instant, as though there was no such thing as separation in life. And to think I had imagined there would be no letter— how sceptical I am even though I'm so lucky!

Birupaksha walked away, leaning against the wall in a quiet corner. He slit the envelope open carefully with his nails. A large sheet of ivory paper, stiff and crackling—but a little too white, unbelievably colourless. Nothing written on it, not a single ink-mark or pen-stroke—from top to bottom, from left to right, on both sides . . . white, silent, virginal. But what did the words top and bottom, left and right mean anyway since nothing was written; he didn't even know whether he was holding the letter the right way up. Yet the handwriting on the envelope was flawless, the postal mark on the stamp featuring Abraham Lincoln was immaculate—and the envelope, light grey, with the watermark of aeroplanes all over it, made in France, was indubitably from Esha too . . . Then?

Out on the road, Birupaksha wiped his forehead with his handkerchief, slinging his suddenly heavy raincoat over his shoulder he stopped on the pavement. There's a newspaper kiosk—I haven't kept in touch with the world for a long time, let's see how things are. Carefully crossing the road made dangerous by speeding cars, he bought a *New York Herald Tribune* published in Paris, a *Le Monde*, a *Frankfurter Zeitung*, and, at the last moment, a slim guide to tourist attractions in Rome— immediately after buying them he regretted burdening himself with these papers; to tell the truth, am I really curious about the world right now? Crossing the road again and passing the Hispanic steps, he paused suddenly before a signboard: Babbington Tea House. No sooner did he read the name in this unexpected display of the English language than his Bengali throat felt parched for the taste of tea—although many things on the continent were magnificent, no one understood tea there; now he might be able to quench his thirst in real tannin juice in this tea shop with an English name. He liked the place the moment he entered—its tranquil settings were quiet and dark, with just two customers sitting silently and dimly in two corners— that table by the window, tasting the news of the world with tea for a restful half hour—the possibility seemed delightful. He leaned back on the padded bench, ran his eyes over the headlines in each of the newspapers in turn, but it appeared that nothing was happening in the world, nothing new, at any rate—a minister's resignation, trouble at an election, countries at odds with one another, conflicts, pretended alliances—for ages, ages, he had been seeing these same things in the papers, the same news under different names and different dates. Birupaksha sighed, pushing aside the newspapers in exhaustion. A short Italian girl with pink cheeks brought his tea in a silver pot, Birupaksha's heart quickened a little at the sight of her milk-white, ironed uniform.

Was that what it really was? A virginal white? I didn't make a mistake, did I? Making sure no one was watching, he surreptitiously pulled the grey envelope out of his pocket—this time too, an unmarked sheet of paper emerged. Holding it up to his nose briefly, he thought he sensed a faint fragrance—familiar—like the perfume Esha used. What, what could it be? . . . What could it be? Had she written a letter on both sides of a different sheet of paper and then absent-mindedly inserted a blank sheet in the envelope? No, it wasn't possible, there wasn't even a chance in a million of such a mistake—especially for someone like Esha, whom I have never seen losing her composure even under the strongest emotional pressure. But what if that one-in-a-million chance has come true in my case? Who can say with certainty that what doesn't usually happen will never actually happen? But if the mistake did occur, it must have been caught at once, and the real letter also posted? . . . But . . . then . . . why didn't the other one reach?

Birupaksha drank half a cup of tea out of good manners, left a fat tip for the short, pink-cheeked waitress, abandoned the newspapers, and returned to American Express in two minutes.

'Can you please check whether there's another letter for me?'

Checking the pigeonhole patiently, the clerk said, 'Sorry, sir.'

Glancing at his yellow tie, Birupaksha swallowed.

'Will there be another delivery in the evening?'

'The evening delivery doesn't contain overseas letters. Besides, we're only open till three. You can check again tomorrow morning.'

For the first time, Birupaksha realised that, like other things in life, letters also depended on chance. How easily we assume that any letter that's been written is bound to be posted, and that if it has been posted it is certain to reach its destination at the right time. It was true that the majority of letters did arrive at their destination, but don't we hear of letters being lost at times? And this postal network spanning the entire world—international, intercontinental, interoceanic—this highly complicated and superbly controlled system, the finest example of human cooperation, which ensured that a letter extracted from a postbox in an Alaskan village was inevitably delivered five days later to a dilapidated building in a Bangkok lane with its address obliterated—was this too not a wonder, terming which a miracle would not be an exaggeration? So many yawning traps stood in its way—a clerk's exhaustion, a postman's inattention; floods, storms, fire, transport mishaps. Come to think of it, receiving a letter was just as unlikely as living healthily for many years; any letter could be lost, we could die or fall hopelessly ill at any time—and yet we have not learnt to be grateful for being able to live with our organs intact, or for having received all our letters all this time.

But perhaps I'm overdoing it; a wider world exists beyond the circle I am going round and round over an expected letter—not the bubble-like world of the newspapers, but a different, magical world, in which even ruins shine forth as examples of beauty, and the perturbation of existence has a dappled covering which we mistake for permanence. This is Rome, I am in Rome, for the first time, I'll be here only for two days, and yet I've seen none of the sights although it's 10.30 a.m. already.

Birupaksha made up his mind and took a taxi; saw many sights, spent a great deal of money, drank a glass and a half of Chianti with dinner so that he could sleep well—and returned to the hotel at nearly 11 p.m., suitably tired, a little unsteady from the wine that he was unused to drinking. He was sleepy on his way upstairs in the lift, but the moment he unlocked his door and entered, switching on the light to see a neatly made bed, maroon curtains on the window, a bottle of mineral water on the table near the head of the bed—all the routine arrangements for comfort which were available for a price in any country— he was overcome by the kind of fatigue that can almost be called hopelessness, under whose effect he could suddenly fall ill one night while on his travels, switching on the light at his head now and then, tired of trying to sleep, and then switching it off immediately afterwards and turning on his side, and, half-asleep, feeling in the dim darkness that he was in his usual bed in his own home, that someone would respond if he were to call, someone dear to him would come running if he were to scream, when his imagination persuaded him that his country was the best, that the most comfortable bed was the one the maid Haridasi made for him every night, and that the most beautiful sight was the three-storied house with the plaster flaking off the walls he set his eyes on first thing every morning—and remember the very next instant that he was now far away in another country, even if he tossed and turned all night in his sleep no one would come to him. Just like the child whose heart ached (Birupaksha was reminded of the term *pawran porey*, which he had learnt as a young boy in east Bengal) if his mother went away for even a single day, Birupaksha was overcome by unhappiness—he had never felt this way anywhere else—as though he wanted to go back, to do nothing but go back to his own house where his family was, the only place that offered him happiness, offered him security. But the question was: Which was his own country, where was his home, and who was his family?

Birupaksha prepared for bed mechanically; taking off his watch, he piled everything in his pocket on the table, wrapping his dressing gown around his pajamas, he sat down in the chair. He tried to keep alive in his mind all that he had seen that day . . . an unwavering radiance, another free spirit with the same bent of mind, beyond our momentary pains and pleasures—ultimately, was this not what brought comfort to humans—such as his linguistics, or like Michelangelo, Rafael or Donatello, who obliterated the memories of the heinous crimes of the Renaissance, the poison, the dagger, the agony of thousands of people burnt alive . . . But I am only reeling off names, quoting from books, I have not seen anything. My mind is estranged from my eyes, my soul is battling with my body, I am not where I am. Say something, Esha, say something to me—let me see Rome. This is my first time here, I may never come back.

Seemingly disobeying his will, his hand reached out amidst the pile of light, glittering and valueless Italian coins, the wallet swollen with Italian currency notes, the address book, the passport, and the useless scraps of paper. Again that white sheet of paper, turned bluish by the light from the table lamp with the green shade. As though they were there, words, hidden in it, like pomegranate seeds beneath the hard shell—or like the emptiness of the mirror in an empty room, which can be filled any moment if a door were to be opened, if a curtain were to be drawn. Birupaksha held the sheet of paper up to the light, it appeared yellowish white, like the yolk within the eggshell. Stretching it out flat on the table, he examined it more carefully, for better illumination he bent the neck of the lamp much closer to the paper. After a few moments he thought a few letters were dimly visible here and there. Birupaksha rubbed his eyes, concentrating all the power in his eyes, trained by years of reading ancient manuscripts, on those spots; a few more letters became visible.

Suddenly he remembered reading about invisible ink in a detective story a long time ago, the letters appeared as soon as the paper was warmed. Even earlier, when he was in school, someone had said that the same effect could be achieved by writing with a nib dipped in lemon juice, he had tested this and found it correct . . . Then . . . that's what it was! Very carefully, he held the paper with both his hands just below the bulb; before his eyes, just like corn popping, or like the blooming of buds into flowers under the touch of sunlight at dawn, the black letters began to appear against the white of the paper—one side was filled entirely. Now for the other side— that didn't take long. And now, the message, the words, the assurance, the drops exuded by the heart of the woman who lived far away, a glass filled to the brim . . . before him, awaiting the touch of his lips. Birupaksha was not the least bit surprised, he felt no excitement—on the contrary, he considered it natural and appropriate, blamed himself for not having caught on straightaway to this small, innocent trick of Esha's. But soon thick creases appeared on his forehead, his breath quickened, he had momentary doubts about his own equilibrium.

The letter was written in a language he did not know.

It was a long letter, filled with letters on both sides, nothing scratched out, no white spaces except between the lines, but even he—an expert in Indo-European languages, someone who worked all the time with several Indian and European languages—could not lift the veil off a single word on the sheet of paper spread out before him. After scanning it for some time, he was convinced that the letter was in code, written in the form of a puzzle, for in it he could see many different scripts—Greek letters between the Roman ones, Cyrillic, Hebrew, Gothic, Devnagari, he suspected some of them of being in Brahmi, in fact there were even Chinese characters, ancient Egyptian hieroglyphs, Bengali letters too, and some symbols that eluded Birupaksha's guesswork. Only at the bottom right of the reverse side, close to the margin, was the name 'Esha' written in large letters (Birupaksha had made her practise this), and only this made it possible to identify where the letter started and where it ended, and only this one word could be read.

Birupaksha laughed in a low, soft voice. She's testing me to find out how good a linguist I am. She used to laugh at me gently when out of sheer bad habit I tried to explain the etymology of words to her, when I tried to teach her Bengali and Sanskrit. 'Even after twelve years in America I haven't mastered English,' she would say, 'and other languages on top of that!

Spare me!' Her logic was that learning more than one language meant learning none of them, and even after learning several, many more would still be left. I would say, whatever is learnt is valuable. Maybe, but you have to accept that man's ignorance is infinite anyway! The argument would end in amused laughter—but now, she seemed to have written this letter to me just to prove her point, she seemed to be challenging me with bolts of lightning from her lips and eyes—well? Read this if you can! . . . Give me a little time, a little time—look, I've understood your game now.

But could she—whom I had named Esha, who had learnt a few Hebrew and Yiddish words from her grandmother as a child, and a little Russian from the time she had spent with her former husband, but who, to tell the truth, didn't know any other language besides German or Russian—possibly compose such a global puzzle? But then how can I say she could not, for many ordinary dictionaries do include the Hebrew, Cyrillic and Greek alphabets, she could have picked up a few Devnagari and Bengali letters from books that I had left behind, and what I thought of as Chinese, Egyptian or Brahmi scripts might well be her own improvisations—maybe they had only been used to embellish the manuscript, the way many people doodle in the margin while thinking of the next sentence . . . But what if it turns out that the entire letter is meaningless, merely an artistically assembled chest with nothing inside? Just look—the handwriting appears synthetic too, the Roman letters are like printed text, interspersed

with capitals—not quite recognisable although similar
to Esha's script. It seems this letter's taken a long time,
a great deal of patience, to be written or drawn—but
how did she get so much time, how did she manage to
be so patient when she knew how much I yearn to hear
her voice?

Why do you mock me, Esha?

Mock? Did she then not really give all of herself
to me, did she hold something back? Is she then trying
to take herself back at this final hour, before the last
farewell, to reject her relationship with me—she, who's
the torrent in my heart? . . . No, it isn't possible, it just
isn't possible. I must believe. There's her signature—
clear, my most favourite letters in the language most
familiar to me—am I so weak as to ask for more proof?
She's not lying, she's not mocking me, I will decipher
the meaning—I have to.

An hour passed, but still the lines on Birupaksha's
brow didn't smoothen out, his eyes began to ache
from glaring constantly at the letter. Despair crowded
around him again, his body was ready to collapse with
fatigue, but there was no sleep, it was impossible to
sleep in this state of mind. Tell me, Esha, explain what
this means—if it's rejection, tell me that too. In two
days the distance between us will become immense—
tell me your final word before that—tell me, is this
agonising vigil of mine real? Is it not real?

The telephone on the table caught his eye. His
watch showed one-thirty. Eight-thirty in the evening
in the Midwest in USA—she was probably at home

now, after dinner, the dishes done, she was flipping through *Life* magazine by herself, or listening to the news on television—what else did Americans who lived in the suburbs have to do in the evening? After a few moments, Birupaksha placed a long-distance phone call.

Successive female voices wafted over the ether— Rome, New York, Chicago—a wave travelling at the speed of thought—a few moments of silence, and then, he heard clearly, 'Hello.'

For an instant, Birupaksha could not breathe. Esha's voice—exactly like hers, a little deep, as though she's standing before me, as though I'll see her face in a moment. It took a little time for the echo of the impersonal 'Hello' to die in his ears.

Again from the other end, 'Hello.'

'It's Birupaksha, from Rome.'

'Oh, it's you! How strange—I was thinking of you. How are you?'

'Did you write to me . . . in Rome?'

'Yes, of course I did. Didn't you get it?'

'I did—but I cannot understand whether it's a letter.'

'Cannot understand?' A gust of laughter.

'I cannot understand a word, Esha. What have you done?'

'I am writing a letter to you, all the time.'

'All the time?'

'All the time. In my head. Not everything can be written down, you know.'

'But this letter—listen—what did you write in it? Which language is it in? Tell me, Esha, answer me— what did you write? Which language?'

'You're asking me what I wrote? In which language? You, of all people.' That drizzle of laughter again.

'Esha—I beg of you—tell me what you wrote.'

'I wrote . . .' a strange sound followed, as though it wasn't Esha's voice any more, but impotent, half-spoken gobbledygook from the throat of someone being strangled.

Birupaksha heard himself shout, 'Tell me! Tell me! What did you write?'

'I wrote . . .' Again those peculiar, distorted sounds. As though the sentence was being bent and mangled the moment it was begun, the shriek of a broken record on an old-fashioned wind-up gramophone, or a monkey trying to imitate a human voice. Every time Birupaksha called out, 'Esha! Esha! Can you hear me?' he heard the same sounds.

Then the line was disconnected. After a few moments Birupaksha placed another call to the same number, after several attempts the operator told him there was a storm on the Atlantic, she wouldn't be able to get through till the next morning.

Birupaksha realised he was trembling, sweat was pouring down his face. Drawing the curtains, he opened a window pane, after several gulps of mineral water he sat down with the letter again.

What had they talked about on the telephone? Nothing at all, all he had found out was that Esha did indeed write him a letter. But . . . even that was a lot. Yes, she did write, but what proof did he have that this was the letter? 'Cannot understand? . . . You're asking me what I wrote? You, of all people!' Faint laughter, affectionate, but blended with a touch of amusement, as though she was surprised that I cannot understand, as though she has reposed enormous faith in me, but I am proving myself unworthy of her. If only I had been able to talk a little longer, if only that mechanical failure hadn't swamped us suddenly, if only nature's whim had not cut us off! But she had said, 'I am writing a letter to you all the time—in my head. Not everything can be written down, you know.' What could be clearer? Not everything can be written down, since there's no end of things to say. And besides (this might be the real reason), how much can language achieve? A tight, ill-fitting outfit—does that describe only a foreign language, as English is for me or Russian, for Esha? Isn't the concept of language itself constrained, a sort of guesswork—even if it's what we refer to as our mother tongue? The only difference is that we are more at ease in some languages than in others. Consider the nations that speak English, or Spanish, or Bengali or Hindi or Tamil—how many of their people can really speak it in a way that you can talk about? Instead, language is being eroded by their usage, it is their thousands of newspapers that are becoming filthier by the day, the adjectives are crumbling, the proverbs and humour and apt phrases are being converted to clichés. Do none of those acclaimed pieces that are acknowledged as the best examples of a language reveal the occasional stitch of a blunt needle, a strand of loose thread, or passages held together by a pin—which we do not notice because of the gems that sparkle in between? What is perfect and dazzling and complete in itself in the mind shrinks—or swells, bursting and losing its intensity—to become a compromise when it is put into the mould of language—no longer absolute, but relative to place, time and situation. Yes, relative, but language changes continuously over time—even the flesh-and-blood Shakespeare can no longer be read without notes now; eighteenth-century Bengali prose is incomprehensible to the everyday reader. Consider two contemporary individuals from Chittagong and Bankura—both places situated in what was once the single state of Bengal, both the individuals speaking 'Bengali'—but bridging the linguistic gap between them is almost impossible. Texts change so much in translation—they have to, for not all languages are equally endowed, every language has its subtleties, compound words, pulses and rhythms, light and darkness, which are unique to it, beyond the reach of any other language. And what we refer to as original writing, that is translation too—from thought to language, from imagination to embodiment; this translation is the most difficult and arduous—and perhaps the least successful. How wonderful it would have been if we could have woven several languages on the same loom, if there were a retort flask in which we could have distilled the different qualities of different languages! Perhaps in this might grow, not this language or that, but just language, the long awaited language in which everything can be said. And perhaps that is what Esha is trying to do—on a small scale, on her own initiative, she wants to create just for me a special, secret, assimilated, symbolic language that no one else may understand, but that I will easily be able to get to the bottom of—at least, that's what she assumes—since I am a linguist, and since I love her. Then . . . what I had thought at first is right, after all.

But how is that possible? Esha isn't a book-eating creature like me (thank goodness!)—how would such a plan occur to her? The doubt rose in Birupaksha's mind for the second time, but this time he dismissed it deliberately, the proposition that it was impossible for Esha to create such a script no longer seemed worthy of consideration. He viewed the whole thing from a different perspective now; he asked himself: How much do you know about Esha anyway? No, do not protest; you have to admit that you were busy with her in another way—choked by the constraints of the body and of time, the days and nights growing more passionate under the threat of your imminent parting, you had neither the time nor the inclination to look for anything beyond this. You tried to hold her in arms too eager, far too impatiently, that is why she slipped through them; when you think of Esha you recall her laughing eyes, the scent of her hair, the trembling you felt at her touch—nothing else, just these. You have to admit that you could not accommodate anything larger in this love of yours, you only nibbled at the corners with your small appetite.

But now this error would be corrected. This letter was the means.

Birupaksha trained his eyes again on the coded sheet of paper; he did not realise when his head fell back against, when his thoughts dimmed and disappeared in the darkness. He woke up with a start to realise that he was sleeping in his chair, his neck ached, and the glow from the table lamp had paled in the glow of the sunlight reddened by the maroon curtain.

~ 2 ~

He didn't receive a letter at American Express that day, but then he hadn't expected to. He spent the day wandering about the streets—dishevelled, aimless, desultory. Numerous lanes, several piazzas, many statues and palaces and churches and fountains and gardens; but all his other curiosity was dead, he had eyes for nothing else. The thought that he was in Rome did not disturb him any more; he didn't even remember that on the plane he had decided that he simply had to see Bernini's sculpture Fountain of the Four Rivers at Piazza Navona (because one of the rivers was the Ganga); indeed, he didn't even feel the urge to visit the graves or the memorials of the two poets from his childhood whose lines had still not been squashed under the weight of his linguistics studies. A different task, one specific task, seemed to have captured all his attention, he could have no respite until it was complete.

It was August, as the day progressed the sun grew stronger, at one-thirty in the afternoon he took refuge in a cafe. First a glass of Campari with plenty of ice, moistening his parched throat, he spread the puzzle out again—for the first time that day. Something unexpected happened. As soon as he glanced at the paper three words leapt out of it to lodge themselves in his brain: 'fern' ('distant' in German) in Gothic letters, in the next line the Greek 'oyaks' ('home'), and, a few words later, the word 'alo' (Bengali for 'light')—surely it was Bengali?—in Cyrillic script . . . so simple? He almost laughed aloud, but because of his familiarity with the rigorous techniques of research, he controlled himself at once, exercising caution . . . Where were the verbs hidden? Which of the words were prepositions and conjunctions? What kind of grammar linked the words? Nothing could be conjectured, an entire sentence had not revealed itself yet . . . Still, a start had been made, three holes discovered in the wall, like the false dawn before sunrise, the sky would soon be filled with light. That one of the three identified words was 'light' also seemed a good omen; 'distant', 'house', 'light'—perhaps she had written, 'A light shines for me in that distant house'—in other words, 'Your absence is making me unhappy' . . . But it could also be 'I want to return home from that distant light'. In which case the meaning would change entirely. These three words could be part of hundreds of different sentences— which of them was it? And besides, what was the certainty that they were part of the same sentence? The punctuation is unclear, and I'm not used to reading handwritten Greek or Gothic or Cyrillic, could I be getting confused, the way Bengali children confuse compound letters? If only I could get some help, if only a multilingual dictionary were at hand, an expert or two . . . is there anyone in Rome? He remembered Enrico Carducci, Italy's finest linguist, but the field of his research is Mongolian, my problem doesn't exactly belong to his area . . . Should I go to Geneva, home of Charles Dubois, whose huge accomplishment is the compilation of a ten-volume comparative dictionary of the ancient Indo-European languages? Birupaksha toyed with the idea—I met Dubois just a few months ago at the international conference in New York, he had expressed his approval for my short monograph on 'The Evolution of Nasal Words in North Indian Languages'—I don't think he will turn me down. But . . . what shall I tell him? This letter . . . so personal, intimate—how can I show it to anyone? But . . . I could pretend amusement and say, 'One of my American students has sent me a riddle—can you tell me whether it makes any sense, or whether it's a hoax?' . . . And besides, to a scholar it's all a question of knowledge, and knowledge is never personal; an authority like Charles Dubois or Joachim Tsin from Tubingen will analyse this letter with the same detachment with which a surgeon uses his scalpel on an unconscious and naked beautiful woman. Moreover, their probing skill will only reveal the literal meaning, the implied message will remain a virgin just for me. The more he pondered, the more Birupaksha found himself drawn to this idea; he felt that before he returned home he had to somehow shed this burden of disquiet that had taken over his mind. There was no difficulty, his holidays had not run out, the return ticket was valid for three weeks more, he had some money too. Nothing would go wrong if he were to delay his return . . .

He rose with his ravioli half-eaten, took a taxi to the airline office, cancelling the next day's ticket, and sending a telegram to Calcutta, he took the train to Geneva in the evening.

But Charles Dubois was in hospital, ill. At Tubingen he was told that Joachim Tsin was in Portugal for his summer vacation. From Tubingen to Hamburg, where everyone was surprised when he enquired about Professor Helmut Schnell, for the octogenarian scholar had been buried a year earlier. He went to Paris, but Henri Pere from the Sorbonne was in Quebec, and not due to return before October. For a moment, Birupaksha gave up in disappointment, he felt as though ill luck was dogging his footsteps, perhaps he would have to spend the rest of his life burdened by this turmoil.

His last night in Europe passed in a cheap hotel on the Left Bank in Paris. Before going to bed he counted his remaining foreign exchange—he had been travelling third class on trains all these days, had not taken a taxi in any circumstances, eaten frugally, travelled through the night wherever possible to save on hotel bills—but what he had still managed to spend was by no means insignificant in Indian terms. He was a good husband, a good father, dutiful, he was taking back for his family whatever money he had saved from his income as a teacher in the United States—he did not consider the money his own; which was why he felt a stab of remorse at this whimsical and speculative expense on the last leg of his journey. And it had come to nothing. Perhaps I should forget this letter, or conundrum, or joke, or whatever it is, it's not as though I have nothing else to do and can devote all my time to such a trifle.

He had almost fallen asleep when a new thought suddenly set his mind ticking. That he had not found anyone to help him despite so much effort might also be intended, planned; she does not want me to seek anyone's help; her demand of me is that I should pass this test alone and unaided. As soon as the thought occurred to him a wave of pleasure washed over his heart, sleep made his eyes heavier, he felt he had discovered the vital clue in this complex game. Slowly, he drifted off.

When he awoke, he found it was not light yet. His plane was to leave at ten, he had plenty of time. He had slept barely three hours—but still he felt light on his feet, without a sign of exhaustion from all the travelling. Switching on the lamp, he sat down with the letter again; after a couple of hours he arrived at a certain conclusion. The first three letters were in medieval Pig Latin, possibly they said, 'After you left . . .'

He returned to Calcutta ten days later than scheduled, rejoined his job, began to shoulder all his responsibilities again. He repaired his ancestral house with the money he had managed to save and bring back, bought his wife a refrigerator, a radiogram, and new furniture; he re-entered the orbit of his old, familiar life—easily, without resistance.

Over the next ten years, he published several slim volumes of research in linguistics, inducing active interest among international scholars. But what was normally discussed only by experts abroad made an astonishing impact on people at home. Needless to say, issues such as the influence of Sanskrit on conjugation in Tibetan, or which Hebrew and Greek words had been imported from ancient Persian, or how closely the Tagalog language was related to Tamil and Sinhalese, and how much of Pali and Magadhi-Prakrit featured in it, were equally irrelevant to the daily life of people anywhere in the world; but since incomprehensible issues can also provide the ingredients for excitement, and because the incitement of patriotism and the possibility of compensating for our inconsequentiality makes us Indians exaggerate assumptions of genius, one morning—as a result of two long and admiring discussions in *The Philologist* from Oxford, England and *The Journal of Linguistic Studies* from Cambridge, which some people chanced upon—one of Calcutta's highly circulated newspaper ran a special article on Birupaksha Ray, the other newspapers followed up with a number of reports—

journalists bestowed such flowery appellations on him as 'Mr Eloquence', 'Born Under the Star of the God of Speech', and 'Twentieth-Century Mithridates', in an unguarded moment a harmless-looking but cunning young man took a photograph of him reading and had it published in an illustrated magazine from Bombay. Things became more convoluted after this; suddenly becoming aware of his existence, the gods of Delhi conferred the title of Padma Vibhushan on him; the following year, competing with Delhi, the leaders of West Bengal awarded him the highest honorary title of the university, which was normally preserved for highly ranked scholars on the verge of death.

Birupaksha was considerably disturbed by these unexpected and, for him, completely unnecessary events. Crowds of uninvited socially conscious men and women at home and in the workplace; appeals from many unknown and, occasionally, a few famous people through the post and over the phone, requests for interviews from one magazine after another; he was asked to participate in myriad agitations, to become the president or vice-president of—or advisor to—a variety of organisations, to sign a multitude of petitions and address a host of meetings; he was immensely surprised at his opinion being sought on such diverse subjects as the Suez crisis, spaceflight. Sino–Indian relations, artistic freedom, and even the architecture of a proposed temple and the desirability of displaying kissing in Indian cinema. For some time attempts were made to drag him into the centre of the debate on the national language of India; north Indians assumed that he would support Hindi by virtue of being an expert in Sanskrit, and south Indians were hopeful that no Bengali could be anything but anti-Hindi; as a result, flattering statements began to be showered on him from both sides. Invitations piled up from foreign embassies; requests to join different programmes in Delhi and Bombay and Jalandhar and Ernakulam, or to head cultural delegations despatched by the Indian government to east Europe or southeast Asia. How was he to cope with all this, what would he do with them? Birupaksha felt helpless at the first onslaught—confused, beleaguered, powerless, and because of this, as though unable to maintain his balance, did one or two things which were both inappropriate and unbeneficial. He signed a couple of petitions (simply to get rid of strangers quickly, without properly reading what they said); responded to repeated requests (since refusing over and over again was a waste of energy) by delivering pedestrian speeches at one or two meetings—but a trivial incident amidst all these developments made him determined to exercise self-defence. One day, one of his colleagues (older than him) told him, 'Let me tell you something Birupaksha-babu, you're in the good books of the bosses now—why don't you take the opportunity to grab a fat grant for *Speech* magazine, in fact if you make an effort you might even be able to get your hands on a plot of land for our linguistics society.' Each of the words and phrases like 'good books', 'opportunity', 'grab' and 'get your hands on' seemed to make Birupaksha quiver inside, but his senior colleague used precisely this language, and in a tone, accompanied by movements of the eye, which suggested that it would be foolish of Birupaksha not to accept his advice. And at once Birupaksha knew what he should do in this situation; he realised that the only way to survive was passive resistance, like a vulnerable insect he would have to hide in his hole, withdraw into a shell like an immobile snail. After this he began to reject each and every proposal indiscriminately— gently, firmly, deferentially, sometimes a trifle rudely, even evoking the ire of ministers and popular leaders. The harsh glare of publicity, which had fallen on him unexpectedly, moved away smoothly, no one could see Birupaksha Ray at meetings any more, he was not the member of any committee in Delhi or Calcutta because of his silence on all manner of topical affairs, his name never appeared in newspapers or magazines. For some time, he was criticised in some quarters for his unsocial behaviour; but because candidates always outnumbered posts, his absence was not felt anywhere (some people breathed a sigh of relief at his exit); influential men shunned him, the public forgot his name; Birupaksha was freed of the demon.

Meanwhile, there were some changes in his family life too. His daughter married a young artist of her own choice; his son moved to Ranchi with a job in the government's geology department; and his wife Suhasini created a happy and independent life for herself. After the initial passion of youth had been spent, Birupaksha's relationship with his wife had begun to sag—the reason could be his excessive fondness for linguistics, or an unconscious aversion on the part of his wife; for many years (barring the weeks with Esha) his life had been devoid of physical relations with women, and that was what he had become used to. So he was not upset when, shortly after his return from Europe, his wife reached her menopause, though somewhat early. And now, when there were virtually no inhabitants at home other than the husband and the wife, they grew distant from each other, with almost nothing in common. Under the influence of her daughter (or of her son-in-law, via her daughter), Suhasini began to consider herself an art expert; she visited exhibitions with them, entertained young artists at home. In addition, her South Calcutta Women's Organisation kept her busy too; as its secretary she was invited to the Governor's residence on Independence Day and Republic Day, she discussed issues of women's welfare on the radio sometimes. Then there were visits to her son twice a year, motoring around the beautiful hilly tracts of Manbhum-Chotanagpur, the unmixed pleasure of becoming friends with her grandchildren. And since Birupaksha did not participate in any of this, his distance—not just with his wife but also with the rest of his family—kept growing.

It wasn't as though there were no conflicts over this at first. Soon after her daughter's wedding, Suhasini had made a strong accusation to the effect that since Birupaksha was a learned man, whose opinion might

be considered valuable, he should not be silent about
Asit Samanta's paintings. 'I'm not saying this because
he's our son-in-law, but really, his work is very good—
extraordinary!' Now, to Birupaksha, paintings referred
to creations in which the subjects could be identified
clearly, where the water, the mountain, the animals, the
people, the gods and goddesses all revealed themselves
at a single glance, all told it was like a narrative—
viewing some samples of which on his visit abroad
had made him feel as Duryodhana did in the demon
architect Moy's Indraprastha—he was about to pull
out his handkerchief to wipe away the fresh blood
oozing from the wounded soldier's chest, it had taken
him some time to realise that the flash of bright sunlight
was not a natural phenomenon but the result of
applying colours. Of course, he wasn't indifferent to the
depiction of Radha's tryst or to Holi as seen in Mughal
or Rajput miniatures, although the figures looked
like dolls you could tell immediately what was going
on—but Asit's work, he felt, could easily have been
the work of a child; broken, straggling brushstrokes,
arbitrary splashes of colour, on the whole nothing like
the things we know—in fact it wasn't even possible to
tell whether the painting was upside down or not. His
intellect tried to convince him that this was the new
style (for he had seen similar work abroad)—but be
that as it may, none of this made any difference to him,
all this was a thousand miles away from his life. That
was why he preferred silence; lest his wife or daughter
or his artist son-in-law himself try to explain the

mysteries of these paintings, the fear of which prevented him from speaking his mind. At this time, Suhasini and he might have had private conversations such as this one:

'Asit's exhibition opens at the art centre on Saturday. You're going, aren't you?'

'Let's see.'

'What do you mean let's see. Asit's first solo exhibition—how can you not be there?'

'I don't understand art.'

'Art is to be seen, not understood.' (Suhasini said this a little self-consciously, and Birupaksha told himself, 'Khuku's words, Khuku heard Asit says this, and Asit must have read it somewhere.')

'I . . . er . . . I'm busy, you know.'

'Everyone's busy. That doesn't mean they have no diversions.'

'Very well, I'll go.'

'Can you tell me why you aren't interested? Do you know what *Abhijan* said about Asit this week?'

'What?'

'They wrote, we congratulate Asit Samanta wholeheartedly for his painting *Starry World*.'

'Wonderful!'

'I'll show you Asit's file.'

'File? What file?'

'Clippings of all his reviews, that's all. You'll see how much praise he's getting.'

Birupaksha sighed.

'Lady Pramila Chatterjee is coming to the exhibition on Saturday. Do you know who's inaugurating the show? Shankarananda Sinha Roy!'

The name sounded vaguely familiar to Birupaksha.

'Just imagine, such a great film director, so famous all over the world—he's inaugurating the exhibition! Asit is hoping to do some work in cinema—paintings don't sell in this benighted country, but there's money in films—if Asit can be the art director in Sinha Roy's next film . . .'

'Of course! Of course!' Birupaksha interrupted. 'That would be wonderful.'

'Everyone admires his work so much—but you don't say anything even though he's part of the family—do you think that's appropriate?'

'What do you think I should say?'

'You want me to tell you that too!' Suhasini said acerbically. 'They're your own daughter and son-in-law—you don't have the slightest feeling for them. You're not just his father-in-law, you're an important person too, don't you understand how delighted Asit would be if you were to encourage him?'

Suhasini continued her lament for some more time, but Birupaksha didn't say a word.

Or, a few years later:

'So you aren't going?'

'I told you . . .'

'Leela requested you so fervently, she wrote . . .'

'I have things to do here.'

'Very well, take your books along. Debu's got a huge bungalow—you'll get a room to yourself just like you do here, no one will disturb you.'

After some thought Birupaksha said, 'But I cannot tell beforehand just which books I might need.'

'Don't you even want to meet them at least?'

'But I do. They visit from time to time.'

'It's not the same thing. Just think how happy they'd be if you went. You're becoming more and more peculiar by the day—we have a lovely granddaughter, you haven't even bothered to play with her.'

'There's no dearth of people to play with her.' Absently, Birupaksha made an unwise statement.

'Incredible! Are you even a human being!' Suhasini hissed a rebuke, her eyes furious.

But even this sort of bickering was now a thing of the past. He was selfish, he was self-centred, he was stuck in his own little world, he did not care for his own children, he loved no one but himself—Birupaksha had become used to accusations like these, and Suhasini had tired of levelling them too.

No one protested any more about the fact that Birupaksha did not join celebrations and didn't deviate an inch from his daily routine even to please the nearest members of his family, no one expected anything of him, everyone had accepted him. Accepted him exactly as he was, a zero with the label of 'husband' or 'father' or 'grandfather', as though he was missing from this house even while living in it, as though, despite the natural circle of love, any contact between him and his family was now beyond the realm of possibility. Sometimes Suhasini told her children pityingly, 'The man's heart has died rummaging through dead languages all his life—he wasn't like this before, you've seen for yourself . . .' and the others exchanged glances and changed the subject, for everyone knew there was no use talking about it any more.

~ 3 ~

But still, despite being so unburdened and detached, despite the unbroken leisure, free of distractions, at his disposal, Birupaksha had made almost no progress in his real work over these past ten years. Continuous hard work and round-the-year efforts, defying the seasons, had yielded only those three short monographs, from whose dangerous worldly repercussions he had managed to protect himself carefully. Those were nothing—merely the preliminary shoots, with nothing in them to suggest that he would eventually be able to sink his teeth into the succulent, blood-red apple. The certainty—distant. The proof—none. The letter was still as impenetrable as it had been on a summer morning in Rome ten years earlier. He had covered a great deal of ground around it, emerged from his Indo-European circle, learnt some Hebrew and Chinese; hunched over books for days on end at the National Library; familiarised himself with several extinct scripts after much research; leapfrogging obstacles like his own lack of money (for fate had not endowed him with the ability to walk the path of wealth), the unavailability of foreign exchange in India, and the reduction in the import of foreign books, he had procured from London many dictionaries of obscure languages, he had not slept for more than three hours on many a night; but still he had not been able to pierce the obscurity of the composition.

He had, of course, encountered several points of light. Many moments when he had clutched his pen with the ardency of the adulterous wife at the moment of meeting her lover to write down what at that time had appeared to be a literal translation of the letter. But after the first few sentences he had been stupefied by doubt, a tortuous and unending worry about which corner of the universe the next sentence was concealed in, and how he would find it, making his grey head droop over the desk. He had written nearly three hundred and fifty fragments over ten years, besides innumerable notes and comments—meanings of words, the possible syntax, minute details of the probable grammar—a dozen thick notebooks filled with scribbles, whose meaning was unclear even to himself now—every time he felt that the secret key was within reach, his perplexity grew even more. The principal reason was the inappropriateness and inconsistency of his surmised or imagined translations, terming which laughable would not be an exaggeration. One sentence seemed to yield a description of women's fashion for autumn that year ('The cheetah and peacock from your country will steal women's fashion this time.'); another appeared to offer an intricate analysis of the Cold War between the USA and Russia; a third seemed to be the beginning of a scientific treatise on migratory birds. One revealed an unbelievable degree of vulgarity, while another was like the Sunday sermon by a Methodist priest. Clearly, none of these could possibly be the message he was seeking; obviously, all of them were wrong. He had not been able to close the distance even by a hair.

In moments of exhaustion, he had decided to write to Esha, asking her to unravel the mystery, but this had not seemed the correct course of action for various reasons. First, Esha may not have kept a copy of her unusual letter, and he was unwilling to be parted with it even for a moment—or else he could have had a block made and had as many copies printed as he liked. Of course, Birupaksha had made about fifty facsimiles on the pages of his notebooks—he believed the last three were absolutely flawless, therefore there could be no objection to sending one of them to Esha. But . . . a long time had passed, what if Esha herself had forgotten the solution to this puzzle? Suppose she has indeed forgotten, and wants to know from me what she wrote? Possibly that's it, possibly that's just what it is. She rummages through her post-box every day with just this hope. She jumps when the phone rings. 'How strange! You can't decipher it? Not even you!' How infinite her faith in me, she will not allow me to seek anyone's help, she has made me so lonely, self-dependent. If I ask her for the answer now, will

I not be proven unworthy—not just unworthy, but also a fraud? Whatever else I may be, I am not one of those who cheat at chess, who copy from their books in university examinations, who buy lottery tickets to become overnight millionaires. Even amidst such uncertainty, Birupaksha remained steadfast to two of his convictions: (1) This letter was an expression of Esha's eternal love for him—so that he did not forget her, till his last living breath, that was why she had tied him up in knots, and therefore (2) deciphering the letter was not only his personal responsibility, but also possible. An unformed but strong feeling took hold of him—since he had been held to this vow, it must be assumed that it was within his ability of fulfil it. There's no difficulty—it's just that I'm not able to concentrate hard enough; charmed by the decorations on the chest, maybe I have forgotten to lift the lid.

That was why, with considered thought, Birupaksha had refrained from getting in touch with Esha. It would not have been impossible for him to revisit the distant country where he had discovered her in an unknown town. At one point—when the Indian government and foreign embassies were looking upon him favourably, the possibility had even risen once; but he had deliberately (or, perhaps, battling against his inclination) brushed aside the possibility. No—it will not be right, I do not deserve to meet her until I have accomplished the task she has given me. She— my gentle, soft-spoken, lover—is waiting patiently for me to explain the meaning of her letter to her.

She is waiting—for me to remind her of what she has forgotten herself. Day after day, year after year.

~ 4 ~

But who was this Esha, to whom or to whose memory this middle-aged scholar had dedicated his time, his health, his complete attention? For that matter, what did 'memory', that ponderous, glittering word, mean? Does my pulse quicken when I say her name in my mind? Do I hear her voice any more when I press my ear to my pillow before going to sleep? Can I recollect her face clearly? In fact, if she were to knock on my door suddenly, would I recognise her at once? Questions such as these rose in his mind from time to time, he brushed them aside at once. And this was probably the deepest reason that he had never attempted to meet her face to face again. What if the old melodies were forgotten when they met? What if the hours go by making small talk, as though we are mere acquaintances? What if a letter brings forth a reply that anyone else could have written? No, not that way, not through any easy road—I will not take this route to my destination. What does it matter who Esha is, what she is, what she's like? What difference does it make if she has retreated to a distance that cannot be bridged? It is that very distance that I touch, just like the waterfall touches the sea the moment it begins its journey. The letter, I have this letter. Her final message—the very last gift with her name—this is enough. This was how, as the years went by, this was what Birupaksha had thought. As a matter of fact, the waves of time had washed away all the facts—sometimes he couldn't even recollect the name of the tiny town in the American Midwest; to determine whether Esha's house number was 1302 or 1203, he had to turn the yellowing pages of his notebook—but through this continuous erosion, a single idea—the core of his existence, as it were—remained strong, even grew—that this letter, these different scripts, was indeed a message.

On some nights, when Birupaksha opened his notebook and flipped through the pages gouged by his own pen, his heart swayed like a pendulum between the two extremes of enthusiasm and despair. Sometimes he hunched over the mysterious letters, holding the sheet out flat in the glow of the table lamp, just the way he had in Rome after receiving the letter, as though with the hope that a hitherto undiscovered new letter would appear suddenly, or a new relationship between the visible letters would emerge. There must be some principle beneath all this, a mathematical law—surely it was all quite simple, just like the way substituting numbers with symbols automatically revealed the working of algebra. But why have I not been able to find this underlying principle despite all my efforts? Birupaksha was annoyed with himself because his notes and explanations were haphazard, he had written down whatever had occurred to him, without following a rigid methodology—should he have prepared a card index using the American method, creating an alphabetical listing, had he drifted further away from his objective by studying the Tibetan and Sinhalese languages, neither of which was connected to the letter? But method—was that everything? Wasn't vision the main thing, don't all mysteries reveal themselves if the power of vision is sufficient? A few years ago, I found it difficult to read small letters, they were indistinct, as soon as I began to use glasses everything became clear. Only after Galileo used the telescope he had made himself did he see the mountains on the moon. X-rays made it possible to see the skull, the lungs, the heart of a living man. But where is that miraculous ray which can pierce this paper to reach the distant place where a certainty beyond all argument awaits me?

The night deepened, one o' clock, one-thirty, two o' clock, Birupaksha sat uncertainly, dazed with sleep and uneasiness in his heart, immersed in the silence of the night. Drowsiness made his thoughts incoherent; even the conviction that he had considered deep-rooted all these years seemed to disappear now and then, a horrifying question assailed him: Is there really anyone named Esha? Was there, ever? Did I ever see her, did I touch her? If she is not a figment of my imagination, if she does exist, why doesn't she appear? Why doesn't she say something? She must come, she must prove she exists, she does not have the right to saddle me with all the responsibility and remain dormant herself. At times the form of a woman pushed aside the curtain of sleep closing over him—sitting in the armchair next to his desk, her face indistinct because that part of the room was in the shade, but the contours of her body were not mute, as though she were saying something with all her being, silently. But what? Birupaksha listened carefully, tilted his head to pay more attention, there was only a buzzing, like the continuous hum of a small insect, as he listened sleep came in a rush, waking up suddenly he saw the sheet of paper beneath the lamp. Hebrew letters, Greek letters, Devnagari. His research, his lifetime quest, his examination. If I ask for more proof, will I not be proving my own poverty? Pushing his notebooks aside, Birupaksha rose to his feet, he felt as though he had returned to his focal point, switching off the light he went to bed—but sleep eluded him for a long time.

So he swung from one end to the other—all day and all night—simultaneously with everything else he had to do, hidden behind them.

Ten more years passed. Meanwhile Birupaksha published yet another book; about a hundred and fifty pages of the main text, with eighty-seven pages of notes—dense with symbols and scripts—titled: *A Proposition Regarding the Relationship of Sanskrit with Chinese, Russian and ancient Persian*, it offered a new theory regarding the origin of the Indo-European languages. It created even more of a sensation among foreign experts, a great deal of debate ensued over his hypothesis, several people protested vehemently, some labelled the monograph 'revolutionary', while others rued the fact that, like many other Hindus, Mr Ray had also regrettably abandoned science in favour of mysticism. German and French translations appeared within six months, but because India was in the grip of a political crisis, there was no repetition of the unwelcome incidents referred to earlier; delectably meeting his expectations, this new effort went completely unnoticed in his own country. He retired from teaching the day he turned sixty-two—although nothing would have prevented him from clinging on for three years more, and Suhasini had pleaded with him to do just that. On the same day he handed over editorship of *Speech* magazine to a younger colleague, and ignoring all protests he resigned from the post of president of the linguistic society. Now all his time for research was under his own control. But—his family observed in astonishment—his daily routine changed in ways beyond everyone's imagination. He no longer spent his entire day with his nose buried in his books, his chair in the second-floor library was often empty, his connection with the National Library had become tenuous too. The thick journals that came from abroad—which he would eagerly leaf through as soon as they arrived—were often put away without being unwrapped. Even more surprisingly, he joined family gatherings now and then, took part in light conversation and banter with his children and their spouses—he even seemed curious about pop art and The Beatles. It was noticed that when his daughter's or daughter-in-law's female friends visited, he—provoking ill-concealed discomfort in everyone—spent some time uninvited with these young women, gazed at them with a degree of wonder, made unnecessary conversation with them, even made racy comments not befitting his age or status. His son had been transferred to Calcutta with a promotion some time earlier; Birupaksha had made friends with his granddaughter after she turned eleven, the same granddaughter whom he had not paid any attention to earlier, he took her for strolls along the river and the Dhakuria Lake, his enchantment with her childish babble became evident in his expression. One morning, he grew excited after seeing a photograph of Madhubala, who had died recently, and reading her biography in the newspaper; he expressed such intense regret at having to die without the chance to watch such an extraordinarily beautiful actress—whose talking, moving figure on the cinema screen had captured the heart of the entire nation—that his daughter-in-law could not suppress the laughter rising in her throat. 'All right,' she consoled her father-in-law, 'if I hear of *Mughal-e-Azam* playing anywhere I shall take you.' 'Who are the most beautiful actresses today?' he asked eagerly. 'Most beautiful?' His daughter-in-law reeled off several names, explaining the unique qualities in their acting styles, Birupaksha listened attentively. 'There's a Saira Banu film on, would you like to go?' she asked, using the Bengali word 'boi'—book—to refer to the film. 'Boi? What do you mean, book?' His son answered, 'That's how films are referred to nowadays.' 'Not just nowadays—for a long time now,' added his daughter-in-law. 'I've been hearing it since I was a child.' 'Really? For a long time now? How strange! And I had no idea. Just imagine . . .' unconsciously echoing something he had heard many years earlier, Birupaksha said irrelevantly, 'Just imagine how difficult it is to learn even a single language properly—leave alone several!' Meanwhile, his daughter-in-law had been scanning the entertainment columns in the newspaper, looking up from the paper, she said, 'It's playing at Bijoli, I can send for tickets if you like.' 'Are you mad!' his son objected firmly. 'What's the use of torturing Baba this way?' But astonishing everyone, Birupaksha accompanied the women in the family to watch not one but two films in a single week—featuring Saira Banu and Tanuja, respectively. His daughter declared, 'I can guarantee Baba will be forced to leave in ten minutes . . .' but nothing like that ensued; on the contrary, after their return Birupaksha conducted a long comparative analysis of the two actresses' looks and acting skills.

This strange transformation—which should have pleased his family—did not generate the expected joy in anyone's heart. Out of long habit (and to tell the truth, because his absence had never created any difficulties), everyone felt that it suited him better to spend his days in his second-floor library, detached and indifferent; he seemed to be descending to a pedestrian plane from the highest peak of punditry that he occupied; he seemed to be unfairly destroying the pride that they had felt in his being an 'extraordinary man', despite all the pain he had caused them. His daughter felt a fresh bout of pique at the thought that her father had never commented on Asit's paintings, but now appeared childishly obsessed with cheap Hindi films, which was why she couldn't protest when Asit chuckled, 'Your father's brain is turning to jelly.' Meanwhile, Suhasini casually told her daughter-in-law, 'Don't you go inciting your father-in-law to watch films, he might turn senile.'

~ 5 ~

However, Birupaksha continued to wage his secret war, it was only his strategy that had changed. He now viewed the entire problem from a different perspective; what he had sensed sometimes, on a late, drowsy night, had now been converted into certainty; he had accepted that the so-called 'scientific approach', which he had tried to follow assiduously all this time, was not applicable in this particular instance. I have attacked the script from so many different angles; left to right, right to left; top to bottom, diagonally; I have improvised many different symbolic alphabets, constructed a mixed framework of many languages, but the results have all been unacceptable, all of them have misled me further. By and by he began to think that his knowledge of linguistics was only a façade for ignorance; life was so short (once again he echoed someone else unconsciously)—how many languages do we have the time to learn anyway? There are innumerable languages about which I do not have the slightest idea, whose very existence I am unaware of, and even those in comparison to whom I am but an insignificant labourer, even those geniuses are nothing but infants, just like me, before the enormous Tower of Babel. Bantus, Swahilis, Eskimos—all these people are articulate and eloquent; despite being surrounded by an alien and powerful language, American tribals apparently still speak in nearly five hundred different tongues. Then how futile, how meaningless our efforts—we who consider ourselves linguists, with our capital of ten or twelve or, at most, twenty languages. Besides, language doesn't belong to man alone; cats have their love songs, chimpanzees are argumentative, domesticated dogs can communicate hunger, fear, love and the intrusion of thieves simply through inflections in their barking. But wild dogs do not have this range of notes—it is said that the domesticated dog has learnt the 'language' of man by cohabiting with him and copying him. But is this assumption valid in all cases? Take the bat—blind by day, living far away from the company of human beings, an actual sound from whose throat we might hear once in a lifetime— fifty years ago a German expert had published a complete notation of their language. And recently a team of scientists in California have recorded the language of the hippopotamus, the range of its sounds is apparently extraordinary considering that it is not human. Until now, human society has believed that only human beings can 'talk' in the real sense—since he can stand upright, since the power of his tongue and vocal cords is unique, since the structure of his brain and nervous system is exceedingly complex . . . with logic such as this man has proved his own pre-eminence. But who knows, maybe fish are not dumb either—it is our eardrums whose capacity is limited, and no instrument exists yet to capture the very low or very high sounds that fish might make. Since we are human beings, we look at the world only through the eyes of human beings, we observe the behaviour of other creatures only with our own minds and senses (we don't have a choice)—in these circumstances, how can it be certain that all that has been conjectured about the languages of other animals, or about the origins of human languages, is not as blurred and ephemeral as cobwebs floating in the air?

Birupaksha could no longer accept all the theories he had read about the origin of language—from gestures, from dance, from war, from screams or hisses—in his imagination the family divisions between languages had disappeared too, he had even become sceptical about the universally accepted proposition that Chinese had nothing in common with English. He felt that the Puranas were right where these things were concerned. The echo of one particular articulated sound, like the first pulse of life in an animate world, had tumbled over centuries and millennia to compose all those other collections of sounds, vowels and consonants, nasals and aspirates, whose diverse symmetries we refer to as language. It's just like the numerous concentric circles created when a pebble is thrown into a lake, only its

surge was unending, the waves never ceased. A cascade
of echoes, a reverberation of resonance—not the real
thing, different kinds of counterfeits, in other words,
all languages are only corruptions of the original
language—the so-called primitive languages like those
of the Bantus or Mundas as much as the so-called
evolved languages such as Sanskrit or Greek, English
or French. And that is why we do not understand one
another's languages, do not understand each other
even when speaking the same language or dialect; the
minds of the monkey or the bat or the hippopotamus
remain unrevealed to us, whatever interpretation we
have of this world and this life are all woefully partial
and subject to revision. But St Francis of Assisi used
to converse with birds, Gunadhya wrote the *Brihat
Katha*—Ocean of Stories—in 'barbaric' Prakrit and
read it out to wild animals, Orpheus's song entranced
trees and stones and beasts. Don't these legends
all point towards a single world language—not a
synthetic Esperanto or a commercial basic English,
not something limited to a particular continent or a
means to a limited end—but universal in the widest
sense, the natural mother tongue of all of nature, the
connecting link between the innumerable and distinct
existences on earth? Just as the fraction may be infinite
but is still contained within the whole number, so too
are the separate language fragments of man and beast
subsumed within the original tongue, which in itself
is unique and infallible, but beyond the reach of our
specialised sciences because it is manifested in many

different languages. If one of its rays were to give itself up to me, no language in the world would remain unknown to me, and in an instant the message would become lucid, the message which I have exhausted myself over with my literal quest over all these years.

Birupaksha was electrified by the courage of his imagination, almost feeling afraid at first. Will it be right for me to step off the path which I have long been accustomed to, and which so many experts have walked on? Logic does not support my line of thinking, after all. But was it logic that had dreamed up X-rays? If a ray capable of penetrating flesh and skin to unravel the inner mysteries of the human body could have been discovered, why can't we discover at some time in the future an invisible beam that can penetrate the covering of script and meaning to unveil what lies at the heart of any language? This see-through ray, which was beyond imagination even a short while ago, was actually hidden in nature since the beginning of time, and it is now considered a natural property of the universe. Similarly, the original language is waiting too—one of us will suddenly part the veil to reveal it. It's easy—quite easy—only a thin curtain lies in the way, it seems as though it will be drawn any moment, it virtually wants to give itself up.

As he mused about this, it occurred to Birupaksha that man's biggest superstition was the perceived difference between the miraculous and the natural. We cannot invent anything, we can only discover things. They exist—everything exists simultaneously in the universe—all that we desire, the subjects of our wildest hopes, even all that is beyond our ken right now—are all present; it's just a matter of finding them. Am I then on the verge of some such discovery, which people will dub astounding and epochal? Birupaksha felt his heart beat faster, overcome by wonder and humility, he pressed his hand to his chest and lowered his head. A different thought sprang up at once from the bottom of his mind, as though he could see a clear path before his eyes. Enough of attacking—it was time to surrender. What I am looking for is self-illuminated (for all the languages of the world are only weak reflections of it)—why should intelligence, knowledge, analysis or exertion be necessary to find it? The world is lit up as soon as the sun rises—do we have to make an effort to realise this? The locked, abandoned room that has been dark for many years and the room that became dark five minutes ago because of a power failure will be illuminated simultaneously when a match is struck. One pinpoint of light is sufficient to dispel even the darkness accumulated over centuries. Then what use is knowledge? An illiterate itinerant forest bandit had unexpectedly articulated incantations bound in rhythm. A clever thief had built the first veena from the entrails of dead animals. I will now have to forsake all my learning. I will have to pretend I have forgotten my vow. I will have to start afresh.

This was the reason that Birupaksha's daily routine had been broken so spectacularly, or perhaps he had broken the very concept of the daily routine.

He was waiting—he would have to pass this period of waiting easily, without making demands of himself, without pondering, without pride. He would have to fill his days with whatever diversions were at hand— and it would be a serious mistake to assume that anything that was at hand was necessarily trite, or irrelevant for him. No—everything was connected, they were all part of the different fractions of the whole number. Every last thing was important now. He would have to observe young women's gestures, the cultivated seductiveness of beautiful women on cinema screens, how the little girl's shy smile spread from her lips across her entire face, how sadly his daughter-in-law's pet dog raised his eyes to the sky, how the beam from the setting sun which fell on his bathroom window made the walls glow . . . he would have to listen closely to the splash of the rain, to the sound of the streets being watered, to the trundling of the first tram at dawn—the essence of all these ingredients would have to be stored like a secret stash of food within himself, where there was growing, little by little, unknown to him—like a foetus incubated for years on end in the womb of a gigantic mother— the message which he had been searching for in vain all this time. As though the radiation from a distant star had covered millions of light years to approach earth, to approach mankind . . . to approach him. There's nothing I have to do—besides allowing what is imminent to materialise. There's nothing I have to think, I am prepared.

~ 6 ~

This new realisation of Birupaksha's had some other results too. The sheet of paper with the symbols—which he had taken great care of all these years, spreading it out flat and inserting it into a clear plastic folder (so that it did not tear along the folds), never forgetting to spray insecticide on it once a month—he put away in the iron safe in his bedroom, adding the notebooks with the notes and comments that were the fruits of years of labour. He could no longer believe that they would prove useful; he was amused when he recalled the nights that he would go to bed with the plastic folder beneath his pillow, and his notebook, pencil and the bed switch within his reach; those moments from the past appeared tragic—moments when he had sat up in bed and switched on the light, written line after line in a feverish hand, drawn a number of diagrams, mouthed the presumed sentences silently, only moving his lips, and then, suddenly stabbed by the dagger of doubt, had plunged his face into his pillow and tried to go back to sleep. He had scanned the letter so many times that a perfect and complete facsimile had been etched sharply in his mind; he could hold on to the image as long as he liked, and if he ever told himself, 'Not now, I'm sleepy,' it would slowly disappear. Before he went to sleep, or at the moment of awaking, he played a game like this with his mystery letter.

Because his work always involved sitting at a desk, Birupaksha had long suffered from constipation, of late its severity had increased, he had to allot a quarter of an hour for the preliminary moving of his bowels. To keep annoyance at bay, he went in with a light novel or magazine, but one day he remembered that whatever original ideas he had had about linguistics had been revealed to him for the first time, long ago—not in his library, nor while teaching—but in the pleasant solitude of the toilet. Immediately, he felt a desire, after a long time, for a look at the original manuscript; he took it out of his safe and into the toilet. It was just the same—in other words, just as he had seen it six months earlier. For quite some time now it had become obvious that the physical existence of the script could not be depended on; once pitch black, the letters had turned brown long ago, but even that brown had now become yellow and faded, despite all the care a few creases had appeared on the sheet, even its whiteness seemed grey now. Birupaksha tried to look at it afresh, as though he were seeing it for the first time, but the pretence didn't last; at first glance the letter seemed to grow heavy in his hand with all its past history. No—there was nothing new to see, he knew it all, he had come through all the battles, burnt a great deal of incense, but not for a moment had he set eyes on the goddess of these letters. Birupaksha sighed, he spent longer than usual sitting where he was—so long and so absent-mindedly that there was a knock on the door, he was informed that his tea was getting cold

('Actually they're worried that I might have fainted—it happens all the time these days.')—to reassure them, Birupaksha said, 'Coming,' and rose to his feet, and suddenly, out of haste or carelessness, the letter slipped out of the plastic folder. It fell directly into the commode where he had recently emptied his bowels. Without a moment's thought, he dipped his hand into the dirty water and picked up the letter, blindly turning on the tap in the basin and spreading the sheet of paper out under it. The cleansed—far too clean—yellowish letters melted into the water, all that had been written was obliterated, and the sheet of paper crumbled into dust and into the basin, where it passed effortlessly through the drain into the metropolitan underworld through which flowed the excretion of innumerable people. And all this took place within just a few seconds, before his eyes—Birupaksha had no opportunity for second thoughts, he could not save a single fragment as a memento. By the time he had turned the tap off, not a sign remained.

The first impact of this accident gave rise to two different feelings in Birupaksha's mind. He felt guilty—as though a loved one had died because of his carelessness, someone who had been his lifelong companion. But just as, after someone's death, we think mostly of the dead person, just as they come alive all over again in our minds, so too did Birupaksha recollect, strongly, the real person, whom he had named Esha, the way he had seen her, twenty or twenty-five years ago, in a small town in the American Midwest.

Astonishing him, almost overwhelming him, Esha's face, the form of her body, her voice, all came back to him clearly. Suddenly the desire to see her again, to touch her again, reared its head. He remembered the sunlight, the drizzle, the light breeze, the cobbled lane and the wide, generous piazza—he saw himself at American Express, waiting behind nine or ten people for his letter; his heart was twisted once more with the hope, the anxiety, the failure, of that moment. And then, shaking with restlessness, he slowly found his answer, he went forward towards that quiet ending, which time prepares us for without our knowledge, so that a man does not suffer too much.

Birupaksha did not even realise when the wave of memory and desire, which had been resurrected by the disappearance of the letter, subsided. What had been a reality in the distant past was converted into a pure idea now, his thoughts found a new equilibrium. He was no longer repentant because the original letter no longer existed; on the contrary, he saw a certain aptness in its sudden disappearance. It was natural for an inanimate object to dissolve into the five elements—it wouldn't be wrong to call it desirable either—because something remained even after that, and this remnant became evident only when it moved out of the shadow of the physical object. Is there anyone who doesn't know that the idol has to be immersed so that the goddess can seep into our lives? Or perhaps there's no need to make an effort, it works as automatically as the air we breathe. When it's humid, when not a leaf on the trees stirs, the breeze still exists—for everyone, all the time. Is this—what I've thought of all this time as the 'letter'—'my letter'? Isn't the word 'my' presumptuous, isn't it incorrect? Can anyone really live without a task such as this, a responsibility, a constant companion? People live easy lives, passing time on some pretext or the other—until they're called away to their real work. 'Here's the letter—your letter—read it to find out what it says.' The same letter for everyone, yet everyone thinks it's only for them—and that is why the mystery runs so deep. It will not be unravelled in any meeting, by any committee, at any conference, pedantry and judgement will be of no use, each one will seek an answer on their own—only within themselves, nowhere else. Birupaksha looked out of the corner of his eye at the other people in the house, he observed people's expressions if he happened to go out—had the letter reached any of them, or would it reach soon, did any of them know of the expectation that kept each of them moving about restlessly? He thought that this was why his granddaughter was growing up, why his daughter and daughter-in-law did their make-up with such care, why his busy son's eyes sometimes grew wistful, why his son-in-law played with his paint and brushes. They wanted it, they wanted the same thing that had been growing within him all this time, which had filled him to the brim year after year. That was what they wanted too—but they hadn't realised it yet. Now and then he wished he could call one of them and reveal his secret, wished he could ask, 'Have you got it?

Have you got the letter?'—but he restrained himself at the last moment, lest they thought he was going mad.

For the first time in his life Birupaksha seemed to consider himself happy; that he was alive was enough, there was nothing else he had to do, nothing else he wished for. He may indeed have suffered from a mental problem at this time; sometimes he didn't understand the meaning clearly when he opened a scholarly book, he thought to himself, 'Why do people write all this? What purpose does it serve?' One day an old essay of his happened to fall into his hands, reading just two pages so exhausted him that he had to lean back on the sofa and close his eyes. Another time, his daughter brought him a clipping from a French magazine—a brief discussion on Joan Miro—in the process of reading and explaining it to her, he had to stop several times and check the dictionary. He was surprised, but not upset—instead, he was pleased to think that he had finally been released from the iron grip of his own learning. His vision was weaker, he had to hold the page close to his eyes to read, but he felt no urge to change his glasses, for books had retreated from his life. And the incident had retreated even further—quite indistinct by now—the incident which could be said to have given birth to all the others, and which had seemed oh so important once. Perhaps it was incorrect to call it an 'incident', for the word held the sense of an ending, while actually it was still taking place, it took place every day, there was no assurance of its ending. It was like a game, and the game was everything—it was irrelevant why and for whom. And that was why the person who had introduced him to the game was almost wiped out from his mind, he forgot her real name, he even forgot the name he had given her, Esha. And the lost letter, which he had assumed was imprinted in his memory, no longer appeared frequently in his mind's eye; after spending many sleepless nights, he now fell asleep the moment his head touched the pillow, sleeping through the night without waking up; in his dreams he sometimes went back to his childhood, now and then he saw his mother's face, she had been dead thirty-five years now. The last year of Birupaksha's life passed this way, in utter happiness.

~ 7 ~

An April morning. Birupaksha had just woken up after a pleasant night's sleep. He was awake, but hadn't got out of bed yet, not even opened his eyes. He didn't know why, but he considered himself extraordinarily happy that day from the moment he had awakened, still in bed, he was enjoying the sensation, half-asleep, without opening his eyes. A breeze ruffled his thin hair—not from the electric fan (he realised this clearly), it was blowing in through the window, a zephyr, a vernal breeze. He seemed to taste the phrase 'vernal breeze' with his tongue, with an air of amusement, he thought he got a sudden fragrance of cloves, and the scent was translated into several of the poet Jayadeva's smooth alliterations. A woman's voice wafted in from the dining room—he recalled that the house was full of people, Khuku and Asit had dropped in the previous night and stayed over, a niece was visiting from Bhagalpur—not exactly visiting, her parents had sent her to Suhasini so that the entire country could be combed to arrange a match for her—'she's not doing anything much after passing her B.A. exam!'— and the girl had already made some progress towards striking up a romance with Asit's younger brother. Birupaksha recollected the faces of everyone in the family—how nice they are, how nice they are all—I really have been unfair to Asit, I have hurt Suhasini now and then, Leela too—and yet how they all love me—amazing! He was pleased by the thought that he lived with all of them, that he was alive with all of them around him, he was pleased by the thought that his niece would soon get married, two individuals would once again discover the age-old mystery, like fresh blades of grass children would come again, the youth of the world would remain intact. I had been somewhat detached when Khuku got married, when Debu got married, but this time I will play the uncle of the bride to the hilt, welcome the guests, supervise the wedding feast. There was a tinkling sound—the tea was being laid out—everyone would wake up now, one by one, the dining table would turn noisy. He heard his granddaughter say, 'Make my omelette please, didani, all right?' She couldn't bear to have an omelette unless it was made by her grandmother, even if it was burnt, she would still bite into it and say, 'Delicious!'. How sweet Debu's daughter was, she would probably grow up to be a real beauty. Suddenly a face floated up before his still-closed eyes—a woman's face—the body took shape slowly beneath the face—who was it? Where am I? The sea, infinite from one horizon to the other, an unending succession of waves, the froth racing over the blue, breaking and flowing back constantly—and the woman was walking along the shore of this sea, in a sheer dress, triumphant, radiating youth with every step, beneath the enormous sky, as though wrapping the sunlight around her, and making the ocean her witness. Did I ever see a scene like this in a film? Or is it someone else whom I know, whom I have seen somewhere? Who can it be, what is her name? Suddenly he remembered—Madhubala. Madhubala . . . Madhumala . . . Madhumati . . . wasn't it a different name? But not all his efforts could make him recollect another name, identifying the woman correctly appeared impossible, and yet the feeling that he knew her, that he had seen her somewhere, grew stronger. He concentrated all the power in his vision on the woman—she was walking towards him, she wasn't very far away now, but the little distance that remained simply could not be bridged, he was surprised, wondering how the woman could be in motion and still be so immobile. And then he saw that there was no woman there any more, the sea and the sky had disappeared, and in their place a single letter appeared before his eyes, a dazzling symbol against a dark background. And immediately an uneasiness took hold of his body, his chest seemed constricted, and then a marvellous sight took his breath away. Rows of letters—aligned and organised—surrounded him on all sides, in the same disciplined way in which a band of soldiers wrested a fort from the enemy. All those letters—now he remembered—long familiar . . . unfamiliar . . . but unfamiliar no more now. The letters seemed to enter his body on their own—spreading like germs in his bloodstream, in the marrow of his spine, piercing his flesh like needles; their meaning, their sense, their subtle allusions brought forth a response from every pore in his body. 'Ah! At last! Then . . . it's true, all true!' He tried to say this out loud, but all he heard was a sound like a faint cough. He felt as though he was being unfolded by this unexpected attack, he was spreading out in every direction like a waterfall cascading down to the plains—swelling in every direction, with love for everyone, he was going far, far away. Where am I going? The question flashed in his mind and disappeared at once. Joy—he was overcome by unimaginable joy—happiness, as unbearable as pain, was grinding him to pieces, his heart beat uncontrollably, the sea that had disappeared from his sight a short while ago now roared in his ears, but not devoid of meaning; amidst this roaring he seemed to hear the sounds corresponding to each of the letters. But his senses had not left him completely yet; he felt an indistinct need—although he could not determine whether it was a wish to pass urine or to quench his thirst, or was it to write down for others what he had just heard? His body twitched with the desire to sit up.

A little later, Birupaksha's daughter-in-law entered the room with his bed tea to find that his head had slipped off his pillow, one of his legs was dangling from the bed on the floor, his body was motionless, his face, peaceful, and the lines of his mouth suggested that he wanted to say something.

Restless Was the Night

The steamer sliced through the cloudy water of the Meghna; on both sides the water rose, fell, swirled and then broke in a head of foam, white as the naked body of a water nymph, clear like grape juice. The intimate green of trees on one side, the blurred blue tint of the distant horizon on the other.

The wind blew furiously, I couldn't tell from which direction. The small boats scattered across the river moved speedily; all of them had their sails up, patched in various colours like the attire of bauls. Our steamer moved ahead among them like a queen surrounded by her attendants.

The sun had just set. We could not see the sanguine magic of the demure evening to the east in front of us—we saw an enormous portion of the sky, indistinct like fog, its hue not identifiable—someone seemed to have wiped all the colour off its face—the sky in our country didn't often look as discoloured, plain, and downcast.

We were sitting next to each other in two deckchairs without saying a word. A festival of colours might have been in progress elsewhere, but the grey shadow of evening fell on us here like the wings of a cruel nocturnal bird spanning the skies of the entire world. The cloudy water of the river turned dark—like a single jewel, a star appeared in the colourless sky.

I turned my head to look into her eyes—how strange, I had not been able to determine their colour yet. She seemed to change by the moment. Sometimes they were grey like this evening shadow, sometimes green like that distant star, sometimes black like the water of the river, sometimes blue like the incomparably beautiful form of the horizon.

Chuckling, Neelima said, what are you looking at?

I brought her head close and pressed my lips to her enchanting eyes in silent reply. Finally, Neelima's eyes closed. I took the opportunity to run my own eyes all over her. Exquisite. How much of their affection, their grace, their compassion the artist of the world must have poured into creating this woman's body. She was like a veena—it didn't play on its own—a lover of music must gather the instrument in their arms to worship its melody, and therein lay her fulfilment. I could restrain myself no longer, I drew her to my breast quietly and embraced her with great passion.

Freeing herself slowly, Neelima shifted her chair closer to mine and said, aren't you going to tell me about that thing of yours?

What thing of mine?

You told me one day—have you forgotten?

She was trembling ever so slightly with excitement. He breasts swayed with her sharp breathing—swelling at times to defy the constraints of her blouse. It was like wine overflowing its glass.

My eyes fixed on this movement, I said reluctantly, hmm?

Neelima exclaimed, like a little girl making a demand, no, please tell me.

Suddenly, the trance was broken. Trying to sound as normal as possible, I said, my only request, Neelima—don't ever ask me to tell you about this one thing.

Her liquid eyes conveyed both a plea and a complaint at the same time.

Glancing at an easy chair on the other side, I said, very well, I'll tell you. But don't blame me when you realise it would have been better not to have heard this story.

Leaning her head back a little, Neelima said, blame you! You're my bridegroom after all.

My words slipped out, I may be your bridegroom—but I am not your husband yet. And after what I tell you, the chance of that happening may vanish altogether.

Which is why I want to hear it all the more.

* * *

When I went to Calcutta for the first time six years ago, we didn't have a house there yet. So I had to accept the hospitality of a barrister who lived in Bhawanipur. He and his family were old friends of my father's. Must you know their names, Neelima?

How can there be a story without names?

Other stories, maybe, but mine will do fine without.

Very well, go on.

Summer holidays had begun. I had just taken my IA examination at the college. I was tender in years, the freshness of youth had added colour to my mind and body. Many things in this world were mysterious to me then, and the greatest mystery of all . . .

. . . were women?

Yes, women. Remember, Neelima, I was of the age when the sight of the end of a sari made the blood flow faster in my veins, the heart longed to hear the jingling of bangles—it was the age when people give up mathematics to pursue poetry, when the bioscope and its actors seem preferable to physics experiments.

Should I tell you the truth, Neelima? Whenever I saw a girl of my age, as green and tender, I wished I could run up to her and bring her home, and then—talk to her, kiss her. The girls' school bus used to go up and down the road next to the house—I tried in vain ever so often to exchange meaningful glances with some of them. You wouldn't be pleased to hear of the thoughts that crowded my mind constantly at that time.

Living in this house with my newly awakened thirst was like plunging into a deep lake. My father's friend had for three generations been living in western ways— all the customs and practices in his house appeared perverted, given the habits I had inculcated since birth. I had been born into a pure Brahmin family, after all. At first, I felt discomfort at every step, like a fish out of water. But gradually I got used to everything, till it felt as though I had grown up in this very environment since birth. For the sake of the truth, I must say my days passed pleasurably.

I fell silent abruptly. The water of the river was no longer visible—the night had turned everything black. The eastern sky, where there was just the one glowing jewel earlier, was now filled with stars; were they dewdrops on the brow of a radiant dawn at the entrance to Amaravati? The electric lights on the deck were swaying. I heard Neelima say, go on, why did you stop?

I cannot see you, Neelima. Why don't you sit in the light? Why must you hide yourself in the darkness?

Taking my hand in hers, Neelima said gently, here I am. I didn't go away. You only have to reach out to touch me.

I breathed a sigh of relief. I felt as though I had been sinking into the depths but had managed to come up to the surface for a breath of air, which tasted ambrosial. Leaning across the handles of our chairs, I took my face very close to hers and said, ah, here you are, Neelima. So close. I can get the fragrance of your hair, I can see my eyes reflected in your blue ones. I am afraid no more—ah, Neelima, how lovely you are.

Calmly Neelima said, what happened after that?

Like a wound-up gramophone, I began to speak with unnatural energy, it wasn't so much a house as an exhibition of beauty. Like a garden of flowers, with blooms of all varieties—their magnificence eclipsed even a full-moon night, their maddening scents made the very air drunk. As I said, I arrived in the midst of all this with my newly aroused infinite desire—and promptly lost the bearings of my existence.

The head of the family had seven daughters, three of whom were of marriageable age. And besides, there was no small number of female relatives newly arrived at their youth also living there. With friends added, there must have been twelve or thirteen of them. Every day they would tell me how many it was, but I don't remember the number clearly any more.

This group of young women began to play reckless games with me. Perhaps they had not yet found as suitable a boy to dance to their tunes. And besides, I came from a wealthy family, wasn't bad looking— and it wasn't as though none of them nurtured any particular intentions where I was concerned. They didn't keep themselves from conveying this to me with occasional flashes of lightning in their eyes. There was no end to their playful moves and artful ways. They would bring their faces very close to mine and suddenly withdraw; brush the keys tied to the end of their saris against me while passing; or call me from behind the door while doing their hair in the dressing room to whisper something meaningless in my ear before disappearing—all of this was an everyday affair. I will admit that their ploys did not go in vain. Trapped in their joyful machinations, I was quite lost—I didn't even try to understand what was going on, I let myself be swept away without support in that wild flood. What could I have done, tell me. I had no control over myself.

* * *

Lowering my voice, I asked quietly, want to hear more?

I do, said Neelima in a muffled tone.

Several days had passed since my arrival in Calcutta. One night I woke up, very, very slowly. Very, very slowly—you know how? Not the way in which someone wakes up from a terrible nightmare in the middle of the night and gasps for air. You know how when someone else talks or moves about in the bedroom early in the morning, it blends with your dream at first—and then gradually turns real and wakes you up—and you emerge from your sleep, smile quietly, turn over on your side, and close your eyes again? Something like that. I too woke up the same way, ever so slowly. Opening my eyes, I looked out the open window—and as soon as I did it seemed to me . . .

It seemed to me the movement of nature had come to a halt abruptly—as though in eager expectation of someone or something. Just as theatre audiences suddenly become still, silent, before the curtain is about to rise for the first act, so too did all of nature appear to have become stock still. The stars were no longer twinkling, the leaves of the trees weren't whispering, all the strange and unprovoked sounds that normally fill the night had muted themselves at an unknown signal, the moonlight seemed to have gone to sleep in the blue sky—even the wind had turned inanimate like an exhausted animal, unable to blow any more—oh Neelima, I have never seen such a beautiful, such a marvellous, such a terrible silence ever again. Unknown to myself, I mumbled, is someone coming?

At once the curtain at the door parted. The air in the room swooned, the faint moonbeam that had fallen near my head shifted a bit and went out suddenly—my body and mind grew languid with delicious lassitude—it was as though I could see nothing, hear nothing, feel nothing—an intense wave of drunkenness swept me away like a storm—and then—

Why is your face so pale, Neelima? The flowers in your hair are rolling in the dust, the end of your sari is on the floor. Neelima . . .

And then?

It seems like a reverie all these years later. Like a dream I had aeons ago—a thousand years, a million—a memory from my previous life. Was I in my senses? Did I understand everything clearly? Who knows? But none of it seems real today—it's all indistinct, drab, like stale flowers, blurred like something seen through tears.

Yes—then some things rough to the touch descended on my face—I felt a tingling all over. Cheeks as soft as butterfly wings, lips like rose petals, the lowered chin so very desirable, a captivating neck as submissive as a leafy bough, a pair of cool, alluring breasts—you will never understand, Neelima, what that arousal was like, how ruinous that pleasure.

Then, encircling me slowly like tendrils with her arms, someone ground herself against me—my entire body spasmed at intervals—I felt the blood might burst through my veins and begin spurting.

Perhaps nothing is more draining than the fatigue that comes after great passion. Her arms loosened slowly.

I'm telling you the truth, at that time it did not seem to me for even a moment that there could be anything remarkable or unnatural about this incident. My curiosity was intense by now—who was this? Which of them? Was it her, or was it her? I ran through all the names in my head then like beads on a rosary, but I don't remember a single one now. As soon as I reached out for the light switch, a hand fell on mine to stop me. My voice was no longer hesitant—I asked quite intelligibly, will you not let me see your face?

A muffled reply came back, no need.

But I want to.

I have been created to meet all your wants. Except this one.

Why? Modesty?

Modesty about what? I have already given my modesty to you.

You don't want to identify yourself?

No, let the mystery behind my identity deepen.

There were some moonbeams on the bed . . .

I've closed the window.

I see. But it can be opened again.

I'll run away before that.

What if I hold you back?

You cannot.

Not even by force?

You will not force me.

The soft sound of laughter. Like the water in a narrow stream touching the bank for a moment.

Are you not satisfied with what you have got.

There's no question of satisfaction or dissatisfaction for what I have neither asked for nor earned, but received by chance, far beyond my imagination.

And yet?

Must my hope to see your face die in vain?

Is a woman's face only to be seen?

Of course not. It is a bottomless cup of ambrosia.

Well then?

I accept defeat.

I reached out again with my arms and felt her vine-like frame with my entire body. She lay on my breast in silence.

Somewhere over our heads the moon had risen. The black surface of the river had turned yellow—streaked silver in places. Neelima sat in silence with her hands gathered at her breast. Had she heard everything I'd said? Her lips were dry like wilted petals. Why was she looking at me that way? There was something she wanted to say, but she couldn't say it. I was afraid to ask, who knows what she might tell me. Gazing at the spot where the water and the moonlight had met in a maelstrom, I took a cigarette from my pocket and lit it. The smoke rose like smooth blue lines. The steamer was making a raucous noise. Would it go on forever? Would it never stop? Neelima's face was parched like the sky overhead.

She asked, does your story end here?

Like a student answering the teacher's question, I said, no, it's just begun. But there's nothing at the end, so you can consider this the end.

Neelima said no more. I continued, I fell asleep as I was. When I awoke, the bed was bathed in sunlight. On the pillow and the sheets, all over the bed, her fragrance remained like a cherished memory.

Oh, the humiliation that lay in store for me the next morning! Like every day they gathered around me—like every day torrents of their words flowed like the sweet tinkling of a xylophone, waves of their laughter made the still air in the room whirl with ardency, the pleasant sounds of their bangles rang out as they always did when they moved their arms— everyone looked as beautiful as flowers, as tempting as jars of honey, but my voice was silent, the source of my own laughter was blocked. Assuming that the signs of the previous night's madness still clung to my face and my eyes, I couldn't raise them to look at anyone. But still I examined each of their faces surreptitiously, in case I could identify the person. Each one I looked at seemed to be her. Every time one of them spoke, it seemed to me it was the same voice that had whispered so many things to me the night before. And yet, I didn't spot any change in any of them that could make me certain. All of them were warbling, laughing. Who was it, then? Which of them? Had I dreamt the whole thing? At that point, I could indeed have believed it was a dream, had it not been for the deep exhaustion that persisted, wrapped around my entire body like unexpressed agony.

Seeing the state I was in, one of them said, didn't you sleep well last night?

Another one said, that's right, you look so haggard.

I looked around quickly as though struck by lightning. This was my chance! If one of them turned pale or reddened a little—if someone looked away or laughed uneasily, nothing would be left to the imagination. But all of them were smiling the same way from the corners of their lips—it was impossible to single out any of them. It seemed to me all of them had found out my secret and were having a little fun collectively at my expense. But what sort of joke was this? Was I a plaything for them—a doll? Every glance that each of them threw, every word they said, every gesture of theirs made my suspicion go from strong to stronger. It felt unbearably warm inside the room. I dashed out into the garden rudely, without excusing myself, so that I could spend some time in fresh air.

I have no wish to recall how the time passed till the afternoon. Even Raskolnikov's agony was probably not so intolerable, despite his being a murderer. No matter where I went, I felt myself impaled on a bed of thorns. I couldn't converse with anyone—whoever came near me appeared to be the one.

My suspicions about each of them grew stronger. I couldn't confine myself to my room either. From the carpet on the floor to the plaster on the walls, everything laughed at me mockingly—and yet I had to keep myself away from everyone's eyes. I wandered around on the streets of Calcutta all day on the pretext of having things to do.

But from the afternoon onwards, a new doubt began to grow. Would she visit me tonight too? Everything within me that was decent and cultured said in unison, no she won't come again. Ah, what a relief. My injured pride said, thank heavens, I'll be spared the humiliation. But my forefathers' blood told in a state of agitation, no, she will come, she will certainly come. Go back, go home.

In my head I protested faintly, no, I shan't. Do you believe in the existence of the soul, Neelima? Do you think it was possible that Jane Eyre heard the desperate call of her lover across the great distance separating them? Now of course I do not believe it—but back then, I did feel all the barriers of brick and cement turning transparent, and through them I could see someone beckoning to me, a faint but beguiling invitation rose above the hubbub on the street to drift to my ears— even now my heart trembles on recollecting how extraordinary, how enormous, how momentous it was. I ran back before daylight was snuffed out, I raced back to my room, I could not ignore the enticement, Neelima.

My voice choked all of a sudden. I didn't dare look at Neelima, I kept my face averted deliberately. The wind blew directly at us, my hair flying into my eyes across my forehead—Neelima's sari was probably fluttering too, I couldn't see it, but I could tell. She sat stock still with her arms on the handles of her chair—I caught sight of half of the aekadashi moon in the sky, like the golden horn of the divine Kaamdhenu. In the dining saloon, the white men and women were having their dinner—the sound of wine bottles being opened, soda bottles breaking, the clinking of forks and knives, snatches of conversation—all of these floated in, and I listened.

Neelima loved eating dinner on a steamer—should I ask her? I wish I knew. I had already hurt her enough, now should I go all the way and demean her too? But wasn't it just today that I told her before the sun went down, I have never loved anyone the way I love you, Neelima.

Somewhere in the distance on the horizon a light came on. Another. And one more. Five-nine-thirteen—I couldn't count them any more. What were all these lights? Had the mythical snake Basuki risen from the depths and turned on the million gems in his hood? No, these seemed to be the lights of the Goalanda steamer jetty. The steamer was slowing down—we were almost there. There was no time.

Abruptly, I said in something of a frenzy, since you've listened to the story so far, Neelima, will you be kind enough to listen to the rest? I beg this favour of you, Neelima. I will go mad if I cannot tell you the rest.

Tell me.

I was startled. An utterly unfamiliar voice. Was it Neelima's?

I had expected to stay awake all night. It wasn't usually easy to go to sleep in this state of mind. But whether it was because of extreme mental agitation or the physical exhaustion of having wandered around on foot all day, my body collapsed in sleep soon afterwards—I sank into slumber like a newborn child. And then—once again I woke up slowly—once again I saw nature stilled in anticipation, without a sign of movement—once again the curtain at the door parted—the air in the room swooned at the fragrance—the moonlight went out—again the madness of the pleasure of that touch on every molecule of my body—the seductive rapture—the same wearing down of lips by lips—the same friction between chest and breasts—and then the cooling exhaustion—the furtive love murmurs—and then waking up in an empty bed at dawn to exchange glances with the morning light.

And again the indomitable desperation to know the identity of the secret visitor of the night tore me apart till the afternoon—and then, as soon as the sun declined, the same heartless craving, the inviolable invitation, the unconquerable attraction. Day after day passed this way—night after night. My appearance changed so much in the course of these incidents that I was startled at my appearance in the mirror. The comeliness, the grace, the gentleness had all dried up and dropped off, and my normally serene eyes glittered incessantly like a beast maddened by a grotesque appetite. I tremble now to think of that look in my eyes.

Gradually, I went into a state where my entire being was trapped within that short period of the night—only during those brief moments did I live, at all other times, I had no awareness of my own existence. In those hours, no thoughts of what anyone was thinking or saying about me came anywhere near my mind—it was as though I was made to sleep all day long. Every notion in my head, all the fervour in my heart, my entire physical limits were motionless in anticipation of the desired moment—as though they were bound within its folds till eternity—that moment alone held the image of the entire universe. Outside it, time did not exist, the world did not exist, the sky did not exist, the air did not exist, life did not exist, death did not exist, joys and sorrows did not exist, even emptiness did not exist. The vestiges of the eagerness to unravel the enigma of the mystery woman that had been flickering in my head in the form of a mildly independent thought, a faint sign of existence, vanished as well—the curiosity did not survive. Today I firmly believe that I must have gone mad. If this wasn't insanity, what was?

I do not remember how long this frenetic sport went on, but I will tell you how it suddenly ceased forever one day. That night I stumbled on the doorstep as I was entering my room and feel flat on my face—my entire body was wracked with pain, a captivating darkness closed in around me. Fatigue, Neelima, impossible fatigue. I didn't even have the strength to climb into bed. I lay my head on the carpet and fell asleep right there. I did not wake up that night.

* * *

When I went back home to my family, I was told that I had bled from my head all over the carpet that night. I was unconscious for two full days—so weak that the doctors had feared my heart might stop functioning any moment. Apparently extreme physical weakness was partly responsible for my falling unconscious to the floor. In addition to this, mental agitation and shattered nerves had debilitated me so much that I came perilously close to fracturing several bones.

I recovered slowly. When my mental state returned to a normal one, I tried in a thousand ways to learn the identity of the stranger woman, but all my stratagems, all my tricks were in vain. I could make no headway. I still haven't.

And then—the steamer blew its horn monstrously. I couldn't speak any more.

We had arrived at Goalanda. Our steamer advanced slowly through a narrow channel, making sure to protect itself. A gigantic flat appeared in front, the anchor was dropped with a deafening grinding, metallic sound, steam emerged in clouds—the vessel seemed to be exhaling in relief after covering a long distance, lurching slightly and making us lurch too. The gangway was lowered loudly, the seamen rushed about, the porters, a collective epitome of foolhardiness, ran up the uncertain steps to fight for the right to carry the luggage of first-class passengers, the third-class travellers waited with their suitcases—we had to get off too. The moonlight could not break through the line of innumerable steamers. The black water of the river seemed aflame in the gas light—the leonine roar of the train could be heard from the land—oh—what a racket all around.

Finally, I rose from my chair. Summoning two porters, I loaded the luggage on their heads and sent them on ahead. Going closer to Neelima, I told her, there's a train in fifteen minutes, we'll arrive early in the morning if we can catch it. It's Wednesday tomorrow, everything has been fixed for Sunday. We have three days in between. Will you still say what you had said when we left?

Neelima's lips quivered, but I couldn't hear what she said. At that precise moment, the steamer horn went off impossibly loudly. The chimney cast a shadow on Neelima's face.

I took her hand to lead her away from the darkness.

One Red Rose

First he took off his coat, then his tie and shirt, then the socks and trousers. With his back to the mirror he quickly put the dhoti on—whenever he was in a hurry it took him longer—sometimes too short, sometimes too tight, it could take him six or seven minutes at times, bringing perspiration, bringing tears—but although he was afraid of just such a thing happening, how amazing, nothing like that happened, the dhoti gave him no trouble at all, didn't disobey him even once, he put it on perfectly at the very first attempt. Good omen! Pleased, Protap went up to the washbasin to splash water on his face, his hair; wiping his hands on his handkerchief he took his silk kurta out of the attaché case, pulled it on, extracted his comb from the pocket of his abandoned coat and stood before the mirror. It wasn't as though he standing up straight would work; only after bending at the knees, just the way frogs are drawn in children's books, could he see his face reflected, for Mr Ghosh was short, and the mirror in his bathroom was fitted to his convenience. It wasn't possible to maintain such a pose very long, but despite the physical discomfort he examined his own face, seemingly carefully, in the dim light, trying to tell himself, after a thousand scans, a million scans, 'I'm not all that unpleasant to look at.' But the imaginary words stuck in his throat, despite a thousand attempts, a million attempts. Nothing had changed, just because it was his Maya boudi's birthday, and just because he had been invited to the celebrations, his appearance hadn't changed; the same protruding forehead, sunken cheeks, snub nose, pockmarked skin, and the same thin sparse dying hair. Someone seemed to have plucked his hair out in handfuls—and he was barely twenty-seven. But then what could he do about it—medicine was just quackery, you cannot hold back someone who's determined to go—quick clean baldness was the best option now. He would look respectable—quite elegant, in fact—what you might call affluent. They wouldn't keep him waiting in shops, college students might actually make room for him in trams. Some sort of hope shimmered in his heart sometimes; perhaps he'd look quite presentable if he turned bald. But his cheeks would still remain sunken, wouldn't they? And the pockmarks wouldn't ever go away, would they? Why did he have to have both? If he had had only one of them—the sunken cheeks or the pockmarks—he could still have managed somehow, with a bald head he could have appeared a gentleman, but the pockmarks, and on top of that the sunken cheeks . . . it was too much.

With a sigh, Protap straightened. Now the mirror reflected his scrawny neck, the collarbones sticking out, thin jutting shoulders, a pigeon-chest, long thin legs. Let the face remain as it was but couldn't his body be a little . . . a little more like everyone else's? 'Be careful, there's a lot of TB going round in Calcutta these days.' How often had he heard that. He would get tuberculosis any moment—that was the first thought that came to people's mind when they saw him. He himself was scared—some nights he half-died at the thought of getting tuberculosis. He had himself x-rayed not once but thrice, spending his hard-earned money—but nothing. Still—medicine, injections, vitamin, calcium, calories—regular meals, not working too hard—he had tried everything—but to no avail. He didn't gain an ounce, didn't look the slightest bit healthier. He would have to make peace with this appearance—forever, forever.

Moving away from the mirror, he proceeded to fold his coat, shirt, socks, tie and trousers one by one and put them away in the attaché case. Although the war had relaxed the dress code, making the bush-shirt the norm, Mr Ghosh never bothered with full-sleeved shirts; Protap always dressed formally, never forgot his tie, nor his socks, wore shoes with laces, although their prices were almost out of reach—as it is western clothes exposed the angularities in his appearance mercilessly, on top of that he was not foolish enough not to hide his arms or neck or feet when he had the opportunity. Considering how ugly he appeared to himself, to others he must . . . no, there was no point fooling himself, he had no hope, no hope. He had fussed over Maya boudi's birthday for nothing, paid thrice the price to have his dhoti laundered overnight, ironed his silk kurta all over again because a corner had been crushed under the lid of the suitcase, borrowed an attaché case from his uncle on the pretext of a business trip to Asansol, after both his brothers—with whom he shared his room—had gone to sleep last night, he put the dhoti, kurta and newspaper-wrapped sandals secretly in the attaché case and hid it under the bed, carried it all the way to office in the morning—in case going back home to change took too long. Pointless! Pointless! Changing into these clothes was no easy task either! After Mr Ghosh had left, he had to loiter for a while, then coax his orderly into a good mood with eight annas in order to use the bathroom for a few minutes . . . Oh! He hadn't been in here too long, had he? Kartik wouldn't start grumbling, would he?

The leather shoes couldn't be stuffed in; with the attaché case in one hand and the shoes wrapped in a newspaper in the other, Protap emerged with long strides of his sandalled feet, dressed in his dhoti and kurta. Kartik was perched on a stool outside the boss's door, and while he didn't actually stand up, he didn't assume a supercilious expression either. Approaching him, Protap put his load on the floor. 'I'm leaving these with you—look after them, will you.'

'They'll be safe,' answered Kartik, without looking at him.

But Protap wasn't reassured. What if they were lost? Or stolen? Thirty-rupee shoes. The check ash suit was only three winters old, looked like wool from a distance. On an impulse he dipped into his pocket, extracting his wallet and pulling out an eight-anna coin and handing it to Kartik after only a moment's thought, saying, 'Take care of them . . .'

Kartik rose to his feet now, saluted fleetingly and said, 'I'll put them in sir's cabinet, if you can come early tomorrow . . .'

Protap didn't wait to hear the rest. There was a wind in his sail now; a wind that bore him like a king across the huge empty hall of the office, where he occupied a corner eight hours a day to work on figures. It propelled him down the staircase—the very same stairs he climbed up and down every day, muttering invectives against his fate—blew him out to the road. Never mind the other things, he was nearly six feet tall, after all, just how many Bengalis were so tall? Mr Ghosh, with his salary of sixteen hundred rupees, only came up to his chest, he towered over everyone else walking along the road. Even the arrogant Kartik, who didn't baulk at arguing with the cashier, had been forced to offer him a salute, hadn't he!

Filling his lungs with air, he looked around. The winter afternoon had been shivering earlier, it was night already. The West-End clock blinked before him, twenty-to-six; he had to be there at six-thirty. It would take twenty minutes at most by tram to reach Maya boudi's Elgin Road flat, and besides, it was better to be a little late—make a better impression? To the trams overladen with home-bound people, he pretended that he always travelled by taxi, that he was walking on a whim. With long strides, towering over the rest, he wondered what to buy as a birthday present. He was ready to spend up to fifteen rupees, that would only leave five rupees for the rest of the month—but what was a few days' financial discomfort compared to today's happiness? Nothing, nothing at all! If it was wonderful on any given day to take a seat in the luxury of Maya boudi's drawing-room, to gaze at her moving about gracefully, to listen to Sami da's eloquence, how much more wonderful it would be on this festive evening! The very thought made happiness wrap itself around him, a soft warm opulence enveloped him like the colour of clouds; and as the colour melted, a light flared up, the most wonderful amongst all that was wonderful. Protap could see her face, her eyes, her eyes so very clearly in his mind's eye that he felt an ache in his breast. Her name was Chhaya; what a beautiful name.

At Esplanade, Protap paused. His eyes moved past Curzon Park and alighted at Chowringhee, a necklace studded with many-hued lights, the gloss was back after the war, it glittered invitingly, come along, come along, come along—Protap felt intoxicated. Walking swiftly, he reached Chowringhee in a couple of minutes. There was an incredible crowd outside Metro cinema, dazzling with a hundred lights. The three o' clock show had ended, the six o' clock show was about to begin.

It all looked incredible, incredible clothes, incredibly large cars. This was life . . . life was pleasure. What else was man alive for, if not for pleasure. A thousand cars raced along in search of pleasure, a thousand shops had laid out pleasureware. Come in. Come in, come in. Protap heard the invitation; a keen appetite for life awoke him, awoke someone else within him, that one among many, his youthfulness, his life force. He existed, he too existed, these pleasures were his too, a life as bright as a hundred bulbs lit up—that was his too.

For the first time Protap understood the meaning of being alive, the purpose of being alive. Partly from the shock of this realisation, and partly because of the jostling crowds on the pavement, his footsteps slowed; mingling with the people waiting to watch the film, he breathed in the caress of contentment, the perfume of pleasure. But the scent of happiness wasn't enough, he wanted all of it—its body, its touch, its warmth, its satisfaction. An undefined, infinite appetite for life manifested itself to him at that moment in the form of the smoky aroma rising from three restaurants, converting itself into an appetite for food so powerful it whipped his belly.

Should he enter? It was best to eat something now, or else he would end up devouring the food over there to satiate his hunger at the end of a long working day . . . Late? Why not! Maya boudi would say, a smile dangling from her lips, 'You're early, aren't you?' while someone else would have a plate ready . . .

In one prawn cutlet always lay the wish for another—but no. He would have to eat something there, after all. What if she came up to him to say, 'But you aren't eating at all.' What if she said, 'That shondesh . . .' Protap's nerves rang out like sitar strings. What a lovely voice. What lovely diction. How could everything about a person be so lovely. Had god decided to give everything to just the one person? And nothing at all to me? . . . What do you mean, nothing at all? He has given me the one whom he has given everything, hasn't he.

After a few sips of tea, leaning back in his chair and lighting a cigarette, Protap ran these words over in his mind without blushing, without feeling bashful: God has given me the woman whom he has given everything. The shyness he used to experience at the very thought of her was now like dead skin at the end of winter; for the first time he surrendered himself to his heart, the same heart whose covert explorations used to leave him afraid to dream when asleep. For the first time he was able to think of Chhaya without turning giddy with excitement. He could picture her standing, sitting, walking, laughing, talking—Maya boudi was a lot like her, but she was like no one. Perhaps she had been there since morning since it was her sister's birthday; after Sami da had left for the studio, the sisters must have had so much to talk about in the intimacy of the afternoon, so much to tell each other. The best things to talk about are the ones that stay only between two people, two people, two people . . .

Of course, during these past seven months he hadn't exchanged even seven sentences with her—but so what. She didn't even look at him properly—but what did that matter either. Who could tell she wouldn't look at him one day, who could tell when she would look at him. If such impossible things as Protap's being accommodated in the famous film director Samiran Sanyal's drawing room, addressing his wife as boudi, and being invited to her birthday celebrations, could have taken place, then why could something even more impossible not take place too? . . . Of course, had he not been fortuitously present at the right time that Sunday morning, he may not have received the invitation, but then fortune always has a role to play in life, and maybe fortune had smiled on him because it intended to smile some more. When he arrived on Sunday, Amar Mitra was leaving, and Sami da was saying: 'Don't forget about day after tomorrow, all right?' 'How can I forget Maya's birthday.' And a couple of minutes after Amar babu had left Sami da said, lighting a cigarette, 'You must come too, Protap—in the evening, all right?' He had overheard, so Sami da had invited him too—so very well-mannered of him.

Protap had never been exposed to such good manners, such immaculate behaviour. His father bellowed at home, his mother didn't even bother with her chemise in summer, his brothers kept themselves busy gossiping at the roadside shop. Sometimes it was unbearable to get back home from the Sanyals'—but no, why call it unbearable, at least he still had something else beyond his horrible home and even more horrible office. Who would have thought on that Saturday, when he had accompanied his colleague Subodh Bagchi to watch a film being shot in a Tollygunge studio, that fate held such a wonderful something else for him. It was a special occasion of some kind, several guests were present with their wives, Maya boudi was there, and so was—he uttered the name clearly in his head—Chhaya. Subodh was a relative of theirs, during the conversation he said, 'This is my friend, Maya boudi . . .' There were so many people, but even amidst all that confusion she exchanged a few sentences with him, alone. Protap was charmed by her courtesy, and beside himself with joy the day he visited them at home along with Subodh. Thanks to Subodh, he addressed Mrs Sanyal as boudi the very second day, and a couple of months later, after Subodh had gone off to Bombay with a better job, for the first time he went by himself, a little apprehensively, but, reassured by Maya boudi's behaviour, started visiting quite regularly.

Sami da was large-hearted, and Maya boudi was, after all, Maya boudi; there were frequent gatherings of people at their house in the evenings; some wrote, some painted, some were brilliant with the camera—so many talents! A few film actors visited, too, at times, though actresses never did—but then Protap had no fascination for actresses. Was there an actress who could . . . who could be compared to her, imagine comparing a film star to a real star.

He didn't visit very frequently, sometimes once a week, sometimes twice. Lest . . . anyone was annoyed. In that crowd of such gifted people, he was . . . definitely a bit of a misfit. He never spoke, only listened, observed; when people burst out in laughter at something, he didn't laugh loudly, only smiled behind the cover of his palm, his face turned away. Was he even worthy of laughing with them as an equal! Those expert writers painters photographers didn't even consider him worthy of their attention, why should they, still, it did hurt him a little initially, he had even bought a copy of Rabindranath's *Sanchayita* after receiving his salary, even buckled down to writing some poetry—he had almost managed to finish a poem, eleven or twelve lines along the lines of 'O distant sky / pray tell me why / you look at me / so bewitchingly'—but then Ghentu woke up suddenly, growling like a beast, 'Switch off the light.' He had made another attempt the following night, but Bhentu reared his hood that night. No, it was impossible to write poetry with a couple of wild cats for company. He hadn't tried any more, stoically accepting his own insignificance, he had been at peace.

As he drained his tea, he felt like laughing at the thought of those attempts to write poetry. How childish he had been just the other day, even yesterday, even a short while ago! But something had happened suddenly, all the doors had opened, gifts lay stacked behind every one of them, for him too, for him alone . . . He had tried to write poetry to be worthy. But was Maya boudi a poet? Or a painter? It was true she was beautiful, talented too, but among the visitors were many women whose beauty was prouder, whose talents were louder. But was any of them like her? It wasn't her beauty or her talent, it was her niceness that made everyone like her so much, wasn't it? She always found the time to talk to him, touching on those very subjects that he was comfortable talking about. If, once in a blue moon, he managed to spend five minutes with her alone, it was like a spell of refreshing rain. She was so very nice—that was her greatest qualification. And—he almost said it aloud as he rose from his chair—it's my qualification too; I'm nice as well. He was shaken from head to foot by a giant wave of niceness, at the head of Corporation Street, suddenly, amidst that December crowd on Chowringhee.

With Christmas approaching, New Market were simply bursting with people. English, Bengali, Parsi, African, Chinese—the shops as well as the shopkeepers were finding it difficult to cope. Very well—Protap strode ahead, thrusting out his reedy, hollow chest—he would buy too. But what? Entering through the gate halfway down Bertram Street, he sought the answer with his eyes, with his heart, while maintaining the spare determined gait of someone headed towards a specific shop with a specific intent. Going past the Christmas cards, the petticoats and chemises, the woollen clothes, the pink and purple conical lingerie, he arrived at the hub of the market with the weighing machine situated in the centre, and turned right; arrayed before him were silverware, silks, precious stones of different hues, ivory dolls, scarlet shellac tables. He suppressed the desire in his eyes—he couldn't afford any of this, but he didn't have any idea what he could afford, either; he walked towards the Lindsay Street end of the market—and instantly he was riveted by rows of flowers to his left. Yes, flowers. He paused, then turned towards the nearest flower shop, where a group of English girls were gathered—how they chattered! Protap waited a little absent-mindedly behind them, with his six-feet-tall glory . . . Roses, red roses. As red as the fresh flow of blood when you cut your finger. And also the darker hue that it acquired afterwards. Each one as large as an electric bulb, the light shining from the folds in the petals, the wick was green, it lit up the illuminated market, the city, the winter night in Calcutta.

They were discussing flowers one day, Protap remembered. Sami da voted for the magnolia. Ananga Nag—a painter—said with a laugh, 'Too fleshy. It's almost like it wanted to be a fruit and became a flower by mistake at the last moment.' 'The essence of the flower is the jasmine,' said writer Amar Mitra, 'all of Bengal lies within.' 'Maybe,' commented Maya boudi, 'but it dies at the slightest touch, while a fistful of bokul remains fragrant for a month.' 'I see,' responded the writer, 'even when it comes to flowers you prefer the hardy, the durable.' Everyone laughed at this, and when they stopped, Chhaya said softly, 'But I like roses the best.' . . . With his ears, Protap saw her words were a warm red; with his eyes he heard the song of the rose.

Yes, a bunch of roses—ten, fifteen, twenty—as many as he could afford.

The English girls bought nothing at all, and though they had seemed young from the back, their faces were aged. Both these factors heightened Protap's enthusiasm. Approaching, he asked, 'How much are those—the large ones?' pointing at a magnificent bunch of roses.

'Twenty-five rupees.'

'Twenty-five for a single bunch of flowers!' Protap frowned like a veteran.

'Not the bunch—each.'

'Each!' It sounded like a cry of despair.

'Twenty-five rupees for each flower.' The shopkeeper's announcement was heartlessly cold.

Protap was shattered. During the war years prices had risen to absurd levels: forty-eight rupees for a cotton kurta, twelve rupees for a tin of gold flakes, two-hundred-and-fifty rupees for a tea-set—but still, twenty-five rupees for a single flower! A flower! Just one! Twenty-five! He had once seen a puppy frolicking on the street when it was suddenly hit by a car—how it had squealed! But he was a human being, he could hardly whimper.

A couple came into the shop. They weren't English, they didn't seem Bengali either, but you never could tell these days. The woman with short curly hair, dressed in navy-blue slacks and a red jumper, took ten roses, and the man pulled out two hundred-rupee notes in the twinkling of an eye, then they walked out without looking at each other.

'If it's two hundred for ten it should be twenty each,' Protap blurted out the words without looking at the shopkeeper.

'Twenty-five if you take just one,' came the answer.

'Twenty?'

'No.'

After a few deep breaths, Protap said, 'Can't you let me have it . . . I have just twenty . . . I really need it . . .'

Finally the shopkeeper looked at him. 'How many do you want?' he asked after a pause.

'Just the one . . .' sensing a ray of kindness in the shopkeeper's eyes, he added quickly, 'a large one—yes, that one please.'

He went out into the road quickly, holding the blood-red rose wrapped in tissue paper. The tower clock of New Market rang a quarter to seven! He was late, very late. By the time he would reach the room would be full; the tea would be half-over. Cracker-bursts of conversation, rocket-trails of laughter would leave no room to draw one's breath; Ananga Nath, Amar Mitra, the actor Suresh Banerjee, the cameraman Naren Chanda, Indu Das—something or the other, but Protap had not yet succeeded in making out what—and Lotika Debi, Sunanda Debi, Anuradha Debi—all the ladies were debis, goddesses—in Sami da's drawing room. Who else? Many more people. Amidst this dazzling, glittering gathering, he would appear suddenly, lanky, reedy, gauche; holding a single rose after all the expensive, carefully chosen gifts—no one would look at him, or everyone would look at him, he would stamp on a lady's feet as he tried to sit down, the smoke from the strong tobacco in Naren Chanda's pipe would make him cough, he wouldn't say a word, but still he would remain, he would have to, for he didn't even know how to take his leave all by himself, before everyone else.

Protap trembled as he walked towards the tram tracks. His shawl was seven years old, faded, with holes in it—but still he wished he had it with him. Who would notice him, after all? But what if they did? Although no one noticed him ever, maybe the holes in his shawl . . . But so what? How could he conceal his poverty? How could he conceal his ugliness? The hope, the joy, the wave of pleasure that had driven him mad just a few minutes ago now left him like a receding fever. Breaking his tooth of arrogance with a couple of resounding slaps, a cold north wind lodged in his brain the truth that he was Protap, the very same Protap, whose salary, including dearness allowance, was a hundred-and-ten rupees, whose cheeks were sunken and skin was pockmarked, too, who never caught anyone's eye despite being nearly six feet tall, who looked like a TB patient when someone did notice him. He hadn't become a different individual just by virtue of addressing Samiran Sanyal's wife as boudi; he hadn't been reborn because he had been invited coincidentally, for form's sake only . . . no, no, no . . .

Noooh . . . screeched the tram as it came to a halt. He found a place to stand directly beneath the electric fan, if he stood upright, he would knock his head against it, but he had to save the rose too—luckily there were straps to hold on to, at least. That he was so tall was also a joke that destiny had played on him; without any other kind of development, he had suddenly shot up abnormally. Half his legs stuck out of his dhoti when he was dressed in one—and the less said about the legs the better! He would have preferred to have been short, he wouldn't have looked like a reptile, he would have fitted into his surroundings too, would have felt a sense of comfort at being able to blend into the crowd.

The closer the tram got to his destination, the more his interest in arriving fell. He needn't have become so impatient about getting to this birthday celebration on time: he could have gone home, had the bread and tea set out for him, changed into these clothes and arrived at a leisurely pace. He would have bought a powder-case, or a bottle of perfume, or a book of poems, for three or four rupees at the neighbourhood shop . . . The sheer arrogance of competing with the others had made him carry a sack of clothes to the office. For a rupee he had purchased half a salute, for twenty rupees, a rose. He had spent twelve annas on food, now all he had left in his pocket were a few annas; tomorrow he would have to find a way to borrow five rupees. How stupid, what colossal stupidity . . . shame! Coming to terms with the extent of his own foolishness, he felt like leaping out of the tram.

He needn't have accepted the invitation. That is what he should have done. First, he hadn't really been invited, Sami da had included him for form's sake because he happened to be present. Secondly, irrespective of what it was like on other days, today he was definitely a misfit in that gathering, like a mangy jackal in an assembly of majestic creatures like the tiger, the leopard and the peacock. And thirdly, was he affluent enough to spend even two rupees on anyone, leave alone twenty? His father claimed seventy rupees from his salary, and he himself barely survived on the remaining forty; no lunch towards the end of the month, so many good films skipped, having to agonise for six months whether to get a couple of new kurtas made or not. Really, why hadn't he wriggled out on the spot on some pretext or the other? But as if he was capable of saying as much to Sami da, to Maya boudi! If only he was, he would have been a real man. And suppose he had actually said that, how then would he have been able to turn mental somersaults in sheer elation?

The tram went past Theatre Road. Theatre Road, Circular Road, Elgin Road. He would have to get off in another five minutes. It took him a minute's effort to twist his body away from his position under the fan, he stood near the door gripping the handle, gauging with his eyes the right tactic for breaking through the cordon. Careful, he mustn't let go of the flower. But what if he did. What if he didn't even go, why not just go directly home instead. Having been petrified with anxiety all this while, he suddenly felt reassured at the thought that he could still not go if he didn't really want to. He had been foolish enough already, if he didn't go he would at least be spared this final act of foolishness. Nobody was waiting for him over there. The joys of the evening wouldn't be reduced an iota by his absence. No one would even think of him. Then why bother? Nobody but he knew of the foolish things he'd done, why perform the most foolish act of all before a roomful of people?

He looked tragically at the rose he was holding upright against his chest. A red glow emanated through the flimsy white paper it was wrapped in; the fragrance assaulted his senses, his breath caught in his throat for a moment. Two or three people nearby, noticed Protap, were glancing covertly at the rose, trying to take in its scent as long as it was still there . . . So the flower was nice, after all? But how much nicer, how much more impressive the flowers arrayed in Maya boudi's room would be, and by their side would lie this flower, just a solitary flower, just one. Wouldn't Naren Chanda sneer, wouldn't Ananga Nag blow smoke rings at the ceiling, his eyes slanted?

'Are you getting off?'

'Get off now—or let us get off!'

How uncouth Calcuttans had become. Pushed and shoved, he was forced to get off the tram. He stopped a couple of times as he crossed the road—he hated this crossroads—then tiptoed on to Elgin Road, taking the pavement on the left. One, two, three, four . . . he could hear his footsteps with his heart.

So he was going after all. Couldn't stay away.

The ground floor . . . the first floor . . . as soon as he turned into the final flight of stairs leading to the second floor, he saw the brown door—shut—but even where he was, he could hear the sounds inside. Waves of laughter greeted him as he approached. He paused for a while outside, breathed deeply, but his courage failed him at the last moment though a faint wish remained; dropping the tissue-paper-wrapped flower on the floor, he pushed the door open slowly and entered.

It turned out exactly as he had thought it would. 'Come, Protap,' said Maya boudi, handing him a plateful of food. He had to take a seat next to a rather fat man—not exactly beside him, but behind him— he'd never seen the gentleman before, he discovered he was Maya boudi's maternal uncle, had an important job in Delhi—every time he laughed, Protap had to retreat a little, he kept backing till he came up against the wall, still the uncle kept guffawing and moving backward himself, and the edge of his neatly folded shawl kept tickling Protap's nostrils. The source of all this laughter was Suresh Banerjee, who was imitating the idiosyncrasies of veteran stage actors; during a pause Sami da said, 'Say what you will, there hasn't been another one like them. The way Sisir Bhaduri would call out to Sita . . .' 'Tapankiran could have, if he hadn't died,' said Ananga Nag. 'You're right,' Anuradha Debi exclaimed in a bird-like voice, 'How suddenly he died, and so young too!' 'Twenty-six.' 'Oh no,' protested Amar Mitra, 'twenty-nine.' They argued over this for a while, before settling on twenty-eight. The cameraman was the silent type, but he spoke now, 'I saw him just the other day . . .' he clucked in regret, 'and yesterday I met his elder brother. They're so similar in appearance—if it hadn't been a Calcutta road and the middle of the day, I'd definitely have thought it was Tapankiran's ghost.' 'Don't ghosts appear on Calcutta's roads in the middle of the day?' asked Indu Das. 'Let me tell you a story . . .' 'No, please,' Sunanda Debi raised her hands and twittered, 'spare us, Indu babu, don't tell us a ghost story, please!' Encouraged, Indu Das began his ghost story with great gusto, but seeing that he was losing the audience's attention, he shifted the focus to research, to the difference between banshees and ghouls, to the hierarchy between vampires and zombies, to the question of whether only humans became ghosts or animals too. 'Are you aware of this strange incident?' Uncle said suddenly. 'In 1926, a horse named Aurora won the Viceroy's Cup.' He stopped, whereupon two or three people asked in unison, 'What's strange about that?' 'Aurora had died that morning.' . . . Now the conversation turned to horse racing, Lotika Debi joined in, Sunanda Debi too, but Sunanda Debi's husband—the writer Amar Mitra—trumped everyone here. The clock rang nine, nine-thirty, it was nearly ten. When everyone suddenly fell silent together, 'We should go,' suggested Naren Chanda. 'Yes, time to go . . .' There was a shimmering movement, a rustling of saris. Finally everyone got to their feet at the same time, Protap was grateful for the chance to straighten his crumpled body after such a long time.

He would have left much earlier if he could have, but it was a foregone conclusion that he wouldn't be able to. He passed the entire time in a sort of daze, had no idea what he ate, barely heard half the exchanges around him, raising his cup of tea to his lips, discovered it had turned cold with a film on the surface. His eyes roamed around the room now and then; Maya boudi was seated in the middle of the large sofa, flanked by Lotika Debi and Anuradha Debi—a smiling figure every day, today she was a veritable goddess of happiness—and, a little in the distance, in a small chair near the window at the corner of two walls, sat she, Chhaya, dressed in a light green sari; alone despite the people around her. She was listening to everything, even talking sometimes, but still her attention was somewhere else—where?—on the painting on the wall, or was it on the sky outside the window? Protap hadn't glanced at her too often, lest their eyes meet, lest the idea take root within him, even by mistake, that Chhaya had looked at him during a distracted moment. Truth to tell, he hadn't even been able to look at Chhaya properly even once, he had only fixed his eyes on the dark green border of her light green sari. When she got to her feet at the same time as everyone else, Protap sensed a breeze rustling gently through a leafy tree.

Everyone advanced towards the door, still talking. Sunanda Debi went out, tripped on her high heel. Ananga Nath put out his hand quickly to steady her.

'What is it?'

'I tripped on something.'

'What, let me take a look . . .' Samiran Sanyal stooped, picking up the reason for his lady-friend's losing her footing. 'Oh! A rose! Still wrapped in paper!' He unwrapped it carefully, the blood-red rose, fully bloomed, unveiled itself with a smile, as large as Samiran's fist, looked on smiling, cast a fragrant spell on everyone, then suddenly seemed to tremble under the gaze of so many people and shed one, two, three petals trampled on by a shoe.

'Oh dear, you stamped on a flower,' the writer chided his wife laughingly.

'How would I know . . .'

'Never mind,' Ananga Nath rescued his lady-friend quickly. 'In ancient days some flowers actually didn't bloom until beautiful women had kicked them to life, the modern rose doesn't seem at all dejected, looks happy, on the contrary.'

'So beautiful,' said Maya Debi.

'How sweet it smells.' Lotika Debi took a deep breath.

'It's an expensive rose,' Suresh Banerjee narrowed his eyes like a connoisseur. 'Not less than twenty-five rupees.'

'Really!' The cameraman was stunned.

'Of course. Can anyone even afford roses these days!'

The price tag raised the value of the rose for everyone. How did it turn up here? Had someone left it by mistake? Or had they left it deliberately? It wasn't one of you, was it? How strange, why should it be us— and if we had, we'd have given it to you, wouldn't we. It would have been an honour to present you with a flower such as this on a day such as this!

'I'm sure an admirer of yours has left it for you, Maya,' commented her uncle. 'A silent tribute from one of the uninvited.'

'For Maya? Or for our Chhaya?' Ananga smiled with his eyes at Chhaya.

'Yes, that's right! It's for Chhaya, of course,' a wave of laughter ran through the women.

'Then give it to me . . .' Chhaya came forward at once, taking the flower from her brother-in-law, placed it in her hair with a flash of her right hand. Dark hair turned to light.

Although he was standing behind everyone else, Protap heard everything over their heads, saw everything. Chhaya stood to one side, the breeze rustled again through a leafy tree, a flower had just bloomed on it, a red flower, a red rose lit up the world, a red rose turned to light, dark hair turned to light, darkness turned to light, all the darkness of the day, of life, of a thousand lives, turned to light in an instant, in one red rose.

. . . Down on the road, discussions began on how to distribute the guests between the three cars, but Protap had already disappeared unobtrusively, he was walking along the deserted pavement by himself, tall, trembling. But not in the cold, not in the cold wind, he was trembling in the breeze rustling through a leafy tree, on which a flower had just bloomed, a red flower, his flower, his blood-red rose, his blood-red heart.

And How Are You?

Sometimes I want to know how you are.

When I go to sleep, when I wake up, when I drive at ninety miles an hour, when the weight of time suddenly drops after a few quick vodkas and brandies.

Dawn breaks, night falls; dawn again, night again. The same way, day after day. Sometimes it feels as though something will happen. Nothing does. Day after day.

Believe it or not, I look at myself in the mirror at times. When I shave? No, I think of other things then. But sometimes, alone in the room, after a bath, or before going to bed eventually, I stand face-to-face with myself, eyeball-to-eyeball. Just me, without adornment; a lump of flesh, flab and filth. Completely bald, blunt nose, bags under the eyes, a broad hairy chest, the spitting image of a powerful, aged baboon after removing the glittering false teeth. I enjoy taking off my dentures and making faces, balling up my fists—like two wild beasts poised for battle—when

I open my mouth wide the darkness seems to be the road to hell.

How? I don't even know where you are.

Come, let me introduce the rest of you—this aged baboon you see is Abanish Ghoshal, with engineering degrees from Glasgow and Berlin, learnt the ropes at Ford's factory in Detroit, now engaged in making steel at Pippalgarh. His monthly income is five thousand rupees, more or less, he has been around the entire world thrice at his company's expense, he has to visit Japan or Germany or Sweden or Russia or America once a year. In other words, this aged baboon is a very important person.

But actually I am someone else.

Alas, there's so much ugliness that the tailor can hide, so much pus that formidable degrees can conceal blandly. Fame, honour, riches, influence—all of it may have been achieved, but after that? What lies behind, covered, within?

Was there really a ritual in Athens where young women would emerge naked after bathing in the sea for the ancients to select the most beautiful among them that year? But how else can beauty be judged? All we consider are the adornments. Degrees, learning, 'qualifications'. Everyone wants to know what I can do, no one knows what I am.

You know. Do you?

The population of Pippalgarh is fifty thousand, everyone's livelihood is this steel factory, their lives too, in fact. We are building the new India; creating wealth for the people, earning foreign exchange for the country, with four hundred million by our side, we are marching ahead, marching ahead. Can we ever say that the people involved in such a gigantic endeavour are not successful?

But I remember you from time to time.

Pippalgarh has a reputation around the country of being progressive. We have delivered radios to the homes of the workers; we have swept out cholera and small pox; our huge cooperative store is a veritable showpiece. We have a school, a library, clubs at different levels and of different kinds, doctors, nurses, a free hospital, even a contraception clinic adjacent to the maternity home. Everyone here is happy; they work with healthy bodies, with resolve in their minds and with hope in their hearts: work goes on round the clock, smoothly; our productivity is the highest in India. We affirm life here.

Do you remember that morning—those dewdrops on the grass, and the soft, tender, pink sunshine?

There are hills in the distance here, a sea of earth lies grey beyond the town. There is only emptiness in the vast expanse stretching to the horizon, nothing but emptiness either in the enormous sky above. Nothing at all happens—the sun rises, the sun sets, nothing happens at all.

Everyone says Mr Ghoshal works like a demon. They don't lie; I feel no fatigue when it comes to work, I do not have the ability to rest. My routine stretches from eight to eight; I fell the day with a single blow. Yet the victory does not seem to be complete; sometimes I go back late at night—where the huge fires burn furiously, I walk around supervising things, when I come out I find the darkness thinning. There's no need, of course, there are people specifically for this task—but this is what I enjoy. I like to think that something is happening—this pit of fire, this fierce sound, the mechanical movements of the factory workers—all of these help me forget that I am actually someone else. And I can be seen at almost each of the innumerable parties that are thrown here in Pippalgarh—I always make an appearance, even if only for ten minutes—and if ever I feel like 'letting myself go' I can put away one-and-a-half bottles of Scotch and still continue with my measured smiles, my conversation, my flirtations with the women, without breaking my stride. I am on cordial terms with everyone, but none of them means anything to me. That's the way I like it.

Like it? That's incorrect. There's no question of liking or disliking anything. I work—since I have nothing else. I go to parties—since I have nothing else. Nothing else. I do not have the one thing that would have meant having everything. So I have nothing.

But is it even possible that I am the only one who has come to know this, but no one else has? Is it even possible that I am the only one among this fifty thousand who wonders how you are?

Everyone is happy at Pippalgarh, but the happiest are the women—meaning, the wives of those 'sahibs' who earn more than two thousand rupees a month.

There's a separate club for them—meaning, the 'memsahibs'. There they can attempt self-improvement without the company of men: swimming, sports, hair-dressing, manicure—nothing's missing from the arrangements. Coffee party at ten-thirty, gimlets around one, back home for lunch, a nap in an air-conditioned room, tea after the nap, after the evening cocktail—if there's nothing else to do—dinner at the Cosmopolitan Club, and perhaps an hour of dancing after dinner . . . at least three days a week can easily be passed this way. They're safe for the other four days too: there are different kinds of invitations and events to attend, adorning their bodies, adorning their homes, the responsibility of being graceful hostesses at their own parties, the responsibility of being eye-catching embellishments in this land of coarse soil and steel. Their children? They spend their infancy in their nurses' laps, public school as soon as they turn five, missionary schools—in Darjeeling, in Dehradun, in Ernakulam. The mothers have no time—their lives are busy, happy, fulfilled.

Ah time, cruel time, how ferocious the battle between you and man! Escaping you, avoiding you, defeating you is his objective, his only objective, his only concern. He continuously creates so many unusual, extraordinary, extreme ways to do it, but still no one wins in the final round. Year month week day hour minute; morning noon afternoon evening night morning. And again the dawn, and again the night. Endless. Such torment!

Beasts don't worry about all this. Nor do the gods. What if there really is a God somewhere? Is it entirely impossible?

Don't look at me doubtfully; I have not forgotten I am a very important person, an aged baboon, a beastly lump of flab, flesh and filth.

But actually I am someone else.

You were in the garden that morning. The dew, the grass, the soft tender pink sunlight, the fresh green tender scent in the air. You were brimming over at sixteen, slim, fair—the Goddess Saraswati to my adolescent mind. Your blouse was a deep red, wrapped in a white sari with a red border; you were like light, you were light, you lit up the world.

How did it turn out that I don't know where you are now?

My wife's style is different, she has become a social worker. Adult education among the workers, teaching hygiene to their wives, there are no such things as ghosts and the milk of cows is more beneficial than liquor—imparting such wisdom, along with her disciples, is what she spends her day on. Not just that, she also runs two or three—what's the right word?— cultural societies for those housewives whose husbands earn only between five hundred and fifteen hundred a month. The membership of the women's society in Pippalgarh numbers five thousand, it has its own office, built at company expense; its calendar is packed with the events it organises; playback-singing stars, award-winning writers, fiery orators are invited to its annual festivals; the subjects of the monthly lectures it organises range from the Upanishads to Sputnik. The director of all these activities is my wife—Milu—Urmila. Everyone says it is a worthy match; they are not wrong. Milu has the same capacity for work that I do, she is as indefatigable as I am; but if someone were to force the issue, at least I have the excuse of needing an income, but hers is pure unpaid labour. Noble Milu.

But does Milu know who her enemy is?

Milu is not callous about anything; she writes two letters a week to our son in Chicago, who is a doctor, spends a few days every year with our daughter and son-in-law in Rome, and she does go to all the parties with me. She has to; it is the rule in Pippalgarh for high-valued 'sahibs' to appear at parties as a couple. This gives me an opportunity to meet Milu sometimes. We meet, but we don't talk much—what is there to talk about? And things have come to a point where we are either dining at someone else's house or entertaining guests at our own almost every evening; if we have to unexpectedly dine together at home by ourselves, both of us try our utmost to suppress our unease. No, I don't see much of Milu any more. It is we who are Pippalgarh's 'ideal couple', both of us have been profusely honoured.

Alas, our achievements conceal so many failures; people's respect is a shroud for such ruthless emptiness.

On my way to and from parties, when I drive with Milu by my side, sometimes I think of you.

And how are you?

When did I see you last? Was it forty years ago? Ten? Three or four? Yesterday? I don't quite remember. After visiting so many different countries over and over again, I am confused by places, I am confused by time. Was it in Manila or in Capri that I had seen the sunset from the balcony of the bungalow on the hilltop? Where was that inn with the blazing log fire, the sparse, old-fashioned furniture, the plain but delicious food, the pleasant wine, and the snowy night outside, the exhaled frost in the forest? Was it in Tyrol? In Denmark? Or in Big Sur? And that other time when I saw you when travelling by car—was it on the road to Ootacamund from Mysore, or in Canada, or in Scotland? It must have been some such place—or perhaps somewhere else altogether. I was in a car, there was another one alongside. It was a bright day, there were tall trees on either side, the play of light and shade on the road. A blue Italian Fiat, with you in it. A handsome young man next to you, his luxurious moustache made him look like an airline pilot, or perhaps a famous sportsman. You were brimming over at sixteen, the red blouse was like light on your body, you lit up the day. I looked at you for a long time, then the blue Fiat took a turn into another road.

Just look at the mistakes I make. Can you possibly be sixteen still? By now you must be . . . wait . . . let me calculate . . .

But is it even possible that you too have grown old? You too, who is charm herself?

Milu had been sitting next to me that day. When I could no longer see you I looked at her. A sudden suspicion sprang up in my mind. Milu was not you, was she? Or was it possible that Milu—Urmila—the famous Mrs Ghoshal of Pippalgarh—was in fact you?

Possible?

Sometimes my mind cries out for rest. No work to be done—nothing—I'm sitting on a cane chair in a verandah somewhere, the blue sea before me. The blue green indigo turbulent water, wave after wave, white birds, white sunshine, the hazy distance. I'm in a cane chair, gazing at all this. Holiday, rest; forgetting all the things that make up life. Why don't I? Let me tell all of you the truth, do not laugh, do not look at me suspiciously. How lengthy the day will be when it holds no work to be done. How enormous the weight of that lightness that holds nothing but holidays. Will I be able to bear it? I don't know, I am afraid. We are allowed a month's leave every year; I don't take it. I could take continuous leave for a year-and-a-half right now if I wanted to; I don't. I am afraid.

My health? Don't worry about it. In our hospital in Pippalgarh we have doctors with degrees from Vienna, modern equipment; everything except the soul is examined there at regular intervals; we're eating, or not eating, scientifically; walking, exercising, or giving up exercising; 'feeling poorly' is a term unfamiliar to us. Besides, remember, Milu and I make the ideal couple; although we do not meet very frequently we look after each other flawlessly, although we converse very little we never quarrel. We are beyond annoyances like unhappiness, surliness, differences of opinion, arguments. I remind Milu that she should visit the dentist; in her desire to save me from death Milu encourages me to give up smoking. Apart from such things, each of us is in our own world, engrossed in our own work. We are not dependent on each other, life goes on the same way even without each other; but we are mercilessly imprisoned by the announcement that we are husband and wife. This is the ideal arrangement in Pippalgarh for the 'sahibs'.

I like the discipline of Pippalgarh, its conflict-less class differences, and its unwritten laws which dispel worries. The people here are divided into three classes: 'workers', 'officers' and 'sahibs'. The workers drink hooch, the sahibs, Scotch, and the officers down their deconstipating potions and go to sleep with their wives. The workers are allowed to get drunk at times, there's no objection to their raising a ruckus and getting into fights; but the 'sahibs' are forbidden from losing their poise. The officers are permitted to be devoted to their wives and children (they're 'domesticated creatures', after all); but the 'sahibs' offspring must be either invisible or non-existent, and what their conjugal life must have is not intimacy but faithfulness beyond doubt. They shall make their appearances, as far as possible, as a couple—even if they're merely taking a stroll in front of their house it is unseemly to abandon each other. But if it ever comes out that they enjoy each other's company, that is completely unworthy of approval. If there is attraction, forming an attachment is very easy; but what is expected of the 'sahibs' is that they will adhere to the rules, beyond likes and dislikes, in other words. That does not mean they have to be deprived of tasty morsels of their choice; laughing and joking at parties with women or men of equal rank is their duty—it is a failing not to be capable of this; but you must know where to draw the line. You must not go too far with anything, things just need to be touched upon, you have to float briefly in the shallows, deep-diving is illegal. You must be able to express an opinion on any subject at once, but too much attention to a subject is not in good taste. The existence of the 'sahibs' is in these two worlds of 'social life'—that is what we call it—and, of course, of work, and those who are equally adept at both enjoy the benefit of unimpeded ascent. I, too, am one of those chosen ones.

And yet I am actually someone else.

Did I say something to you when there was dew on the grass, fragrance in the air, and a pink sunshine spread over the face of dawn? Did you say something to me? Do you remember? You don't? You came and stood on the stairs, the morning-sun-coloured dawn was face to face with you—and there I was gazing at you, the touch of dew on my feet, the euphoria of daybreak in my body. You were slim, fair, your hair blue and indigo in the tender sunlight. Your blouse was a deep red, wrapped in a white sari with a red border. Like light you lit up the universe, it was your fragrance that pervaded the fresh green air. My light, my life, my soul, how did it come to pass that I lost you?

That one time I saw you suddenly in the lift in the hotel in Amsterdam. You were dressed in slacks, a bright red woollen cardigan, joy in your face as sixteen brimmed over. Lighting up the grey of the cloudy day spread out outside, you came and stood there. You recognised me, you smiled; you responded at once in German to some trivial observation of mine. You got off the lift before I did; I didn't see you again.

Was I mistaken? Perhaps—yes, definitely mistaken. You cannot have remained sixteen so many years later. And if it was indeed you, why was your hair golden? Why would you talk to me in German even after recognising me? But if that woman was not you, then where are you? Tell me, answer me.

Where? I don't even know whether you still live.

But is it even possible that you have died? You too, celestial beauty?

Yet Pippalgarh runs smoothly. How strange, how terrible, how unbelievable that not one of these fifty thousand people except me wonders whether you are still alive or not. But this is the only thing that is real, important. Yet everyone is happy living by the rules.

Everyone? Who knows whether it's everyone.

To tell the truth, following the rules is quite difficult. Some of the 'sahibs' do have a fall, sometimes literally on the floor of the club, sometimes in the form of some other weakness. Some people actually get friendly at a party—instead of frolicking with everyone they spend the entire evening in the company of a single person—that is a big mistake. Others earn infamy by bringing up serious subjects for discussion. Someone may display signs of excessive attention towards someone else's wife, taking an axe to the root of their prospects in the company. I've even seen one or two people who do not go to parties, reading books of their choice instead when they go back home in the evening—their behaviour is considered illegitimate too. This may not harm anyone, but we term them undependable; the wise principle of Pippalgarh is that those who are personally moved or want to nurture a part of themselves in private, are—even though they are morally innocent—not worthy of being given important responsibilities. But I wonder, why do these people fall? Did they ever see you—and were not able to forget you since then? Like me, do they also wonder where you are?

Perhaps.

However, things that are difficult for many people come easily to me. I am very clever: I do not allow anyone to even guess that I am actually someone else; even though they see me round the year they never suspect that I have known you for ten thousand years. Everyone knows, thinks, believes, that I am only a very important person—an aged baboon. And that is what I am, indeed. Once you can be an aged baboon, there's nothing more comfortable; I am fortunate to have reached that stage.

Milu? Does Milu suspect anything? No, not even Milu. But what if the truth is that Milu is indeed you?

Is that not possible? I do remember a time dimly when Milu was—who knows if she was almost like you. But if that is so, then it must be accepted that Milu does not exist any more. And if Milu does not, nor do I. Is that possible? Certainly. Definitely possible.

But Milu, I—we are nothing. We may exist, or we may not. It does not matter. But the real, important, critical question is: Do you exist or not.

Tell me, answer me. Say something.

To please Milu I had once been to one of her women's society events. The speaker was a renowned professor from Calcutta. Happiness does not make man happy, pleasures do not bring joy, what man needs is ambrosia—he stated this eternal truth in different ways, taking a long time over it. He spouted a great deal of Sanskrit; words like 'love', 'beauty', 'infinite' and 'immortal' were heard over and over again. Why was he saying all this—it suddenly struck me—these were just words, just shells, just envelopes, had he ever wondered whether they held anything within them? Had he not heard of you yet; if he had, then why all this noise? All those words of his—if they did hold any meaning, any substance, an abstract, an essence, then it is you! You—you are everything: But if you are indeed everything, then how can there be a question mark over whether you are alive or not?

One day I will take that holiday—I will have to. I will go away from this place—or, I will have to. I will sit in a cane chair on a verandah somewhere, the sea before me. The blue-green indigo turbulent water, wave after wave, the hazy distance. No work, I am idle; no worries, I am idle; no thoughts, I am idle; and yet I do not fear the morning, the afternoon, the evening. I want to go somewhere where there is no work, and because there is no work there is no fatigue either. I want to go somewhere where there is always time, but where I do not have to wage a war against time. Where is that land, that sea, that blueness? It is where you are. You are brimming over with sixteen, your body smells of the dew, your face glows in the pink sunlight, like light, you light up this universe. You just sat down by my side.

But what if it turns out that you do not exist?

Natu's Final Hours

Bhupati Ghosh found the small, folded slip of paper on the table when he came home from work that day. It was almost evening, and the room was dimly lit; he had to hold it close to his eyes to read it.

'I'm leaving. You won't get me back. Look after Natu.'

After reading it twice, Bhupati crumpled the piece of paper into a ball and, about to toss it through the window, stopped suddenly and put it in the pocket of his trousers. Striding away energetically from the window, he flung his half-sleeved shirt away from himself, switched on the lights, and sat down beneath the fan to dry the sweat from his body. He wasn't very tall but was powerfully built; the sleeveless undershirt revealed the strong muscles on his arms; a sharp smell swept into his nose from the hair on his belly, his nostrils flared briefly. Bhupati was thirty-two, his thinning hair making him look older, but when he took his shirt off, it was evident that the blood beneath his taut skin was red.

'Tea, Babu? Or will you bathe first?' Paresh entered the room to ask.

'Tea.' Bhupati shed the Kabuli sandals on his feet without getting up and pushed them beneath the bed. Natu appeared and nestled close to him.

Bhupati gave Natu a sidelong glance. Black eyes, as though outlined with kohl, whose only expression was a pleading one. His long thick tail was fluttering like a flag. Sniffing and whimpering, Natu conveyed an entreaty of some sort. Bhupati responded by putting his hand on Natu's shoulder.

This little show of indulgence was all it took for Natu to lower his head on Bhupati's knee. He pushed the dog, saying, 'Go away.'

A foolish animal who didn't understand words. Mistaking the push for an invitation to play, he put his front legs up on Bhupati's knees, his long, wet tongue hanging out like the Goddess Kali's.

'Today's the day I'll kill you. I'll kill you today. Do you understand?'

Natu remained standing in the same pose. The patch on his stomach was visible like a white island on his lustrous brick-red skin, the drool of health dripped constantly from his unblemished pink tongue.

Bringing Bhupati a cup of tea, Paresh said, 'Ma has gone out, can I get you something?'

'Get Natu out of here.'

'Natu! Naatni! Nataraj!' Paresh imitated his absent mistress's coy vocabulary. 'Come, eat.'

But Natu, startled by a sound on the road, spun around and raced into the veranda, poking his head through the bars to stare at the road for some time before returning to Bhupati and whimpering again in a low voice. Bhupati didn't spare him a glance, but in his head, he let loose a diatribe meant for Natu.

Do you know boy, I didn't take you in as a pet? Didn't take your mother in either. It's all Srimati Lakshmi's doing, Lakshmi Debi, whose message on a slip of paper I crumpled and put in my pocket a minute ago. I don't love having animals at home, I opposite of love it, but Lakshmi Debi is an independent human being, she can certainly fulfil her own desire. Moreover, when Dinesh Ganguly offered to give her a puppy as a gift, there was no question of saying no. You know Dinesh Ganguly, don't you, the tall and slender man in the perfectly crinkled panjabi, passionate eyes, whose pieces come out in all the English and Bengali newspapers, who has been to Paris, been to Peking, who brought Lakshmi Debi a scarlet lacquer box from Bangkok, with whom she chats till two in the morning while I snore in the next room—or at least pretend to—you know Dinesh Ganguly, don't you? He gave your mother to Lakshmi Debi as a gift, she was a little beauty, her first spring did not go in vain, without informing anyone of the identity of your father she gave birth to five children one day and died within a month after that under the wheels of a lorry. I saw her with a swollen stomach, her teeth bared the way they would if anyone went near her during her meal in the early days. She died happily, but I will not be able to give you such pleasure, you will drown to death, you will suffer. You're so comfortable now, coiled beneath the fan on the cool floor, but I have no choice but to tell you that it is your duty now to prepare for death.

An animal has no idea what death is. No wonder they call it an animal.

You were ugly as sin at birth. The colour of mud, flabby, like one of those bloated rats in drains, no eyes. But so what. Dinesh Ganguly's gift, for starters, and the untimely accidental death of the gift, the excuse of a dead mother, meant even more love and care for all of you. When she was done eating, Lakshmi Debi fed all five of you at the same dining table, like baby monsters you'd sit in her lap or climb up her legs and slurp your milk and rice—the very sight of it was repulsive. When the litter was a little older, she gave away four of them to handpicked families and adopted you since you were the only boy among the five children—the same Lakshmi Debi whom I couldn't persuade in eight years to be the mother of a child, who had of late even abandoned the possibility of becoming a mother, at least with my help. You are almost two now; for two years, she has been taking you to bed, making up for Dinesh Ganguly's absence with you.

She could have taken you away too. I have nothing to be surprised at; I know everything, I had more or less hoped for this, just as well it's happened. But why leave you behind after all the attention she used to lavish on you? Simple—Dinesh Ganguly is not willing to share a bed with you. Mothers even leave their children behind, and you are nothing but a dumb, stupid, tiny dog with a short lifespan. No one can avoid the call when it comes.

Poor you. You're going to die helplessly at my hands today. Now go and have your last meal, eat your fill, I'll bathe in the meantime.

Bhupati put on a milk-white shirt after his bath. He was more or less as healthy as Natu; it only needed water to wash away the stains of labour and the sparkle to return to his face. Running a comb through his thinning hair, he put a clean handkerchief in his pocket, some money too. Going into the small dining room, he opened the refrigerator door.

Putting away the tea things, Paresh said, 'Shall I take Natu for his walk now?'

'I'll take him.' Bhupati sipped his cold beer. 'Feed him first.'

'He doesn't eat now, Babu, he doesn't get hungry unless he's had his walk.'

Natu was close by, stretched out on the floor with his pointed face extended, now he wagged his tail slowly on hearing his name. He knew what 'feed' meant; he never lingered in an empty room, after Lakshmi Debi he was devoted to Paresh.

'There, he's wagging his tail,' said Bhupati. 'Feed him, he'll eat.'

'What if Ma's angry when she returns.'

Bhupati controlled the revulsion running down his spine. 'I'm telling you to feed him. Have you made meat for him?'

'Yes, Babu, I do it every day.'

'Bring it. Give it to him here, I want to see him eat.'

Paresh was a trifle surprised at the head of the family's sudden interest in Natu, and couldn't help being pleased too. He brought Natu's food in an enamelled plate, meat and rice boiled together.

Natu leapt to his feet at the smell, shaking off his drowsiness.

'No. Don't eat.' Paresh couldn't resist demonstrating to his employer how obedient and clever Natu was.

Natu came to an abrupt halt in front of the plate, drool falling in drops to the floor from his open, panting mouth.

'Did you boil it in turmeric?' asked Bhupati.

'Yes, Babu.'

'No salt, I hope.'

'Why would I add salt. Ma has taught me everything already, Babu, don't worry.'

'Very well. Eat, Natu, eat up.'

An undulation ran through Natu's body from the nose to the tip of the tail, but it stopped suddenly when he caught sight of Paresh. Lifting his head, with his eyes almost touching the brow, he raised his right paw and scratched Paresh gently.

'All right, eat now,' said Paresh with a smile.

Natu threw himself at the food at once, the plate turning shiny white in three minutes.

'Swine,' said Bhupati to himself. 'Not enough that I asked him to eat, needs Paresh's permission also. Swine.' He lit a cigarette and looked at Paresh. 'Didn't you say he doesn't get hungry unless he's been on a walk?'

The even-tempered old retainer from Midnapur answered, 'He's an animal, Babu, he will eat whenever you give him food. But he won't eat unless you tell him to, and he won't touch anyone's food except his own.' Paresh went into the kitchen with Natu's plate.

Pouring the rest of the beer into his half-empty glass, Bhupati took it into his own room and sat down comfortably. Aaaah! A bottle of beer quietly by himself in his room, four cigarettes in a row, no commotion, no compulsion to make acceptable small talk with anyone who happens to be present—what could be better. She's actually spared me a lot of trouble. Thank goodness Nehru had introduced divorce to Hindu marriage laws. Can't stand that Dinesh Ganguly. Never could. And that group of theirs—film actresses, businessmen, car-owners, people who picnic by moonlight in their villas. I've had to tolerate a lot—they've spent hours in this house, in this room, friends of Lakshmi Debi's, displaying their teeth politely when they see me, I've often been even more courteous and left the house, sitting by the Dhakuria Lakes and counting the stars. 'You're so ill-mannered, they come home, and you go out.' 'It's not me they come to meet, and the home doesn't seem mine either any more.' 'Very well then, keep your home to yourself.' Their lives separated, and yet things appeared unchanged—this was what was repugnant.

Now the point is, how to kill Natu. Look, he's here again, what is it, what do you want? Are you looking for Lakshmi Debi? As a neutral person, I'd say she should certainly have taken you with her. But how would she? I don't think she'd be unwilling to be the mother of Dinesh Ganguly's child—and then what if you eat up the baby in a fit of jealousy? Or bite the potential father before a baby is on its way? Lakshmi Debi has done the right thing, it wouldn't have done for her to take you. But that doesn't mean she has forgotten you; she has asked me to take care of you. And that's why it didn't take me a moment to make up my mind. Yes, I will kill you.

'When will Ma be back?'

'Do you need anything?'

'We're out of coal, and . . .'

'Here.' Bhupati extracted a five-rupee note from the breast pocket of his shirt with the tips of his fingers. 'Get two packets of Capstans and a matchbox for me, and anything else you need. Bring my cigarettes first. And listen, make chholar daal for me tonight, and some mutton, dry and spicy . . . Take this.' Draining his glass of beer, he handed it to Paresh, collected a couple of things, and said, 'Let's go for a walk, Natu.'

Natu's joy erupted as soon as he set foot on the street. Not a pedigreed dog, lacking the stately gait of a German Shepherd, and full of vigour and strength—all he wanted to do was run and laugh, chase cats, and invite other dogs to fight or romance. When he was younger, Bhupati had taken him on walks sometimes, but he hadn't realised how much stronger Natu had grown in the year since then. He had to hold the leash firmly, and use the leather whip sometimes to restrain Natu, but it wasn't proving easy to control his excitement at being alive in this world of smells and curiosities. He had to sniff at every bit of garbage on the street, approaching a lamp post meant lifting his hind leg whether he needed it or not, and after expelling the waste matter from his intestines not once but twice, his animal spirits kept bubbling over on this October night with the first nip in the air.

Go on, enjoy yourself to your heart's content, I'm in no hurry. I'll have to wait a bit in any case, until the crowd at the Dhakuria Lake goes down, until the night becomes deeper. I need a deserted spot, somewhere near the lily pool. Trouble is you're an expert swimmer. But I have a strong rope in my pocket, I'll tie your hands and legs and mouth tightly, you'll get there in silence. You'll have to suffer a little for a few minutes, but what's the alternative—I don't know where to get poison, and you know I don't have a gun.

You could ask, 'What have I done? Why are you killing me?' It's your duty to ask, and mine, to answer. Don't imagine I'm taking revenge on Lakshmi Debi by killing you. There's no question of revenge, I have no complaint against her. She has done me no harm in leaving; on the contrary, she has done me a favour.

The thing is, I want to start afresh. I'll live quietly by myself, a peaceful life, calm. Paresh is a good man, but I'll have to get rid of him, I won't be able to stand him precisely because he's been there for so long. I'll hire a Nepali, someone who can iron my clothes and make kababs, and doesn't talk much. Having you will be a big problem for me. You don't realise it now, but when it's time for bed, you'll weep for Lakshmi Debi, you won't let me sleep with your barking, Janaki babu from the next flat will give me a piece of his mind tomorrow. Not just tonight, who knows how many days and nights you'll go on crying non-stop. So many strange stories that one hears about you people. Apparently, some of you even starve to death. No wonder you're dogs.

So think what you like, but I can't go to so much trouble. From tonight, I will sleep, I won't have to lie awake in bed reflecting on how I've been humiliated or deceived, I will sleep deeply from now on. That's why I have to get rid of you. I have no concerns; I have a good job that I do well, I have my health, I have plenty of money in my provident fund. I can be transferred to Bombay if I want to, even to London for a couple of years if I pull some strings. I cannot possibly allow my independence to be disrupted by a mere creature like you.

Would you like to go to some other family? Are you suggesting I advertise in the papers? Is that how easily you can forget Lakshmi Debi? What a traitor! You were born in this house, grew up on milk-and-rice and a soft bed, and now you want to go to someone else's house and wag your tail joyfully for them? I'm telling you for the last time, there's no escaping from me today, in no circumstances. You have to die.

Or would you like me to go to Baghbazar or Baranagar and abandon you there? All that will happen is that you, who have never gone out on the streets unescorted, will be run over by a car or bus or lorry in half an hour. Dying will release you, but what if you become lame? Have you ever thought of how you will survive with three legs while competing with all those sly stray dogs? Each of those groups occupies one of the lanes there; if a stupid innocent creature like you tries to enter any of them, they will bite you all over and leave you wounded. You may be strong from all the unsalted meat you've eaten, but you'll never be able to match up to them in cunningness. Even if you survive, you'll be a mangy, lame, half-starved, emaciated animal on the lowest rung of the society of street dogs. You won't have a wife, the neighbourhood louts will taunt you as they lick the paan leaves, they will snarl at you if you try to climb into the washermen's veranda when it rains. What do you want to live that way for? And how long will you live anyway? You have spent these two years in comfort and honour, isn't that much better? And besides, you think I have the time to go all the way to Baranagar to get rid of you? And then no matter how far away I leave you, what if you come back a few days later all dirty and maybe with a disease or two? Lost dogs return even after a month, there are so many stories about it. No, I've made up my mind; I'm going to finish you off today, right now. If I don't do it today, I won't be able to do it later. What do you take me for? I'm human after all.

Past the swimming club, leaving the Buddhist pagoda behind on the left, where a strip of grass runs between two of the lakes—this was the spot where Bhupati stopped. He hadn't been able to smoke all this while, since he was holding Natu's leash in one hand and a playing ball in the other—and considering how turbulent Natu was, walking wasn't easy. Bhupati sprawled on the grass, lit a cigarette, and looked around. The days were shorter now, it appeared quite late into the night already, and there wasn't much of a crowd. But he would have to wait a little longer, maybe a lot longer.

Bringing his nose close to Bhupati's ear, Natu growled, 'Woof!'

Bhupati did not respond with either words or gestures.

Natu moved away, curved his back like the moon, stretched his neck, plumped up his tail, and barked louder, 'Bow wow!' His eyes glittered in the darkness.

What, you want to play now? I haven't mastered Lakshmi Debi's coquettish ways, I can't reach out and kiss you, I can't dress up as a ghost to scare you either. I got the ball for you to play with, but in the dark . . .

'Arf arf!' Natu pranced about from one end to the other, dancing around Bhupati a few times before licking his cheek suddenly.

'Eeeeh!' Bhupati wiped his cheek with the back of his hand. 'I hate these things. How dare you? Scram!'

'Bow wow! Arf arf! Yap yap!'

Pushing Natu away with his arm, Bhupati lay down flat on the grass, and Natu, beside himself with joy, kept leaping across him back and forth, nipping him playfully on his arms and legs, or withdrawing to a distance and then racing up to vault over him. Bhupati rolled the red wooden ball across the grass, and Natu brought it back in his mouth in a flash. Bhupati threw it away harder, and at once, Natu's brick-red skin glinted under the electric lights.

After some more rounds of this game, the ball ended up where Natu couldn't locate it. After sniffing around the bushes, he came back slowly, standing near Bhupati with his head lowered and his tail between his legs.

'Lost it? Good riddance. No more games. Let's go.'

Rising to his feet, Bhupati blew on the bits of grass and the laziness clinging to his body to get rid of them. They began to walk again, but Natu wasn't enthusiastic any more, maybe he was forlorn at losing the ball. Or he was tired. Bhupati's expression was stern, his footsteps were stern, he seemed to be walking to the rhythm of a stern law of some kind, no looking left or right, his eyes fixed on his target. Natu was no longer straining at the leash or leaping up and down, he ambled alongside Bhupati like a docile, well-behaved sheep.

Walking down the grassy slope next to the cannon near the lily pool, Bhupati stopped between the trees at the edge of the water. The shadows were thick here, the light dim, and no one was nearby. He strolled around the area, the benches were empty, everyone had left before nine today. Standing there, he lit a cigarette but threw it away soon afterwards and got down to work.

Natu looked at him in surprise at first and became animate again. Clamping his teeth on the rope, he stood as though poised to pounce. Bhupati had trussed up his hind legs meanwhile. Trying to run, Natu fell on his back. Bhupati tied a double knot and brought the rope round to the front. Natu didn't stop him. A large, strong dog, but he didn't stop Bhupati at all. Did he think it was a new game? Never mind, he's made it easier for me. Bhupati tied the rope quickly around Natu's mouth, wound it around his chest all the way to his hips, and then took it all the way around Natu's body once more. Then he stood up and wiped his moist forehead with his handkerchief. Uff, a lot of work.

I was worrying about it but look how easy it was. As though he knew what I wanted and helped me do it, didn't stop me to make things harder. How inertly he's lying there, as helpless as a turtle on its back, as certain as a corpse. I'd better check the knots once more . . . yes, they're fine, really tight. But aren't they hurting him?

Bhupati picked up Natu in his arms, like a Bengali mother carrying her child, and took him all the way to the edge of the water. He was renowned for his physical prowess at one time—he would be able to throw Natu a distance of ten yards, maybe twenty. To gather momentum, he swung his arms back and forth a few times. And then, just as he paused momentarily, a thin scream rose in the air. A sharp, long, dumb cry. Once, twice, three times, it trembled before fading into the desolate surroundings. And with each scream, the strength in Bhupati's muscles deserted him, it vanished—the pulsing lump in his arms, trussed up with a rope, fell on the ground from his weary, so weary arms. Suddenly, he found himself bending and untying the knots. Fate was kind to him on the way back, he got a taxi near the Marwari club, Natu put his head on Bhupati's knee and fell asleep at once.

* * *

Natu seemed to go mad as soon as he got out of the taxi in front of the house. He raced away breathlessly, without another look at Bhupati, and bounded up the stairs three at a time. Bhupati heard the door being opened with a click, and then, as he climbed upstairs, a woman's voice.

The front door of the flat opened directly into the dining room. The light was switched on, the table was laid for two, and Lakshmi Debi was standing beside it. It would be wrong to say she was standing—she was bent over, stretched back, out of breath. Natu kept leaping on her, putting his front paws around her, licking her everywhere, the force of his devotion simply couldn't be controlled. Lakshmi Debi's hair was undone, her sari was about to slip off her body, she was knocked off her feet repeatedly by Natu, and amidst all this, she kept calling out alluringly, 'Natu! Nati! Natni! My Natni! Nateshwar!'

Bhupati came to an abrupt halt near the door at this sight. Lakshmi Debi brought herself under control on seeing him, summoning something akin to a smile to her lips and said in a different tone, 'I . . . I came back.'

Bhupati rushed into the room; he grabbed Natu by the shoulder with his left hand, picked up a huge bread-cutting knife from the table with his right hand, and plunged it into Natu's neck. The creature made no sound, but Lakshmi Debi screamed. Streams of red blood swept across the floor.

'A hellhole! Sheer hell! Even setting eyes on that face of yours is a sin!'

Lakshmi Debi uttered the words through clenched teeth and climbed down the stairs.

A Life

Gurudas Bhattacharya, Vachaspati, the seniormost teacher of Sanskrit at Khulna's Jagattarini School, had an accident during Bengali literature for Class Nine.

'*Amaar projagawn amaar cheye tahare bawro kori mane . . .*' The pundit stumbled on the sentence. Cheye? Did that refer to the Bengali word for glance? Or for desire? After some thought, he explained the sentence as, 'The king says his subjects want him, they desire his sanctuary, but they respect the king of Kaushal more. Grammar has been distorted a little here.'

The boys on the first bench exchanged glances. Then one of them stood up to say, 'The usage is correct, sir. The word "cheye" in this case is used for comparison, in the sense of "than". My subjects consider him more noble than me. See, it says a little later, "Are you so bold as to imagine you can be more pious than me?"'

'If only I were an Arab bedouin rather than who I am,' the boy next to him recited.

Gurudas did not respond. Accepting the correction made by his students, he continued teaching the poem. The bell rang.

It was the last period. Collecting their umbrellas and books, the other teachers left for their homes, while Gurudas made his way to the school library. The library was nothing but three cupboards full of books in one corner of the staff room, most of them textbooks obtained as free samples. Among the more valuable volumes were several hardbound sets of the Bengali literary magazine *Probashi*, a Philips atlas of twenty years' vintage, a Chambers Dictionary, and three Bengali and English-to-Bengali dictionaries used by students. Clearing his throat, Gurudas said, 'Can you unlock this cupboard, Nabokeshto?'

Not even the servants at school paid much attention to the Sanskrit teacher. And Nabokeshto wore the mantle of bearer, doorman, and gardener single-handedly. 'The library is closed, sir,' he answered with a touch of insolence.

'Never mind, just unlock it. I need some books.'

'But I have to leave for Rasoolpur right away—my daughter's in-laws have invited us . . .'

'That's all right, you can go. Leave the keys with me.'

'All right then. Don't forget to give them back to me before eleven tomorrow. You know how strict the new headmaster is. And lock the door of the room before you go . . . here's the padlock, see?'

Unlocking the cupboard, Gurudas planted himself in front of it; with a glance at his back, Nabokeshto gathered his bundle, wrapped in a homespun towel, from its place beneath the table—he was taking a bunch of grapefruits from the tree in the school yard as gifts for his son-in-law.

No one was allowed to take the dictionaries home; Gurudas spent a good deal of time leafing through the two Bengali dictionaries. The light grew dim, the silence of a provincial evening thickening inside the room. He forgot to sit down, forgot his hunger. His internal senses seemed to soak up the rows of letters. Today's incident had wounded him—he had not been able to capture the meaning of a word which millions of adults and children used every single day without a thought. How could he—he was a teacher of Sanskrit. He had learnt Sanskrit, but not Bengali. But he was a Bengali—that was the language he spoke. He seemed to realise for the first time that the Bengali language was not Sanskrit, not even a corrupt form of it—it was a complete, living, changing, evolving, independent language, the spoken language of seventy million people, their mother tongue. 'A living language, the mother tongue'—he repeated the words in his head several times. But prowess in one's mother tongue was not automatic, it needed nurture.

Gurudas noticed that none of the dictionaries included the word he had tripped over that morning. He

was reminded of other words used in similar fashion—
'thekey', the Bengali word used for 'from' or 'since',
or 'dyakha', used for 'seeing' or 'meeting' or 'looking
after'. This was how the Bengali language performed the
task of the Sanskrit verb-ending. None of this was in the
dictionary. There were mistakes in these dictionaries—
wrong explanations, even inaccurate spelling. How
were the students to learn? And I—how am I to learn?

It was late evening by the time Gurudas returned
home. His wife Horimohini asked, 'So late?' Gurudas
did not answer. He ate his dinner in silence. 'Are you
ill? You aren't eating.'

'I am not ill.' He went to bed early that night.

Jagattarini School began at eleven in the morning,
and the district school, at ten-thirty. Gurudas went
to the district school around quarter past eleven the
next morning, spending half an hour in the library
before breathlessly entering his own class in the nick of
time. The next day was Saturday—from the school he
went to the only college in Khulna. He had a nodding
acquaintance with the Sanskrit teacher there (here,
too, it was he who taught Bengali). They conversed for
some time, and he flipped through three or four books
in the library—but his restlessness did not spare him.

No, he had not found it—he had not found what
he was looking for, anywhere. Could there not be a
complete Bengali dictionary, which had room for
every single word, both Sanskrit and vernacular, in
the language, which included every combination,
every application, every colloquial usage, which would

enable the Bengali language to be learnt, its nature to be understood, its unique creative spirit to be appreciated? The college professor had said there was not even one such book. There were a few good ones among those he examined, but in a workman-like way—where was the dictionary that one could use for real scholarship?

The biggest bookshop in town was Victoria Library. In the evening, Gurudas asked for a look at a major Bengali dictionary and the Oxford English Dictionary. Having leafed through them for a few minutes, he said softly, 'There's something I want to discuss, Reboti babu.'

In a small town, everyone knew everyone else. The owner looked at Gurudas over the rims of his glasses.

'It's Saturday—may I take these two books home? I'll return them to you first thing Monday morning.'

'Take them home?'

'I'll handle them very carefully—won't soil them, won't crease them—I'll look after them. I need them urgently, you see.'

'Someone's already ordered those books, Ponditmashai.'

'I see.' Gurudas's fair, lean face reddened. A little later he said, 'Then I'd better buy them.' He had to wage a terrible war against himself, but . . . he had spoken, he couldn't take his words back now.

'Pack these books for Ponditmashai . . .' Reboti babu made no further reference to the books having been ordered.

'But I can only pay next month.'

'Hmm . . .' Gurudas sent up a silent prayer, 'Let him not agree, o lord.' But Reboti babu's mouth softened.

'Very well. But on the first of the month, don't forget. We run a very small business, you know . . . sign here, please.'

He had got them at a discount by virtue of being a teacher. Thirteen rupees and fourteen annas—nearly a third of his salary.

Gurudas browsed through the two books late into that night by the glow of a lantern. His grasp of English was poor, but he had no difficulty in realising the difference in the presentation of the two books. And yet, this was just a condensed version, he had heard that Oxford had a giant dictionary too.

Before going to sleep, he mused over Panini, considered the sheer extent of the Sanskrit dictionary *Shabdakalpadruma*, and recollected Vidyasagar. An extraordinary talent for grammar, an unmatched enthusiasm for analysis, a vocabulary that knew no limits. He used to possess them all. What happened to them?

Horimohini had planted flowers in a fenced-in corner of the small yard. She was watering them with her daughter on Sunday morning when Gurudas came up to them, smiling.

'Shibani, go check if Nidhu-r ma has brought the milk.'

'Later. Listen to me first.'

Horimohini paused and looked at him.

'I'm about to start on something new.'

A ray of hope flashed across Horimohini's face. Had the match for Shibani been finalised with the Chatterjees of Nimtala then? Their elder daughter, Bhabani, had been married into a high-born family—this was the other daughter. She had turned fifteen, if she didn't get married now, then when?

'Have they sent word?'

'Who?'

'The Nimtala Chatterjees.'

'No, that's not it. I am going to write a dictionary of the Bengali language. I made up my mind last night.'

There was no flicker of expression on Horimohini's face.

'You know what a dictionary is, don't you? A collection of words. The meaning of words in the Bengali language, similar words, usage of words, and so on. There isn't a book like this at the moment.'

'Not a single one? You're going to write it?' Horimohini felt a burst of pride. 'Will it say anything about gods and goddesses?'

'Everything.'

Yes, everything. Unknown to Gurudas, a smile spread across his face. He had fallen asleep last night as soon as he had come to this decision—a deep sleep. And when he awoke this morning, he discovered his mind was calm, his heart, cheerful, and his body, healed and rested. Support for his endeavour radiated from the branching rays of the sun in the sky, as though nature had been waiting these last few days only for his resolve to do this. As soon as he accepted the task, satisfaction spread across the heavens, and the movements in his body acquired an easy rhythm. Gods and goddesses—of course he would have to include them. But all the gods? All their names? He would have to determine which of them belonged to an encyclopaedia and which, to a dictionary. Which of the Sanskrit words could be considered Bengali? What to do with Brajabuli? What were the indications that a word was part of the Bengali language? Would he have to add words which were not in circulation but might be required? There was so much to think about. So much to ponder—even Horimohini's flowering plants were urging him to start at once.

Gurudas had been to Puri once as a student; he was reminded now of his visit. He could see a similar ocean stretching ahead of him—a succession of waves, depressions, whirlpools, effort . . . the horizon in the distance. On this ocean his raft would have to float, this was the sea he would have to cross. For a moment, Gurudas felt his skin prickle.

After lunch, he brought the subject up again with his wife.

'I was thinking of the dictionary.'

'Yes, what about it?'

'The thing is, I need some material. Books and things.'

'Very well.'

'Very expensive books. I was thinking, Chakraborty moshai had made an offer for that acre of land back home . . .'

'You'll sell it?' A shadow fell across Horimohini's face. 'We have nothing else, and the girl's growing up too.'

'We can survive on what we have.' Gurudas could not inject too much confidence into this assertion, so he tried to compensate with a soft smile. 'That is to say, I will survive, and once your son's grown up, you'll have nothing to worry about.'

'The things you say! I think only about myself all the time, don't I? But I shan't let Nobu be a teacher like you. You know Netai, my nephew? He's passed his matriculation examination and joined the Railways. Sixty rupees a month already—and extra earnings on top of that.'

Gurudas did not approve of the final statement, but swallowing his criticism, he returned to the original subject.

'Why stop at the Railways? Nobu might even become a deputy magistrate like my brother,' said Gurudas, throwing a sidelong look at his wife. It was a calculated ploy—he was fully aware of Horimohini's reverence for his stepbrother's status as deputy magistrate.

'Do you suppose I could ever be so lucky? But then, everything is possible if the gods smile on us, isn't that right? That reminds me, I'd sent you sweets after Lakshmi Puja the other day, but Shibani said you didn't have any.'

'I touched my forehead with them—that's better than eating them. Listen, I'm giving the land to Chakraborty moshai then, all right?'

'Giving it? We hardly own anything anyway—and there's not only the girl who has to be married off but also the boy for whom we must leave something.'

'Everything will be done. But I cannot turn back now.'

'Cannot turn back—what do you mean?'

'Wealth is by nature temporary, but . . .' The scholar groped for the right word, and then turned helplessly to emotional appeal. 'I have made up my mind—are you going to stop me now?'

The land they owned was in Nandigram, about an hour away by steamer. Gurudas paid a visit during the Janmashtami holidays. A house, fruit-bearing trees, a small pond, some farmland. Some? It used to be nearly seventy acres in his grandfather's time. After the division, about eight acres had come to Gurudas. He had had to sell nearly two acres for his elder daughter's wedding, and now another acre. Never mind, at least he was getting a hundred and fifty rupees. Rummaging through the books at home, he even found the old Sanskrit dictionary printed in Bombay—it had belonged to his father—and, how fortunate, the Sanskrit grammar textbook that he had borrowed from a schoolmate and forgotten to return. The first thing he did on returning to Khulna was to buy two reams of the cheapest paper, which Shibani laced into a notebook.

On the first day of the Durga Puja holidays at school, Gurudas travelled to Calcutta, where he had to put up for three days at a boarding house in Sealdah. Two more Bengali dictionaries, Suniti Chatterjee's book on linguistics, an ancient (but excellent) Sanskrit-to-Bengali dictionary found after scouring the pavements of College Street and Chitpur, a Bengali grammar book written by an Englishman, *Basumati* published by Tekchand and Hutom Pyancha, Kaliprasanna Sinha's *Mahabharata* published by Hitabadi. He didn't dare ignore Rabindranath Tagore's *The Theory of Words* when it caught his eye—poets were the creators of language, might as well find out what he had to say. All this accounted for nearly fifty rupees. Then there were new clothes for everyone for Durga Puja, for Horimohini and Bhabani a pair each of the bangles that married women wore, a dhoti for his son-in-law, rubber slippers for Nobu costing a rupee and thirteen annas. He had to spend eight annas on his way back on a porter to carry all the books—that really pinched.

They had a wonderful time back home that year during the Durga Puja holidays. Horimohini stayed back with the children, while Gurudas returned to Khulna the day after Lakshmi Puja. He cooked his own meals and read all day. He found the English difficult, but managed to make sense of it, and the more he read, the easier it grew. Drawing one of the notebooks made by Shibani to himself on the day before Kali Puja, he wrote the first letter of the Bengali alphabet, 'Aw' in a large hand. Fifty words were done that day. The school opened three days later, the family returned, and his leisure hours shrank.

Gurudas set himself a routine. He woke up at five in the morning to write for two hours, and then drank his share of milk, went out to tutor students, bought the day's provisions, and returned home. This gave him a little time before his bath. He had to take private classes in the evening too—the exams were approaching—but he didn't go to bed until he had put in a couple of hours of writing. Gurudas was making smooth progress.

Winter came. There was no light before six in the morning, and this was when the pressure of checking annual exam papers intensified. But Christmas holidays were approaching.

He had to visit Calcutta again during the Christmas vacation. The subject was like Draupadi's sari—unfolding constantly, an unending mystery, one whose depths you kept sinking into. How would he prove equal to this task—he, a mere Gurudas Bhattacharya, a minor Sanskrit scholar? He did not know his way on this road, had no clear idea of where he would find the bricks and cement needed to build this structure. In Calcutta, he laid siege to the Imperial Library; the days passed navigating his way through the dense jungle of comparative linguistics. Many of the books were written in German, with an abundance of Greek letters and a thick growth of Latin, Gothic and Persian references, as though the immense vegetation of the Aryan languages had stretched up to the sky, spreading its branches far and wide. Sanskrit alone had never given him this feeling of kinship with the West, with the entire world. For the first time he set eyes on the Monier Williams's Sanskrit dictionary, he discovered

Skeat's etymological dictionary too. Ten days passed cramming his notebooks with jottings.

When he was about to set off for Calcutta again during the summer holidays, Horimohini could not keep herself from objecting mildly.

'Why must you go to Calcutta again?'

'Do you need me here?'

'I was thinking of the expenses. The boarding house costs money too.'

Gurudas had thought about this as well. The examination season was in the past, and not many studied Sanskrit these days. He had no one to tutor. Thanks to a supply of food from the land back home, they managed to survive on forty-five rupees but barely. They could afford coarse rice and daal and their clothes—anything more was virtually impossible. But . . . he simply had to go.

'Doesn't your mother's brother live in Calcutta?' said Horimohini. 'You could always . . .'

'Of course not, how can I stay a month at someone else's house? And he's only my mother's cousin—I haven't met him in years . . . it's impossible. But I'll manage—don't worry.'

'It's all very well for you to say that, but I spend sleepless nights.'

'But why?'

'Have you decided that Shibani will remain a spinster?'

A valid question. He had to accept that his daughter was showing signs of womanhood. It was time for her to be married. But . . . how?

'Why are you so anxious? She's not even fifteen yet. Many people don't even think of marriage till eighteen these days.'

'You of all people are saying this? Your very own family, the Brahmins of Nandigram, didn't allow their daughters to remain unmarried after ten.'

'Why shouldn't I? Didn't Rammohan Roy speak up against idol worship? Didn't Vidyasagar introduce widow remarriage? They were Brahmins too.'

'Those who get their daughters married at eighteen also give them the chance to go to school and college, all right? They don't let them rot at home and turn into liabilities. Do you have it in you?'

Gurudas's lean, fair face grew pale. She was right. He had no response. He must try to arrange a match.

From the matchmaker he learnt that Rameshwar Banerjee of Hatkhola in Calcutta was looking for a bride for his third son. Rameshwar had been a professor at Sanskrit College during the solitary year that Gurudas had studied there. He decided to plead with Rameshwar in Calcutta to provide a safe passage for his daughter.

In Calcutta, Gurudas rented a 'seat' in the cheapest room in a boarding house he was familiar with. His meals were at a 'pice hotel' (which he had discovered on his previous visit; for four paise you could eat so much that you didn't need a second meal). His days were spent at the Imperial Library, at the university library, wandering among second-hand bookshops, and seeking audiences with renowned professors. He had sensed a new requirement: instructions, advice, discussions—he had brought along all the pages in his notebook, in case anyone had any constructive comments to offer. It wasn't easy to meet professors—some had gone to Darjeeling, others were busy. Only two deigned to meet him. Leafing through the notebooks apprehensively, both of them said, 'Excellent, it's coming along very well, you must complete it.' When he enquired whether a detailed discussion was possible, he learnt that both were engaged as chief examiners for the B.A. exams and did not have the leisure even to die at present.

One day, he overheard a young man at a bookshop on College Street. The buyer was looking for a book on the history of Bengali literature; turning over the pages of two or three, the words he uttered were clearly weighed down with nausea. 'Dead! All dead! Rotting and ingested with worms which this swarm of professors picks out to eat. They collapse when they see living literature. Rabindranath was born in vain.' The young man disappeared, his sandals flapping.

Chuckling, the shopkeeper said, 'Subrata Sen speaks as forcefully as he writes.'

'Who was that?' Gurudas stepped forward. 'What did you say his name is?'

'Subrata Sen. You haven't read him? Powerful writer.'

At the boarding house, he normally drank a tall glass of water by way of dinner and went to bed— his exhaustion taking him beyond the hot weather, the stench, and his hunger in an instant. But sleep eluded him that night, the young man's statement ringing in his ears constantly. And you, Gurudas Bhattacharya, engaged in composing a dictionary of the Bengali language—what do *you* know of Bengali literature? Ishwar Chandra Gupta, Bankim Chandra Chattopadhyay, Michael Madhusudan Dutt—and that was it. The young man had named Rabindranath Tagore—some people said he had injected new life into the Bengali language, but you know nothing about him, you haven't read him at all. And these new writers— take Subrata Sen, for example—language lived through transformation in every era. It would die if it were to lose this power. And if a dictionary could not provide a portrait of this evolution, what use was it?

He had to think of the whole thing afresh. A dictionary was not a compendium of explanations for students, not a list or collection, not an immovable, static, ponderous object. Its essence lay in the flow, in movement, in showing the path to the future—to move ahead it had to gather sustenance from the creative work that writers were engaged in constantly. It would have to be replete with hints, allusions, advice, even imagination—just like a flowing waterfall glinting under the light. He would have to read literature— living works, current, changing literature—all that was being written, read, said, heard in the Bengali language. These were his ingredients.

He came back home bathed in a new glow. Within five minutes of his return, Horimohini asked, 'Did you meet Rameshwar Banerjee?'

'I did.'

'What did he say?'

'In a minute.' Gurudas sat down on a mat, leaning back against a post. 'They have many demands. They're well-off, you see.'

'Who'll marry your daughter on the strength of her appearance alone?'

'A thousand rupees in cash. Twenty-five bhoris of gold. All expenses. Provided they like the girl. But . . . can we afford all this? I'd better make some more enquiries . . .'

Sighing, Horimohini went away. Evening fell.

This time, Rameshwar had brought a ream of foolscap paper from Calcutta. It was cheaper there, and available at even lower prices if bought by the ream. He had nearly exhausted his older notebooks. He had to scribble copiously—scratch out bits, make changes, there was new information every day. And yet, he wasn't even done with the first letter, 'Aw'.

Gurudas got down to work calmly. Some of it involved reading. He had avoided reading the newspapers all this time, but now he had to scan a couple of Bengali dailies every evening at the public library. And he left no Bengali book he could get hold of untouched. Happening to read Rabindranath's *Ghare Baire*, he was astounded. Could the Bengali language actually work this way? This was not Hutoom, this was Kalidasa. Not even Kalidasa, something else altogether.

His notebook and pencil were always in his pocket. He took voluminous notes. Most of them would not prove useful, but who could predict what would?

The Bengalis' forms of self-expression became the subject of his discoveries. He listened closely when his wife, son or daughter spoke; with so much interest that he often did not grasp the content and forgot to answer. What he wanted to know was not what they were saying but how they said it. When the younger students raised an uproar during the lunch break at school, he lurked unobserved behind them. At the market he kept his ears peeled for rural dialects. When he went home on holidays, he sought out Muslim peasants and engaged them in needless conversations— they had a unique way of speaking.

And he had to go to Calcutta during the longer vacations. He learnt the Greek alphabet, took help from a priest at St Xavier's School to understand the rules of Latin grammar, even visited madrasas for Arabic and Persian. Hardly any books were available in the provinces— for this too he had to visit Calcutta.

How did he afford all this? Cheap boarding houses and pice hotels, yes, but still? Gurudas had made arrangements, getting rid of another acre of land, this time without telling his wife. He didn't know anyone in Calcutta particularly well, feeling beleaguered if he had to speak in English. Nor did his soiled clothes evoke respect. He had to discover everything he needed all by himself, with the help of that eternal quality— effort, the capital god had endowed every human being with. Effort, endeavour, waiting, patience. It took him four hours to do an hour's work—he was lighting rows of fireflies as he pushed through the darkness. But there were lights at every street-corner—like signals for trains in the blackness of night.

Summer holidays once more, the monsoon once more. The rains were torrential that year. Earthworms burst through the kitchen floor in July. Leech in the front yard. Snakes here and there. On some nights water streamed through gaps in the tin roof—having found dry spots for the children to sleep, the parents stayed up all night. After seven days of incessant rain, Gurudas opened his safe one day to get the shock of his life. Instead of his best books, what he saw were millions of termites wriggling about. Fifty pages of Suniti Chatterjee's book were missing, the third volume of the Mahabharata was in shreds, the Sanskrit dictionary from this father's time crumbled in his hands when he picked it up. The day passed battling the termites—he poured in four annas' worth of kerosene.

Immediately after this accident, a ray of hope emerged; marriage for Shibani suddenly seemed a likelihood. The groom was from Barishal, recently posted here at the Khulna steamer station. The groom's family approved of the bride, and made no demand for dowry—only the cost of the wedding, and accoutrement for the bride. This was no cause for concern—Horimohini still had some ornaments left.

The wedding would not take place before March, but Bhabani was overcome with joy when she heard the news. At long last she would be able to visit her mother. She lived in a large family, surrounded by her in-laws, in Madaripur—she didn't even have the chance to visit her own family during Durga Puja.

Shibani ran up a fever after the rains. When the fever didn't go down even after a week, Gurudas sent for the Ayurvedic doctor. He prescribed plenty of red-and-black pills but to no avail.

On the twenty-first day, the official assistant surgeon turned up. His fees were four rupees, and he stomped about in boots. Typhoid, he said after examining the patient. Give her nothing but glucose. Pour water over her head morning and evening. Here are the medicines. Note down the temperature at four-hour intervals. Inform me after three days.

The medicines were bought with borrowed money. The doctor came once a week—paying his fees was a near-impossible task. Milk and fish were stopped; Horimohini's deity was given a quarter of her regular rations.

Shibani lost weight, the fat disappeared from her cheeks, her discoloured teeth grew bigger and uglier. Then came the day when her hair had to be cut on the doctor's orders. Her scalp needed water, the more the better. Horimohini poured water over her daughter's head every hour, but Shibani was delirious.

When she died, her limbs had withered away to resemble sticks, her breast was like a seven-year-old boy's chest. And the sixteen-year-old girl used to be so healthy, full of grace. The ornaments put aside to pay for the wedding were used to clear the debt to the doctor.

Gurudas returned home at ten at night after the cremation. It was the end of February, winter was on its way out. He felt rather cold—wrapping a shawl around himself, he sat down next to his wife, who was slumped on the floor. The night passed in the same position.

A long night, but the sun rose finally. Horimohini had fallen asleep, while Nobu was curled up on the floor in cold. Covering his son with the shawl, Gurudas carefully slipped a pillow beneath Horimohini's head. Then he went out, spread a mat, and sat down with his notebook. This last one had also been made by Shibani. For a moment, all the letters blurred. Wiping his eyes on the end of his dhuti, he set down more letters next to the blurred ones.

Five more years passed, the dictionary was in its seventh year. He was done with twenty-four letters, up to 'Thaw'.

The words no longer flowed. What had started as an extraordinary, thrilling joy had turned into work now. Work, duty, responsibility, compulsion. The madness of discovery was gone, the excitement of gathering material had dissipated. He had an enormous quantity of information at his disposal now, the roads were familiar. It was time to work, it was time for nothing but work. Daily work, weekly work, monthly, annual, continuous. No likes, no dislikes, no reluctance either. This was an immaculate world, where the individual's angularities were dead.

That year saw the fruition of a long-drawn-out effort on the part of Jagattarini School—the government finally approved grants. Teachers' salaries were increased; Gurudas's monthly earnings leapt to fifty-five rupees—it could even rise to seventy or seventy-five eventually. In that same year Nobu, or Nobendu, vaulted over the hurdle of the matriculation examination. Not just that, he got a job almost immediately. A job with the Railways, as his mother had hoped.

A few months later, there was tragic news: Bhabani had become a widow. And within two months, she appeared in her father's yard with close-cropped hair, dressed in a widow's garb and holding three children by the hand. Her late husband's parents were no longer willing to shoulder the burden of their daughter-in-law, without whom they couldn't survive a moment once upon a time. 'They are not as well-off as before, my brothers-in-law have several children, and he didn't leave anything for us, Baba.'

Her father said, 'Don't worry. Nobu has a job now. I'll look after all of you.'

Gurudas went to Calcutta during the summer holidays that year—after a gap of two years. He couldn't postpone things any more; it was time to find a publisher.

In his canvas shoes, holding a dusty umbrella, he scoured the summer pavements from Goldighi to Hedua with his manuscript stuffed into a tin trunk. Finally, he came across Bharat Press in a lane off Sukia Street. They published old Sanskrit and Bengali books and were inclined towards dictionaries. But the proprietor,

Bipin babu, said, 'We cannot judge how good your dictionary is. If you can get a recommendation from someone important, we'll think about it.'

'Such as? Whose . . .' Gurudas was too embarrassed to utter the word recommendation.

Bipin babu mentioned three or four names. The very first one was that of the vice chancellor of the university.

Gurudas arrived at this gentleman's house the next day. About a dozen people were waiting in a small room. As the day progressed, a crowd of people waiting for an audience filled the open space in front of the house. Dhutis and western suits, Madrasis and Punjabis, even men in saffron robes. Some paced up and down, some leaned against the railing, some peeped over the swing door before ducking behind it. Young men, old men, women, helpless faces, grave expressions—but all of them similarly afflicted by the need for solicitation. The clacking of typewriters, the ringing of telephones, the bustle of orderlies and clerks—it was impossible to tell who had got an audience and who was waiting in despair. From seven the clock moved on to eleven—there was no hope of a meeting today.

Gurudas slipped while getting off the tram on the way back, injuring himself. Putting tincture of iodine on his bruises, he rested on a plank in the boarding house all day. When he awoke the next morning, his hips were aching. But still he got into the second-class coach of the tram with his trunk.

No luck that day either—four hours passed, alternately sitting and standing. Four successive days went by this way.

On the fifth day, he arrived even earlier, in case he could get in before anyone else. He discovered only two people there before him. A man of dignified appearance walking across the yard stopped suddenly on seeing him.

'What's the matter? Here again?'

'I had to come again because . . .'

'You haven't met him yet? I've been seeing you every day. Well, what do you need?'

'I have composed a dictionary of Bengali. It's about this dictionary . . .'

'Oh, a dictionary? Of Bengali?' The man surveyed Gurudas from head to toe, not omitting his tin trunk. 'You've actually brought your manuscript?'

'Just . . . in case he wants a look . . . if he has the time.'

'Very well, sit down. Go straight in as soon as he arrives. Through this door here—there's nothing to be afraid of.'

He really did get an audience, along with a slip of paper with the words 'I endorse this book for publication', accompanied by a signature.

Five hundred copies of each of several slim volumes would be published, each costing one rupee. The books would not be bound. Half of whatever was left over after paying for costs would go to the author, but if expenses were not recovered within a year, the writer would recompense the publisher.

These were the terms of the contract. Bipin babu kept the manuscripts for the first four letters, 'Aw' through 'Dirgho-ee', and Gurudas received the proofs within a week of returning to Khulna.

Six volumes were published in a year; the vowels were done. But Bipin babu welcomed him sombrely the next summer. 'The books aren't selling at all. There they are—see for yourself. An entire dictionary is available at ten rupees, who's going to pay six for just the vowels? And who cares for so many details? I couldn't cover my costs, but I know you cannot recompense me. I can absorb this loss, but if you want to publish further, you'll have to pay half the costs. If the books sell, I'll recover my costs first, plus thirty per cent commission. The rest of the money will be yours.'

'Half the costs? How much?'

'It takes between two hundred and two-fifty to print each volume. You'll get bills.'

Gurudas left another six volumes of his manuscript with the printer. For each volume being printed, he sold half an acre of land. Eventually nothing but the homestead was left, and then that was sold too.

By then ten more years had passed. Gurudas was almost through with 'Baw'; all the letters up to 'Dontyo-naw' had been published. Meanwhile, his hair had greyed, he wore thick lenses in nickel-framed glasses—but despite the spectacles, everything seemed blurred at night. Horimohini was suffering from arthritis, she couldn't do the household tasks any more. The entire family was under the care of the lean, indefatigable Bhabani. She paid a little extra attention to her father, offering him whatever she could—a little milk or fruit, or some juice. When she had a few moments to spare, she leafed through his dictionary. Gurudas had taught her, the first child of his youth, a little Sanskrit and Bengali. She knew her grammar, and had even picked up proofreading skills. There were times—perhaps on the morning of a holiday—when Gurudas sat outside the house, writing, while Bhabani sat beside him, turning over the pages of books, not talking. They never spoke— but they were happy, both of them.

Nobendu now had a salary of seventy-five rupees. He lived in Calcutta; his job was to check tickets on trains leaving from Sealdah Station. His days passed travelling on trains, but he rushed home whenever he could, and he handed over a reasonable sum of money to Gurudas every month. It was thanks to him that they survived even with Bhabani's three growing children. Gurudas could afford to go to Calcutta from time to time, and Horimohini did not come to know that they didn't own any land any more, that they actually had to buy all their provisions now.

Horimohini busied herself in finding a match for her twenty-seven-year-old son. Nobendu wasn't willing, he said he was trying to get the post of stationmaster— it would be better to marry after he had settled down. Actually, it was the state of the family that had made him reluctant to add to his financial burden. But Horimohini insisted, and he was married in May.

Along with new quilts and sheets, a painted box of toiletries, and the fragrance of Vaseline and scent, the new bride also brought a wave of joy into the house. A beauteous girl of fifteen. A little pain was unavoidable too; reminded of Shibani, Horimohini wiped her eyes covertly.

Nine months after his wedding, Nobendu slipped while trying to climb into a moving train and fell on the tracks. When he was pulled out, his heart was still beating in his mangled body, but not long enough to make it to the hospital.

His wife was seven months pregnant at the time. She fell unconscious when informed, and delivered a premature, dead baby four hours later. She never succeeded in getting back on her feet; overcome by childbed fever, suffering for six months, she finally vanished into the shadows like an insubstantial shadow herself.

Gurudas received one thousand five hundred rupees from Nobendu's provident fund, and another two thousand rupees as 'compensation'. And a few months later, just before Durga Puja, the war between Germany and England broke out.

From 'panchambahini'—fifth column—to 'anubidaran'—splitting the atom—Gurudas collected many new words during the six years of the war. These would have to be added to the appendix. But his work didn't progress significantly during this period, he only got as far as the Bengali letter 'Law'. Nor could he publish beyond the Bengali letter 'Raw'; printing had become four times as expensive, and paper was hard to come by. Meanwhile, the landlord suddenly demanded seventeen rupees as rent for the house for which Gurudas had been paying seven and a half rupees all this time. The price of rice vaulted from four rupees per maund to forty. Kerosene became too expensive for lanterns. And his eyes began to trouble him. The doctor said he had developed a cataract in one of them, and that surgery was necessary. This meant a trip to Calcutta and a cost of about a hundred and fifty rupees. He dismissed the proposition as soon as he heard it—it was more important to remain alive, even if on only one square meal a day.

They survived on Nobendu's three and a half thousand rupees. He dipped into it to pay for Bhabani's daughter's wedding, which cost about five hundred. Despite controlling his expenditure strictly, the rest melted during the war years like ice put out in the sun. He had returned his daughter-in-law's jewellery to her father.

It was during the war that Horimohini learnt that they no longer owned a home of their own. But she was not perturbed—she had lost that ability. She had turned inert after her son's death—somewhat deranged. She seldom spoke, just eating her meals and staying in bed most of the time and continued to suffer from her arthritis. Her teeth had fallen off, she was an old woman now.

Bhabani stood like a pillar, resilient. Her sons Amal and Bimal were in school. The elder one passed his matriculation examination and joined Khulna College, where Gurudas intervened with the principal to ensure that he would not have to pay any fees. Bimal gave up studies suddenly and, applying his own judgement, got a job at the ration shop, where he learnt to pilfer. When the sixteen-year-old's mother found out, she used a piece of wood to take the skin off his back.

Gurudas was penniless when the war ended. His salary and allowance at the school amounted to sixty-three rupees, but because of his age, the authorities pleaded with him to retire. After much begging, he secured an extension of two years—he would have to leave after that.

But suddenly the problem of employment became a trivial one. Rivers of blood began to flow across the country, which then became independent. Khulna was allotted to Pakistan. After waiting and watching for a while, Gurudas decided to leave with his family.

It's best not to talk about how the journey was made. Partly on foot, partly by train, occasionally on a boat across a river. Their belongings (such as they were) were left behind; they took only absolutely essential clothes, a few utensils, and his case of books. The published copies, handwritten notes, and . . . and virtually nothing else. All those books he had collected with so much effort since childhood had to be left behind.

Although they were unencumbered, the journey was not an easy one. He had grown old, his vision was dimmed. His wife hobbled. Amal and Bimal actually had to carry their grandmother at times—but how far can you walk bearing the weight of a heavy old woman? They had to pause for rest beneath trees, while Horimohini shrieked with arthritic pain. Rain. Sun. Dust. Droppings. Flies. And hordes of helpless people. Two babies were crushed to death by the crowd at Ranaghat Station.

It took ten days to get to Calcutta. They spent a week at Sealdah Station, eating nothing but puffed rice, and were then transferred on a lorry to a camp at Bongaon, where they were served a lump of rice and daal at two every afternoon. Gurudas recovered a little on this diet, but there was no respite from Horimohini's cries of pain.

Finally, the lord took pity on her. Cholera broke out at the camp, and her heart gave way after she had emptied her stomach out several times. They could not cremate her themselves; government officials gathered bodies wholesale and took them away in a black vehicle.

Two months later, they were given shelter at a refugee colony near Kanchrapara. Rows of one-room bamboo shanties, with a little space to cook in. A pond nearby, a tube well for fresh water at a slight distance. Still, Bhabani set up a household despite the limitations. Amal got a job at a nearby mill, which helped them survive. Bimal went astray, spending all his time outdoors, smoking and watching films, though no one knew how he got the money for it.

Gurudas pulled out his notebooks again. One eye was clouded over with cataract, the other had dimmed too. Every moment of daylight was priceless. He went outside as soon as the sun rose, while Bhabani brought him a cup of tea and a little puffed rice. She had to have her tea with her father—he insisted on it. Gurudas had discovered tea towards the end of the war. It provided energy, and suppressed hunger too. Starting with the first light of day, he worked till the last rays of the sun faded. He sat cross-legged, his notebooks on a small stool, and just two or three books open around him—whatever he had been able to salvage from Khulna. When his back ached, he placed a book beneath the small of his back and lay down for a few minutes. It brought relief.

The next month, Bhabani made him a bolster. And that same day, he wrote a postcard to Bipin babu at Bharat Press.

The reply came two days later. Bipin babu had asked after him, expressing pleasure at hearing from him after such a long time. Demand had picked up for his dictionary recently, the previous editions had almost sold out. It was necessary to publish the subsequent volumes now. The money realised from the sales of the earlier volumes would be enough to publish the new ones—Gurudas would not have to pay any more money. Bipin babu would be obliged if Gurudas could inform him when the new manuscripts would be available.

After a few more letters had been exchanged, Bipin babu agreed to provide a monthly 'assistance' of fifteen rupees. Gurudas saved some of it to get some new books all over again. Several volumes were published in succession over the next two years; he got as far as the letter 'Dontyo-shaw' meanwhile.

The following year, Gurudas finished his dictionary, while it took another two years to publish all the volumes. He had to read everything in print once more: the corrigenda, the appendices, everything. The *Great Bengal Dictionary* was complete in fifty-two volumes. It had taken him thirty years. He was a young man of forty when he began—now the hair on his head was white, his back was bent, his cheeks were like crevices, his veins protruded on his skin. He was blind in one eye and had marginal vision in the other.

Gurudas took to his bed a few days later. The task for which he had conserved the last drops of his energy had been completed, he no longer needed it. He recalled Shibani, Nobu, and Nobu's wife. He recalled his wife. 'Don't perform my last rites, Bhabani,' he told his daughter. 'I don't believe in any of it.'

But he suffered along and incessantly. Death was not at his beck and call.

Meanwhile, there were murmurs in Calcutta about his dictionary. One Gurudas Bhattacharya had apparently composed a dictionary—an outstanding achievement. Word spread by word of mouth—to the university, to literary gatherings, to newspaper offices. Those who bought the dictionary praised it, those who didn't praised it even more.

Eventually, a young journalist appeared in a Jeep one day, accompanied by Bipin babu from Bharat

Press. Gurudas did not speak much—he had no strength. Covering her face, Bhabani answered all their questions in a soft tone. A sensational report appeared in the next day's paper, peppered with magnificent words like 'sacrifice', 'dedication' and 'devotion'.

And so Gurudas became famous.

It was the fifth year after Independence. The government had announced literary awards. Someone on the committee proposed Gurudas for an award. Gurudas Bhattacharya? Oh, the dictionary. Well . . . well, one has to admit he has accomplished a mammoth task, written thousands of pages. And we hear he's in financial difficulties, eking out an existence in a refugee colony—it would be a splendid gesture. Something that would capture the popular imagination. You've seen how *Swadeshi Bazaar* has praised him, haven't you?

Gurudas was chosen to receive the award.

In reply to the official communication, Bhabani wrote that her father was ill and unable to visit Calcutta in any circumstances.

One of the younger ministers said, 'Very well, let us go to him. People will approve.'

Therefore an enormous car drew up at the Kanchrapara refugee colony at ten o' clock one morning, escorted by a Jeep showing the way. A minister of the independent state emerged from the car, accompanied by two high officials, and two orderlies in shining red uniform. The same young journalist, a government clerk, and a photographer with a camera jumped out of the Jeep. The car could not come up all the way to the door. As children and women watched with bulging eyes, they walked along the narrow path between rows of shanties to Gurudas's hut. The tiny space was suddenly filled with people.

There was no room to sit—the ceremonies were conducted with everyone on their feet. The minister said a few words. A silk shawl, a bouquet of flowers, and one-hundred-rupee notes tied with a silk ribbon, amounting to five thousand rupees, were placed on Gurudas's bed. The cameras clicked, Gurudas's weak eyes blinked at the flash-popping bulbs.

He lay still on his back, his hands gathered at his chest. His expression did not betray whether he was aware of what was going on. But when the guests had moved away from his bed, when their demeanour suggested they wanted to leave but were staying back only out of embarrassment, Gurudas spoke clearly but faintly. 'Turn me on my side, Bhabani. This is very funny, but if I laugh, I will be insulting all these people. Make me face the other way.' The eye with cataract was still, but laughter flashed in the other one for an instant. Bhabani turned him over on his side carefully.

He died the same afternoon. His grandsons and the young men from the neighbourhood took him to the crematorium draped in the same silk shawl and covered with the same flowers.

He had made a single statement before dying. 'Keep the money, Bhabani, it'll prove useful for you.'

Lovers

I climb out of the subway on 110th Street. The end of June, the beginning of summer, a glittering Broadway. In the distance, the sun is setting into the arc of the Hudson as it flows into the Atlantic—all of Manhattan is iridescent, the grey houses are pink. I have climbed these subway stairs up to 110th so many times that I have lost count now. I no longer get into the wrong train, I don't have to consult the green arrow any more to take the shuttle to Times Square, I've memorised everything. I belong to this city now. I have no fixed working hours, but I choose to return when offices close, to savour the sharpest taste that the city can offer. The peak commuting hour is past—I was in a paperback store in Greenwich Village (oh God, some of their bookshops turn you mad)—half of New York is done with dinner—but how crowded it still is, how crowded! Millions of people, different races and nationalities and colours, women, men, old people, boys. And among them, me. They are rushing like an army of ants; so am I. They don't glance at one another, but I glance at them—grim, lined faces, expecting dinner back home, each with their secret anxieties, looking forward to meeting their wives or husbands— or sadness. All of them lonely, but I am immersed in an ocean of companionship. Today I took the wrong exit and surfaced on the opposite pavement, I was confused suddenly, for a moment I didn't recognise my hotel. This is one of the contributions of the subway— the same city, the same street corner, the same house and sky can appear in different forms, just like a lover dressed in clothes of a different colour or style. Ten days more, two hundred and forty hours. After that I will no longer climb up these stairs, look at the rectangle of the sky getting larger as I ascend, or be astonished at the sight of an even larger world beneath the sky. The same faces, but they have changed now, this summer evening has spread the light breeze everywhere, people are exchanging glances now, no one is lonely any more. This evening crowd on Broadway will keep smiling and flowing, I won't be there. I will have to leave her—but who is she? She is supposed to be there between quarter to eight and eight: hurry up. Let me call her and tell her not to be late. Here at this drugstore . . . no, the pastry shop is just a minute away; let's go, run. I want a quick look at that girl, at the man too. Husband and wife? No, they're too similar in appearance, must be brother and sister. Danes, both of them tall and slim, perfectly blonde. Indra and Indrani from the Rig Veda. Alas that they have to be shopkeepers despite such beauty, goddesses from heaven pressing buttons to add up prices. There are three customers ahead of me, I keep looking at the girl in rapt attention, why haven't I asked her for a date all this time I have been here, when Dolly was working late at the office—but who knows, what if they are actually husband and wife, I can never tell from the ring, but then I could have found out easily enough by striking up a casual conversation. But I haven't progressed beyond the smiles in their eyes, which they distribute to the entire world, I am leaving in ten days. I ask for a slice of fruit-cake from the showcase beneath the counter, so that she has to bend to get it out. (So slender, like a tender shoot; so flexible, like a strip of cane; my ivory girl, my willowy woman—whose poem is that?) She puts it in a box, I request her to wrap it in paper, so that I can watch her long, tapered fingers at play a while longer. I will have to carry this box now, although I never eat dessert, Dolly doesn't care for it either. In the civilised world, why can't one simply say, 'I don't want to buy anything, I'm only here to gaze at you for a bit, and for another glimpse of your blue eyes'? Near the door I remember—the phone call. 'Bella isn't asleep yet, I'll leave as soon as Martha arrives.' 'When will Martha come?' 'It's time—any moment now, there's the doorbell, that must be her. See you soon then—in fifteen minutes.'

Ah—soon. In fifteen minutes. Run home. The owner of the laundry I use is standing at the door for a breath of fresh air, she munches on some sort of mouth-

freshener all the time, her words are always fragrant.
She smiles at me—should I stop for a bit?—no, two of
the fifteen minutes must be over, there's no time, just
about ten minutes more. How wonderful this city is,
how beautiful this evening, the first real day without a
trace of winter, all the glass doors open, the entire
world out on the streets, the florists on the pavements.
How lovely these twelve—eleven-and-a-half—eleven—
minutes of waiting are. I stand at my third floor
window, looking out, one bus after another comes to a
stop, she will get off one of them—the splitting image
of her, with my favourite face, eyes, lips, and cheeks,
ready for me. I still have a long ten days to go—
unlimited time—a kingdom. I hope she won't take a
taxi, if she comes in a bus, I will see her getting off, her
rolling walk, in this sparkling light, I will see her look
at my window across the road. Thumping, my heart
thumping, I'm trembling with expectation, I'm not
forty-two any more, I'm eighteen. I'm travelling in a
horse-drawn carriage, with Manju by my side. Some
stroke of fortune has handed me the responsibility of
escorting her back to her hostel. What joy, Manju
needn't be back before ten, it's only eight-thirty now. I
have instructed the coachman to take the road leading
away from her hostel—towards Ramna—I've promised
to pay him by the hour, so that he may drive slowly. A
spring morning, a green Ramna, the golf course and
the race course, the houses with sloping roofs concealed
amidst their respective gardens, not a soul anywhere.
Manju by my side, our shoulders touching, never

before have we sat so close together. The carriage trundles along, laziness dripping from the sound of the hoof beats, the occasional rustle of leaves, a dreamy, intoxicating morning. Not too many words spoken, just looking into each other's eyes occasionally; we're alone, the veil of pointless conversation can be torn away; in my eyes she grows lovelier by the minute, my love has made her even more beautiful. Her smile spreads from her eyes to her lips, her lips part, a flash of teeth, tongue, I move away to observe how red I've made those lips of hers. My first time. My first kiss, that is. Manju is panting a little, suddenly it occurs to me that faces aren't visible up close—which is better, kissing or looking? But it is Manju who leans towards me now, we grow bolder, suddenly I spot a boy of fourteen or so on the road, looking at us round-eyed, smiling. We have not even bothered to raise the shutters on the window, we're innocent, we're children, we're heaven on earth. We're children, both of us, I am seven at most, Tunti is probably not even five, I am visiting my mother's family in Faridpur. All my games are with Tunti, I dress up dolls, dig holes in the ground to light a stove, pluck leaves and blades of grass to use as seasoning, I'm trying to be like Tunti, to love everything that she loves, for her sake I'm almost becoming a girl myself, all boys of my age seem to be apes when compared to Tunti. But in the evening my male personality asserts itself, I have taken the responsibility of coaching her, I teach her the alphabet, a lantern sits between us, two large shadows on the wall; instead of teaching her I watch the shadows, both small but one bigger than the other, but because the lantern is so close both are large, they shake their heads when we do, wave their hands, crook their fingers, I love watching them, curling up behind her I merge the shadows into one, I move about to make my shadow touch hers, I shake the lantern to create strange forms on the wall—Tunti laughs coquettishly, she is scared too. This was a mystery, shadows, a primordial evening romance which the easy availability of electricity has destroyed today. But there is no electricity at this Kohinoor Hotel of ours, there's brilliant sunlight all day and at night the world disappears, only we remain— Ila and I—in this tiny room on the second floor, the huge terrace just outside the door, and even larger sky above it, and before us—as big as the sky—huge, powerful, turbulent—waves, one after another, the storm rages all night, but all day long it's just blue, white, frothy, green, violet—the sea. The whole sky is in this room, the horizon is in this room, and the voice, the passion, the breath of the sea—all ours, all for us. Ila's in Puri for the first time, she is afraid of the roar of the waves at night, we spend most of the night awake. I still cannot get used to the idea that Ila is mine now, my wife, every time I feel I am doing something wrong, doing what I should not, and that's why the thrill is unending. Is this real? Are Ila and I really alone in our second-floor room, cloistered in the heart of the night with the sea stretching before us and the star-studded sky over our heads? Which is real? These days, these nights, this upheaval of the waves, this stirring of the blood—or marriage, domesticity, the poky little flat in Bhawanipur, the suffocating smoke from burning coal every evening? We're on the Chowringhee tram, on our way to New Market, I am sitting next to Ila on a seat reserved for ladies, but several nurses in white uniform get on at Elgin Road, I move to the long bench near the door. A young Anglo-Indian woman enters at the next stop and sits down next to me at once, a priest takes the seat on her other side, a thin, tired clerk somehow makes space for himself on the few remaining inches. Four people on a seat meant for three, the priest is quite plump, it's a tight squeeze, I cannot avoid contact with the Anglo-Indian woman's body even if I try, fidgeting makes the contact even more palpable. But her face shows no sign of discomfort, her face hasn't contracted in annoyance, her eyes are quite cheerful, as though she has avoided contact with the priest and is leaning against me, she might even respond without reservation if I say something. Pleasure spreads over my body—the fading winter sunshine on my back, and this other warmth—I am feeling guilty because Ila is on the same tram (even if she has her back to me), and because of the guilt, the sensation is even stronger, as though I am on a swing in a garden, moving very slowly (actually the sideways swaying of the tram), my eyes are closing, I can get a whiff of flowers in the air (actually the lotion in the woman's hair, the powder on her face, the perfume on the handkerchief tucked into her breast)—ten minutes pass this way—no, maybe five, three hundred seconds, an eternity, with my body I sense a young woman, a young soul, a stranger's life—warm, soft, new, undiscovered. She gets off at the same stop as we do, I have to suppress all other desires because Ila is with me (could I not have found out her address at least?), in fact I don't even try to look at her on the road—I do not realise when the mistress of touch is lost in the crowd on Chowringhee forever, gifting me only a flower that lived for five minutes. Everyone is lost this way, no one can be held back, the person you're spending your life with, the person you refer to as your husband or wife, that person has long been lost too. All of us are changing every moment, we do not know one another. A smashing party, liquor is flowing in this city under prohibition, the low hum of the Arabian Sea is drowned in laughter and conversation, film stars are circulating like ferris wheels—millionaires, diplomats, and so on. I am drinking lemonade, I don't want to lose my composure, I've got my eye on the fair-skinned French countess, her velvet dress clinging to her curves, it looks very simple but every weave holds an artist's talent, skill, taste—at least, let's assume that's the case—I must find out whether it's a Dior. As soon I arrived, I got a couple of minutes with this Indophile writer, I asked her without a moment's hesitation whether she was fond of Baudelaire; in response, she smiled with her eyes and murmured the first stanza of the wonderful poem whose title is Invitation au Voyage. The French words fell from her lips like droplets of honey on my ears, I found a new beauty in the creases at the corner of her eyes signalling her age. But I had to move away soon afterwards because of the swelling crowd, and now I cannot approach the siren any more, I cannot even see the slender figure in black velvet continuously, like a jewel in a box, like a sword in a scabbard—how downy black the velvet is, like a poem by Baudelaire, black, a glow bursting out of it. I'm standing in a corner like a fool, guzzling lemonade— how about a Cinzano instead—no, best to avoid these shallow Romantics, classic Scotch is best. No, not alcohol, I need food, I'm ravenous after the exertion of seeing the Vatican, I've just returned to my hotel, it's three in the afternoon. The dining room is shut, I'm at the snack bar in the basement. There's no thronging crowd now, I'm the only customer, besides a broad-shouldered young German drinking beer on the long bench. I raise my eyes as I eat; a girl is standing on the pavement outside, as still as a picture. I am in the dimly lit basement, the girl's one floor above me on the pavement, it's summer outside, I get a clear view through the clean glass window—she's exactly like a heroine taking up position on stage. She's dressed in a thin, white, low-necked dress, I am thinking Boticelli, but suddenly the lady of spring appears to wave, she seems to be signalling with her hand—then, bending, almost flattening her nose against the window, she sends an unmistakable message—come. To whom? Must be the German, but his back is still turned as before, and from his position he cannot see her anyway.

Me? Impossible. I concentrate on my omelette again, but . . . isn't it silly to brusquely reject someone who's submitting willingly? Isn't it cowardice? Isn't it discourteous to life itself? Let me at least find out what this is all about. But when I raise my eyes, she's gone. I abandon my food to go outside—not there. Where has she gone? Black magic? I keep thinking of her all afternoon, and at night when the fashionable crowd on Via Veneto is swelling, I'm wandering around the cafes, scanning the faces—but will I even be able to recognise her now? Did I really see her, or did I only create an object of desire from my sudden arousal? Maybe she was only an ordinary streetwalker (just like my companion of five minutes on the tram to Chowringhee)—she had thought that a foreigner would be easy prey—and for her I had wasted the entire afternoon and evening—and that too, not in any old city but in Rome, where, this very morning, just a few hours ago, I had seen the Sistine Chapel and the opulence of the Vatican for the first time in my life. Was it for the thin white dress, the curve of the neckline, the cleavage which rose and fell with her breath, the cheap array of beauty being peddled that I had forgotten the Eternal City and the immortal Michelangelo these past few hours? Here they are, arranged on the shelf, the books I bought recently; Thomas Mann's novel, Rilke's poetry, a wonderful new translation of Sophocles—and I am restless because Dolly isn't here yet, my days are flying by either in Dolly's company, or waiting for her; the hours that I could have used to reread Philoctetes, to listen to the angels beating their wings, to watch the Goddess ascend from the fires of hell to Faust, have been filled to the brim by Dolly Gordon, who does not understand poetry, who likes going to the Metropolitan Museum only for the pleasure of having lunch by the fountain in its garden, whose lack of time (or lack of interest) prevented me from going to Mozart's Don Juan, making me give up the tickets even after getting them. How cruel this thing is—which people call love. How agonising—this waiting. Half an hour has passed, my eyes are smarting from staring at the clock, ten times I have walked up to the telephone and ten times I have returned without using it. Why should I worry? She's the one who should inform me if she's going to be late: it's her responsibility, her duty. I'm hungry now, lunch was a long time ago, a hamburger (I don't enjoy eating good food alone)— she isn't even bothered that I'm starving because of her. Why don't I go out—let Dolly go back, let her be punished, let her realise that she's no empress, and that I'm no slave either. Dolly does these things wilfully, she hooks me to a barbed wire and enjoys the outcome, savouring her own power. And now there are only ten days to go. Does she really love me? Or, having submitted, does she find herself trapped, is my golden bird now fluttering her wings in a cage? And yet, when I was stuck in Hotel Mascot, unable to go out because I had a cold, it was winter, this same person had brought me food every day—lobster, ham, chicken, apples, Rhine wine, soft and warm rolls she had baked

herself—one day the lift was out of order, she had
walked all the way up to the ninth floor, carrying the
basket of food, a handkerchief tied around her head, a
limpid glow in her Hispanic eyes, snow on her overcoat,
panting because of the cold and the effort of climbing
nine floors, her lips slightly parted, offering me the gift
of her vigour and her joy, the giver of life, the giver of
sustenance. I was gazing at her spellbound—Dolly,
Dora, Dolores, my Dhaleshwari, my dahlia—how
could Jim Gordon have left her. Love: must it be only
momentary, then? Desire, the blooming of desire—is
that all there is to love, does the other side of the
vibrant picture reveal itself as soon as the desire is
satiated? Ah—if only it had been the French countess
instead of Dolly, whose address I hadn't sought, whose
very name I had forgotten, yet with whom there could
have been a mingling of minds, the kind of love on
which the body does not obstinately intrude every now
and then. With her help I too might have discovered
the key to Racine, the fire beneath the ice, the lightning
hidden under the lid of the couplet; I would have got to
the heart of the secret magic that made every cultured
Frenchman and woman besotted with Racine, while
foreigners could not reach him at all. What a triumph
it would have been in my life, like conquering a new
kingdom. But the time comes when we no longer want
conquests, nor happiness—we just want peace. And
this peace can only come from . . . the body. Books
make you think too much, books are bad. The body
offers no argument, the body is good. Even a beautiful

woman sitting in front of me gives me peace, like a pink haze stealing over me surreptitiously, I have to make no effort. And that is why I want Dolly Gordon. Just look at the time—a quarter to nine, the streetlamps have been lit—what is she doing? Fleur de Lis will close in another fifteen minutes—the small French restaurant on 87th Street, never crowded, they serve wonderful oysters and a cold and sweet sauterne—all day long I've been looking forward to dining there with Dolly. Why isn't she here? Is it even possible that her daughter has not gone to sleep yet, or that the babysitter hasn't arrived? Or . . . has there been an accident? Did a drunk run his Chevrolet over her? Did the cable of the lift snap suddenly? I seem to see Dolly at the hospital, covered by a sheet—she is no longer beautiful, she is not a woman any more, she has become a pulpy lump of flesh and blood. No, this anxiety is unbearable, swallowing my pride I pick up the phone: busy. Two minutes later, the moment I hear her voice, I am furious, my jealousy rears its head, unformed accusations and suspicions. 'Sorry, I'm so sorry, please forgive me—Martha only just got here, and Bella simply wouldn't go to sleep.' 'But you said the doorbell rang.' 'That was the janitor, he was here to fix the kitchen sink.' 'Right. But then why was your phone busy a few minutes ago?' 'It wasn't me—Martha was calling her boyfriend.' 'Didn't you say Martha only just got here?' 'Oh, only just in the sense of a few minutes ago. The moment she came in the phone rang.' 'Why was she so late?' 'She had gone to the hospital to see her grandmom.' 'Is her grandmom dying?' The response was brief laughter. 'Wait at the corner for me, I'm coming over in a taxi, okay?'

I have been listening to Dolly a little suspiciously all this while—the janitor, Martha's boyfriend, the grandmom, it all sounds plausible, but who knows whether the truth is something else, I have no way of finding out anything beyond what she chooses to tell me, how much of her days and nights, of her entire past, of her life, do I know about anyway? I am smarting at the casual air with which she spoke to me on the phone, as though these things aren't particularly important for her, she will be happy if she can visit me, but not unhappy if she can't; for some reason, she is oblivious about how wrong it is of her to be so late, uncaring about how much it pains me. But my state of mind was transformed the moment the last word fell off the black instrument bearing our words back and forth. 'Wait at the corner, I'm coming over at once . . .' These words gave life to a different Dolly in my mind— Dolly—Dolores—Dhaleshwari—honey-tongued, clear-eyed, a heart of pure compassion. We have entered a restaurant—fortunately it's still open—high ceilings, a stone building from the eighteenth century, a strapping tall half-asleep young man is our waiter. It's almost closing time, but he isn't hurrying us, his big body is lumbering about lethargically, the corners of his eyes are red, his face is creased, grave. He holds a desultory conversation with us (assuming that Dolly and I are married), perhaps to shake off his sleep, or because there are no other customers. He speaks English haltingly, he comes from Buenos Aires—the loveliest city in the world, according to him—I sigh because I am unlikely to see this city ever in my life, but Dolly begins to talk to him enthusiastically in Spanish. Our broccoli and brain cutlet are laid out before us, the man stands with his back against the wall, Dolly's gaze keeps drifting towards him; 'He's handsome, isn't he? His face is very interesting, isn't it . . .' 'Looks like an alcoholic, doesn't he?' Dolly keeps whispering comments like these in my ears, squeezing my hand at times, as though to reassure me of her devotion, and I am wondering where my gut-wrenching craving has gone, which made every nerve in my body tingle while I was standing at the corner of Broadway and 110th. And when her taxi did in fact stop—it really was Dolly, after this long wait it really was her lovely, fragrant body—how did my joy from that moment vanish so quickly? Is this why Jim Gordon had left her, then? Is it then possible only to love the one who is not near, or who has not submitted? Is love nothing but the phantom of our desire then? Is it better to remain at a distance than to get close? We want to love, our special instants are born of that wanting, they provide only a single glimpse before they vanish into the darkness, into the caverns of time, into the recesses of our dreams—and still new dreams don't cease. Dreams from memories, memories from dreams—unending. Take that waitress in Vienna, ripe of body, red of cheeks, whom I cannot help stealing covert glances at while dining with a professor of Indian studies. This place is known as a 'Greek Inn', centuries old, ivy creeping up its ancient stone walls, uneven rows of caves and grottos inside, some a couple of steps down, others a few steps up, dim lights in brackets hewn into the walls—half-dark, unpolished oak tables without table linen, but with an announcement in four languages printed in large letters, reading which thrills me. 'Beethoven, Mozart, Goethe and Heine used to frequent this inn; many of their compositions were planned here.' I cannot quite fathom what the professor is saying about *Geet Govind*, my curiosity about this inn is growing uncontrollably. How old is it? Seven hundred years? Six hundred and fifty? What was it before it became an inn? Was it a monastery for medieval monks? Or a chieftain's fort? What led to its conversion into an inn? Is there a memorial to Goethe or Beethoven here? The professor does not know for sure, he had heard about this place once, he does not remember now—he has been immersed in studying Sanskrit for the past twenty-five years, he has not had the time to devote himself to anything else. 'Can't we ask the waitress?' The professor asks her a series of questions, explaining the answers to me in English, it turns out she is not very well-informed either, but that does not matter much to me—I get a chance to gaze a little longer at this plump, round, rosy-cheeked beauty with heavy breasts, a figure straight out of Rubens, as though a mythical heroine has descended to earth to pour wine into my glass, as though this extraordinary grotto is the location of my tryst with her—but the moment I leave this place I will never see her again, she will sink into a grey and hazy early morning dream—like the two Negro nurses at my hospital in Cincinnati. They turn frantic as soon as they see me, I don't know why, one of them smoothening the pillow, the other straightening my sheet (although everything is just fine); saying 'lie down, lie down, the doctor will be here any minute . . .' they practically shove me into my bed (without offering any explanation of why I have to lie down because the doctor was coming); they bend over my face from either side, two pairs of silky impenetrable black eyes pierce me; one of them says, 'My name's Jenny, hers is Fanny, call us if you need anything, call us by our names, whenever you like, we're here all night tonight—okay? That's a nice boy.' I turn red, I try to tell them I'm neither a 'boy' nor 'nice', I am forty-two, I am a formidable literary critic in my country, there's not a writer who does not fear my jabs—but before I can open my mouth, Jenny (or Fanny) asks, 'Don't you have a girlfriend?' and bends so far over me that her breasts spill out before my eyes—the colour of clouds, tranquil, like grapefruit, I have to lower my eyes, the doctor enters that instant and my dark-skinned beauties disperse, startled. Knuckles rap my back and chest, everything is alright, but this ward won't be convenient for me, apparently—I cannot make out why not, but in ten minutes I am transferred into a room that I have all to myself, it's far more comfortable but there's no Jenny, no Fanny, I did not even get the chance to bid them goodbye, they vanished after leaving a single black scratch on the sky of my multicoloured imagination. The snow-covered world stretches before my eyes, but in my heart black glows brighter, tender deep black eyes, and unruly waves of curly black hair. Was it not a fresh beauty that had flashed before my eyes for just a few moments? I don't think they were really promiscuous—Jenny and Fanny—perhaps they pitied me because I'm a foreigner, maybe their ability to love is unfulfilled, perhaps they are looking for ways to dispel their loneliness, no matter how briefly. But why am I even thinking of other things when the real life Dolly is here with me, the long day is ending at last, I'll be here for nine days more, the night is deep, Dolly's eyes are shining like stars in the darkness—let us assume nothing else exists in this whole wide world, only the two of us for each other, I am falling asleep, my head on her breast. Ah, this peace, which nothing can match, for which I can forget Michelangelo, Thomas Mann, ambition, effort, responsibilities, the fear of death— everything. Like another round of sleep within the sleep, like certainty that one can sink into—for a few days, a few hours, a few moments. I am falling asleep with my head on Dolly's breast, I am waking up, or am I dreaming? What are those ants doing there? They're dragging a dead dragonfly—from my shelf to their hole in the window sill, their home—a lavish feast. Such power, such momentum, and such speed. The dragonfly's wings seem to be beating faintly now and then—has it died, or have they clamped their sticky legs on its dying—but not yet dead body, should I release the dragonfly from its agony? I press down on it with a book, the dragonfly is flattened, but none of the ants die, their legs are clamped to it as before. One, two, four, twelve . . . exactly fourteen, too small for the naked eye (I had to count thrice), the dragonfly is as big in comparison to them as the elephant is in comparison to us. Papers and books are piled high on my shelf, the window sill is low, they will have to climb down one wall and up another—how effortlessly they are traversing the danger-strewn route uphill and downhill, scaling the peak of the Kanchenjunga before climbing down to the valley—crossing or skirting every obstacle, like a tank on the battlefield, at a hundred miles an hour by our standards—these amazing atom-sized creatures. I try to stop them with a postcard, but it is like trying to stem a flood with a fence—they swarm over it, cross it—they are unstoppable, indomitable. I even kill one or two of them between my fingertips, others take their place immediately, the troops do not scatter. I gaze at this victorious march—spellbound, a little fearful, as though I am exhausted just by the sight of this incredible endeavour, then I become aware of the sound of trams outside, Calcutta's May heat is palpable even at this early hour of the morning—a long, sweltering day stretches before me, I have to get out of bed soon, I have to shave, I have to bathe, I have to wonder how to fill this day, so many hours, till I fall asleep again. I am not as strong as the ants; where can I take shelter?

Twenty-Five Years After— or Before

[A restaurant in an international airport. It must be assumed that the restaurant is huge, with a large number of people eating, drinking and moving about, but we can see only a single table and four chairs around it. On one of the chairs are an Italian ladies' handbag of black leather with brass buckles, and a large, shabby, brown, bulging briefcase. On the back of another hang two raincoats—one red, the other grey.

The other two chairs are occupied by a man and a woman. The man's hair is grey and unkempt, the fatigue of travel is gathered on his face, he is sitting slackly. The woman is middle-aged too, but still attractive, with a well-maintained figure, her face reflecting the aura of good health and make-up. She is dressed in a moss-green nylon sari and a pale green sleeveless blouse. The man is in a blue suit—well-tailored, but slightly crumpled. Long-stemmed wine glasses are set before both of them, between them is a plate of savouries, with a crystal carafe of white wine on one side. The woman's glass is almost full, the man's, half-empty.

The glow from a sloping blue sky and a sunny afternoon is visible through the glass window.]

Woman: (Continuing, as soon as the curtain rises) . . . And that's how the years go by. Sometimes in Cairo, sometimes in Prague, sometimes in Bangkok. Vienna or Washington now and then. And India, once in a blue moon . . . So you're still in Calcutta?

Man: Where else would I possibly live?

Woman: Why, weren't you in Delhi once? I heard you had two stints in America too. Which means we could have met earlier too. (A little later) Why didn't you let me know? Didn't you know we were abroad?

Man: But I had no idea exactly where . . .

Woman: You could easily have found out with just a little effort.

Man: It didn't quite . . . occur to me. There was such a rush before leaving the country. . .

Woman: Didn't occur to you . . . in other words, you didn't remember. (A little later, lightly) You had forgotten me, hadn't you?

Man: (Sipping his drink, smiling faintly) You shouldn't ask such questions, Urmila.

Woman: I'm a simple sort, I say whatever comes to mind. Unlike you, I'm not . . . (Stops)

Man: You're not a brooding type like me. Old hat.

Woman: How strange it seems, when you were in Boston in '61, we were in Washington. Practically next door. (She pauses, the man doesn't respond.) When did you visit Bangkok?

Man: Bangkok? . . . '65, in January.

Woman: There you are. We were in Bangkok too at the time. You've been travelling so much, but not once did you enquire after us.

Man: (Suddenly vehement) But this is best. Meeting suddenly like this.

Woman: Far too suddenly. (After a pause) Did you recognise me?

Man: Of course, why shouldn't I?

Woman: I'm asking if you recognised me at first glance.

Man: Yes . . . almost.

Woman: Almost . . .? (A little teasingly) Now don't say I look just the same.

Man: It's not a question of the appearance. We often look, but we don't see. When we do see, we recognise instantly. Though I don't exactly know what it is that we do see.

Woman: Riddles.

Man: For instance, at first I saw a woman in a sari. The sari caught my eye the most. The woman was walking towards me, looking around her. I was watching the way she walked. Watching in the sense, I was looking but not seeing anything. Her face, her expression, were all visible to me, but still . . .

Woman: But still you didn't recognise me? Have I really changed that much?

Man: It's not the appearance. I was saying that I could see everything, but somehow I couldn't see you. And then . . . what made me recognise you was not your features, not even the way you walk, but everything together, in a flash. As though a bulb lit up in my head.

Woman: But you looked familiar even from a distance. Although I had assumed I was mistaken. But when you came closer, I saw . . . it really is . . . Chinmay.

[An announcement is heard on the loudspeakers.]

Woman: KLM coming in from Beirut. (Another announcement.) Pan-Am's off to New York. Arrival and departure. Over and over. And amidst all this we've met suddenly. After such a long time.

Man: (Sipping his drink) Yes, after a very long time.

Woman: Twenty-two . . . no, twenty-three . . . no, twenty-five . . . exactly twenty-five years after. In this airport restaurant . . . as though you fell out of the sky.

[The man doesn't respond. A few moments of silence.]

Woman: And for such a short time. The two of us travelling in two opposite directions. (Pause) How does it feel?

Man: How does what feel?

Woman: This . . . (Pauses, as though changing her mind) Returning home after a year. How does it feel? You must be excited, aren't you?

Man: Yes . . . well . . . a little. (Sips his drink)

Woman: Your wife . . . daughters . . . they must be very nice.

Man: They're very nice.

Woman: Someone mentioned your wedding in a letter. We were in Cairo . . . Bijon's first job outside India. Manju was born that year. Manju, my daughter. You haven't seen her. You probably remember Bablu.

Man: Bablu? . . . Oh, yes. I used to play with him sometimes. With a red rubber ball.

Woman: Bablu is an established engineer now, he lives in Montreal. His wife's American. Martha's a wonderful girl.

Man: Excellent.

Woman: Manju's married a German, she's going to have a baby next week. I'm on my way to see them. (Pauses, the man says nothing) Karl, my son-in-law, is very accomplished. He paints, he can cook, he plays the violin very sweetly.

Man: Excellent.

Woman: They've named their son Adim. Bablu and Martha. From Adam from the Bible. Do you like the name?

Man: Yes. (Sips his drink)

Woman: As a child, I always thought of grandmothers as old women. But now I see . . . that's not the case at all, it's perfectly possible to be a grandmother and live a normal life . . . Your daughters aren't married yet, are they?

Man: They're . . . getting ready.

Woman: And then—you'll be a grandfather too. Our Chinmay.

Man: Indeed. (Smiling) Living needs courage, Urmila.

Woman: (A little later) You've realised that a little late.

[The man looks out through the glass window. A few moments of silence.]

Woman: (Looking at the man out of the corner of her eye) Why don't you say something? What are you thinking of?

Man: It's a beautiful day. Look outside.

Woman: (After a single glance through the window) I wonder if there'll be any sun in Hamburg. It gets so foggy there.

Man: The sun—the blue sky—the mountain in the distance. I was thinking . . .

Woman: (Eagerly) Yes?

Man: I was thinking that somewhere in the world it's raining now, elsewhere it's winter, and somewhere else, there's a fog. But here, outside the window . . . it's like autumn in Dehradun.

Woman: (Almost inaudibly) Dehradun . . . Delhi . . .

[The roar of an aeroplane outside. The sound is heard for a few seconds before fading gradually. The man listens closely.]

Man: Did you hear . . . the sound?

Woman: Pan-Am's off to New York.

Man: New York? But I suddenly thought . . .

Woman: (Eagerly) Tell me.

Man: As though the sound is going far away, so very far away . . . to a place where we may have been once upon a time, a place we want to go back to.

Woman: (Almost inaudible) Once upon a time . . . a long time ago . . . or was it just the other day?

Man: But the people inside the plane cannot hear the sound. They're wondering when they can take their seatbelts off, when they can smoke, some are reading their newspapers, others are sipping their fruit juice. But later, somewhere else, when some other plane flies past, they'll hear its sound—from a long time ago—which they had heard back then but not listened to.

Woman: Another riddle.

[A few moments' silence. The man sips his drink. An announcement is heard on the loudspeaker.]

Woman: Qantas is off to Singapore. A group of people leaves. Another group is coming up the stairs. They won't wait long either . . . What time did you say your flight was?

Man: One thirty-two.

Woman: Mine's at one thirty-nine. We'll have to leave together.

Man: That's true.

Woman: Mine's leaving from Gate No. 21. Yours?

Man: Mine's probably . . . (pulls the boarding card out of his pocket) mine's No. 22.

Woman: Facing gates, then. We'll go together all the way.

Man: Not exactly all the way.

Woman: (With a light laugh) I meant we'll walk together up to the gates. Climb down the stairs, walk across the lounge, climb down another flight of stairs, and then side by side down a long corridor.

Man: That's true.

Woman: As though we're travelling together, as though we'll get into the same aircraft and sit next to each other.

Man: Yes indeed.

Woman: It's so strange, Chinmay. It's so strange that two hours from now I'll be in Hamburg, chatting with Manju and Karl, and you . . .

Man: And Bijon?

Woman: He's in Ankara. Didn't I tell you that's where I'm coming from? I had to change planes here.

Man: Yes, you did. (Sips his drink)

Woman: Bijon won't get leave anytime soon, I have to go because Manju's expecting. Her first pregnancy.

Man: Why should that be strange?

Woman: Oh for heaven's sake—not because of that. I was saying that two hours from now I'll be in Hamburg, chatting with my daughter and son-in-law. And tomorrow morning you'll be in Calcutta—where your wife, your daughters, your family are all waiting eagerly for you. Everything is all right, everything is running smoothly—and suddenly we meet.

Man: That's true.

Woman: (Glancing at her watch) We have thirty-five minutes more—nearly forty. And then, walking down a long, cool corridor—suddenly we're separated, each to a different plane, on opposite sides. Don't you find it strange?

[No response from the man. An announcement is heard on the loudspeaker.]

Woman: Air India arrives from London. SAS is off to Helsinki. The long table is emptied out. Three Japanese men are coming up the stairs. Two Arab women are coming up the stairs. The corner table over on that side is emptied out . . . interesting place, the airport.

Man: Too restless. So many people, but none of them can be tied down.

Woman: (Smiling faintly) There's no lack of things to tie you down. This is preferable sometimes. Everything is fleeting, temporary. Very interesting.

Man: Yes—nice—for some time. At the end there's the arrival. No danger.

Woman: (Softly) It was you who were afraid of danger, Chinmay—not I.

[The man lowers his eyes to his glass. A few moments of silence.]

Man: (Lifting the carafe, looking at the woman) You haven't touched your drink.

Woman: I will. (Spears a piece of cheese with her fork and lifts it to her lips) You aren't eating anything.

Man: I will. (Refills his glass)

Woman: People talk too much when they drink. You're growing quieter. You haven't said anything about yourself yet.

Man: What else is there to say, tell me.

Woman: We've been sitting here for nearly half an hour, you haven't yet told me anything about me.

Man: (After a pause) You're still the same, Urmila.

Woman: What do you mean, the same?

Man: You haven't grown older.

Woman: (With a smile at the corner of her lips) All these trite statements have turned stale. (Eats a small sausage) But you know what, I never think of age—I keep myself busy, I get about, I never let things get me down . . .

Man: Never?

Woman: As much as I can help it. Take us here, now—I seem to be doing all the talking, and you look as though you're bent over with worry at the sight of an old friend. Back then too I used to say we had completely different natures. But how, in spite of that . . . (Stops)

Man: Perhaps because of that very reason.

Woman: What do you mean by reason. No one knows why these things happen.

Man: Or, when it does, we don't understand.

Woman: There's nothing to understand. It's a sort of madness. How else could I have been prepared to walk out—Bablu was just four, and I'd only been married six years.

Man: That's exactly what I'm saying. You can't always keep yourself from worrying.

Woman: But how often does something like that happen in a lifetime! If you count the hours and minutes, how long does it last? All these things are so short-lived.

Man: Are they really short-lived? Didn't you ever feel afterwards that . . .

Woman: There's no 'afterwards'. All these things live and die with the moment. Tell me truthfully, how many times have you thought of me during these past twenty-five years?

Man: It's not as though I never have. Sometimes I even wished I could see you again.

Woman: Which is why you never made enquiries while you travelled half the planet.

Man: Exactly. I did not want to see you at home with your family. You're a different person there—you're a wife, a mother, an eminent lady.

Woman: (Throwing him a sharp glance) I seem to remember being the same back then too.

Man: It was because you were that . . . (Stops, doesn't finish) I had wanted to see you somewhere where you'd be—just you. I wanted to match you to the picture in my head.

Woman: (After a pause) Are you able to match me?

Man: I'm trying to.

Woman: Meaning—you can't?

Man: If only you'd help me a little. Tell me—what were those days like, when you'd thought of walking out?

Woman: (Looking at him coolly) I was prepared. You backed out.

Man: I was asking what those days were like.

Woman: Such thoughts. As though something extraordinary was about to take place in my life. Something amazing.

Man: (Softly) Someone else was involved too, Urmila.

Woman: Bijon. My worthy husband. (Laughs softly) Do I need you to remind me of him? I'm sure you didn't think of me as an unhappy wife.

Man: You wanted for nothing. I created the want.

Woman: (Drawing her words out) Oh . . . I . . . see . . . eee. You went away out of kindness for me? Out of pity for my well-constructed, neatly arranged, inflated, exaggerated happiness? You wanted happiness for me, Chinmay—you didn't want me. (Laughs softly) Fine. Fine.

[The man doesn't respond. He sips his drink. The woman eats an olive absently. A few moments of silence.]

Woman: You're just the same. Your tie's still crooked. Your hair still sweeps over your forehead.

Man: (Brushing his hair away) But—what did happen? What happened between you and me?

Woman: You're asking?

Man: I know the facts, but what . . . what exactly did we do?

Woman: You're asking? Asking me?

Man: I was occupied with what was actually happening. I didn't understand any of it. Can you describe it?

Woman: (Smiling faintly) As if it can be described.

Man: Why not. What was that room like? That town, that house, the scene outside the window? What was the garden like—the one in which you strolled at dawn while I gazed at you through the window?

(Continues after what seems to be a moment's reflection) Roses, weren't they?

Woman: (Almost inaudibly) Dehradun—Hillview Hotel—where we first met.

Man: And dahlias, I think. Or was it sunflowers?

Woman: We met virtually every day, exchanged a few words. One day I discovered you were in the garden already.

Man: I think I counted five different shades of roses. Red, white, yellow, pink, and the fifth . . . the fifth was halfway between red and pink—darker than pink, lighter than red (after a pause, ardently). Tell me what that particular colour was—did it have a name?

Woman: We returned to Delhi together after the holiday. Bijon was working at the Secretariat, you were teaching at Delhi College. The light colour deepened gradually.

Man: A solitary tree—directly in front of your Raisina Road bungalow. Was it a deodar or a gulmohar, or . . . see, I can't remember.

Woman: I hope you haven't forgotten Feroze Shah Kotla. The sunset on the Yamuna.

Man: Didn't a lot of birds flock to the tree at sunset? Or was that a different tree—was it in Delhi or Mussoorie or Dehradun?

Woman: There's no place on earth without a tree like that.

Man: But that tree, which you and I would look at together. Those birds, whose cries you and I would listen to together. The things that lie beyond what the eye sees, what the ear can hear . . . see, I can't remember.

Woman: I hope you haven't forgotten Qutub Minar on a winter afternoon. You and I climbing up, Bijon lagging behind, the staircase growing narrower as we climbed.

Man: The smell of moist earth—can you tell me exactly what it was like? Like the smell of ancient stone, something that's faded but still clinging to it.

Woman: And at the top—such a strong wind, how large the earth seemed. I was afraid I might fall. But the fear was like a joy.

Man: Tell me, Urmila, does whatever has happened live and die with the moment? Why can't we capture it—that precise moment? The smell in the staircase—I seemed to get it a minute ago, but now it's gone.

Woman: The light, the wind, the smells—they were everywhere, just for me. Seeing, hearing, speaking, not speaking—waves washing up continuously. But sometimes I saw a shadow on your face. Sometimes Bijon looked grim. Once it so happened that there was no sign of you for ten days. And then at a concert . . .

Man: You're right. Hirabai was singing . . . Jayjayanti, wasn't it?

Woman: You were listening with great attention, you turned pale the moment our eyes met.

Man: Go on—and then?

Woman: (Looking at him coolly) You seem to think this is a story, that it has nothing to do with you.

Man: That's true—it has everything to do with me, I was deep inside it at the time, that's why I didn't understand what it really was. How I felt—when I was listening to Hirabai with my ears, thinking of you in my head, I considered slipping away but I couldn't avoid your eyes . . . how I felt then . . . I don't remember.

Woman: You took me home from the concert. There was no more of hide and seek between us.

Man: I remember a road—narrow, winding, dense foliage on both sides, dimly lit—I walked with you on that road after darkness fell—when was it, where was it . . . (Fervently) Where was that road, Urmila?

Woman: There were many such roads in old Delhi back then.

Man: No, not many—one, just one—the one along which you and I walked. Bushes and hedges on either side, no one else on the road, no sound from any of the houses, we didn't say anything either. But where— where exactly was it? I don't remember.

Woman: Surely you haven't forgotten your flat in Dariyaganj. Where the curtain was brought down on this drama.

Man: Perhaps that road still exists, but we aren't walking along it. So it doesn't exist any more. Even if we walk along it again, it will still not be the same road. And yet it feels as though we're still walking along that road—you and I from back then.

Woman: You were startled to see me. 'I was going to your house anyway, why did you come?' I said, 'I came to Chandni Chowk to buy something, I suddenly felt very thirsty.' You brought me a glass of water. Looking at the glass, I said, 'This won't quench my thirst, Chinmay.'

Man: Incredible! You shook your head the same way now, spoke in the same tone.

Woman: Do you remember your response?

Man: The same smile on your lips. That very moment seemed to be back—and then it vanished.

Woman: 'Let me go, Urmi.' You were looking so forlorn. Poor thing. (Laughs softly)

[A few moments of silence. The woman sips her drink for the first time. The man is gazing at her steadily.]

Man: And then?

Woman: (Her voice sharper) This isn't a story, Chinmay, this is life. Red blood beneath the skin, a throbbing engine beneath the breast—which you were afraid of that day. (A pause) Tell the truth, weren't you afraid?

Man: Perhaps.

Woman: I was ready with everything I had, you went back from my doorstep. I hadn't imagined you were such a coward—so impotent.

Man: Or courageous, perhaps.

Woman: You could certainly say that. You do need a little courage to make advances to a married woman.

Man: (After a pause) There's something you probably don't know. Bijon and I had a conversation one day.

Woman: (Coldly) I see. Bijon.

Man: There were tears in his eyes that day.

Woman: Really? A tall, strong, powerful man— with tears in his eyes! Why, exactly?

Man: That sounded cruel, Urmila.

Woman: At least I'm crueller than you.

[A few moments of silence. The woman sips her drink.]

Woman: (Drawing out her words) So . . . you melted at the tears in Bijon's eyes? And as for me—whose happiness, whose peace, whose sleep you destroyed— you didn't think of me at all? You really are generous.

Man: I didn't think of myself either, Urmila. I hurt myself too.

Woman: What do I care whether you were hurt? I was roasting in my own hell. (A pause) So—you made such a big sacrifice—for Bijon! The same Bijon, who was toying with Rukmini Chauhan not six months ago—practically under my nose. Encore! (Laughs softly)

Man: (In a pained voice) Why are you blaming Bijon suddenly, Urmila?

Woman: You wanted to know exactly, ex-act-ly, what happened, didn't you? Then listen.

Man: You were in a turmoil. Maybe you misunderstood many things. Maybe you imagined some of it.

Woman: (Sharply) Why should I have to imagine anything? Did I do anything wrong, for which I needed an excuse?

Man: But if you blame Bijon you blame yourself too, don't you see?

Woman: You mean to say that it's wrong to want to punish someone who does something wrong?

Man: I want to say that whatever happened, happened on its own. There was no other reason behind it.

Woman: What if I say you were mistaken?

Man: (Smiling affectionately) Mistaken, Urmila? Were you pretending with me, then?

[A few moments of silence. The woman takes a long sip of her drink.]

Woman: (Softly) Why be surprised if I did? You need to, sometimes.

Man: Impossible. I never saw in your eyes what you're saying with your lips now. I still don't.

Woman: (Tenderly) You're such a good person, Chinmay, such a good person. But still—listen. Just like some people catch a cold when they travel, Bijon had that illness. Sometimes it was Rukmini Chauhan, sometimes Jayeshwari Shukla, sometimes someone else. I was forced to think of a cure.

Man: You shouldn't humiliate yourself, Urmila.

Woman: I was humiliated by Bijon. But the medicine worked.

Man: You won't succeed. Not even you can blacken the picture in my head.

Woman: The picture in your head? Imagination? A beautiful, dazzling, wonderful dream? You're right, you're right. That's all that a person like you needs. But I had a different sort of demand.

Man: (Ardently) Then you accept that there was no pretence for you?

Woman: (After a pause) How do I know—it's been such a long time. Maybe it began with pretence, but that too was a delusion—it wasn't really pretence but I was trying to pretend that it was, or perhaps pretence stretched out over a long period becomes real—or appears to be real.

Man: (With a faint smile) There you are—you couldn't call it pretence despite your best effort. The truth came out.

Woman: The truth . . . how can I say that either. You left Delhi suddenly—I was in such a state. I thought I would die. (Smiles faintly) But gradually—everything became all right. While you were there I used to think of Bijon as bad—horrible. But later I discovered—not at all, Bijon was quite nice, wonderful. And all the turmoil—it seemed to have been nothing at all. (A pause) No one knows how many different ways we fool ourselves.

Man: No, Urmila, no. There you are—I can see that glow in your eyes again, as I listen to you it's all coming back to me—all the roads and the rooms and the gardens, all the windows and the evenings and the nights—all that we had one day—that we still have—that continue to be, taking the you and I from back then along with themselves—we're not aware of them, but it isn't as though we're never aware of them.

Woman: (Slightly miserably) Just memories. Suddenly—unexpectedly—now and then. They're not enough to live with, Chinmay.

Man: But it feels as though it's possible to return. Now and then—suddenly—momentarily.

[A few moments of silence. An announcement is heard on the loudspeaker.]

Woman: There comes your Air France. (Shifts in her chair) I feel a little sad, you know. Not for you or me—but for what happened. So many hopes, so much joy, such suffering—but eventually—nothing. Nothing?

Man: What we had felt—still feel—is that nothing?

Woman: Feelings? Beating heart, tearful eyes, missing someone? What do they add up to? I had wanted love in every sense, Chinmay. I had wanted from you every last thing that life can offer.

Man: But . . . and what could have happened then, what usually happens . . . that's nothing but routine. But the things that really happen are outside the routine.

[An announcement on the loudspeaker]

Woman: My flight's boarding too. Thank goodness. We'll set off in opposite directions once again. Everything will fall into place again.

Man: But still . . . what about this time in between, Urmila? We'll have this too. Or, we will remain in this.

Woman: Just a little time. It's always just a little time. But we have to live a long time—a long long time. That's why we can't do without routine.

Man: But still—this meeting today. This restaurant—the sky and sunshine and the glittering aeroplanes outside—this will go on too, taking along with it the you and I of today—it will go far, far away—to a place where we may want to go back someday.

Woman: And now—back to our respective routines—let's go back.

[They rise to their feet, take their respective belongings and leave the table—ready to proceed. The handbag hangs from the crook of the woman's elbow, the red raincoat is slung at her shoulder. The man carries the briefcase, his grey raincoat folded on his arm.]

Woman: Hamburg in two hours, Ankara again a month later—my happy, married, family life—for which I am grateful to you.

Man: I am grateful to you too, Urmila, for you have just taught me that what has happened once never dies.

[They're ready to leave.]

Woman: [Stopping as she is about to start walking] Just a minute.

[They stop for a moment, look into each other's eyes.]

Woman: Your tie's so crooked. (Straightens his tie, touches his hair fleetingly) Let's go.

[Side by side, they begin walking.]

The Strange Course of Love

Ila is pacing up and down restlessly in her room when Shobhon appears outside the door. The only information about them we need is that Ila is twenty and Shobhon, sixteen.

Ila: (Brusquely) Who's that?

Shovon: It's me.

Ila: Ah . . . Shobhon? (Gently) Come in. (Shobhon enters) Sit down. (Shobhon sits down) Have you heard what your Amal babu's done, Shobhon?

Shobhon: What's he done?

Ila: You haven't heard? (Acerbically) He's getting married, you see!

Shobhon: Then so are you.

Ila: (Suddenly stops pacing up and down and faces Shobhon) Look, Shobhon, I'm warning you, you're becoming cheekier by the day . . .

Shobhon: I'm sorry.

Ila: (Quickly patting Shobhon on the shoulder) Well, so'm I. Please don't mind—I'm not in my senses today.

Shobhon: So I see.

Ila: Listen. Your Amal babu is marrying Pamela Mitter—can you imagine! Pamela—ha ha! (Ila laughs drily.) What do you think of Pamela's looks, Shobhon?

Shobhon: Ug-ly.

Ila: Ah, Shobhon. You have discerning eyes. Pamela . . . her face is exactly like a halibut's, isn't it?

Shobhon: (After some thought) Very much like a halibut's.

Ila: Not very much, Shobhon, exactly like a halibut's. Take a good look when you can.

Shobhon: I will.

Ila: And he has to pick halibut-face to . . . have you brought my cigarettes, Shobhon?

Shobhon: I have. (Takes the packet out of his pocket and gives it to Ila)

Ila: (Rips the cellophane wrapper off the packet and opens it with such force that the entire foil-covered tray slips out on the floor.) Damn!

Shobhon: Here you are (picks it up and hands it back to her).

Ila: (Putting a cigarette in her mouth) Want one?

Shobhon: No.

Ila: Have one. Never mind, don't, you're still a child. (Tosses the packet on the dressing table, then picks a lighter up from the teapoy nearby to light the cigarette) What I simply cannot understand, Shobhon, is how he could choose this halibut-face—ugh, what taste Amal has! Just as well, Pamela will suit him just fine. Do you suppose, Shobhon, that I would marry him, that I would even consider marrying him, even if he threw himself at my feet and licked the soles of my boots and sobbed?

Shobhon: Why are you pacing about that way? Please sit down.

Ila: If you run into him, Shobhon, tell him that Ila is ashamed today, that she feels sorry for herself, for having consorted with someone whose taste runs in that direction . . .

Shobhon: I will.

Ila: No, don't tell him she feels sorry for herself. You can tell him instead that . . . never mind, there's no need to say anything at all. If you run into him, say nothing about me. All right, Shobhon?

Shobhon: All right.

Ila: And if he tries to say anything, if he tries to say anything about me, Shobhon, just give him a resounding slap. Can you do that, Shobhon?

Shobhon: Of course I can.

Ila: No, don't say anything, there's a good boy, don't say a word. There's no use making a scene. Let him do whatever he wants, what relationship do I have with him any more? (Remains silent for a while, then throws the cigarette out through the window) Let him die, let him go to hell, let him be ruined—what do I care? And yet and yet and yet, Shobhon, yes—you know that I loved him, Shobhon—can you tell me why he didn't marry me? Yes, of course I would have, I was ready to. If he asked me even now, at once I'd—you're laughing, Shobhon?

Shobhon: Oh no, why should I laugh?

Ila: What do I do now, Shobhon, tell me. What use is it to stay alive? Now I wish . . . if only I'd died earlier . . . but who would have thought such a thing would have happened. No, it's no use staying alive. I'm going to kill myself, Shobhon.

Shobhon: You're determined to?

Ila: I'm telling you in confidence, Shobhon, don't tell anyone else. Tomorrow . . . by this time tomorrow I'll be dead.

Shobhon: How will you kill yourself?

Ila: With poison—no, I'll shoot myself. Can't you get me my father's pistol without anyone knowing, Shobhon?

Shobhon: Do you know how to fire it?

Ila: That's true, I've never fired a gun in my life. What if I miss—how terrible! There'll be a bang, everyone will get to know, such a scandal—but I won't have died. I'll have to die of shame instead. No, I'm going to poison myself—opium, strychnine, potassium cyanide . . .

Shobhon: Where will you get all this?

Ila: You'll get them for me.

Shobhon: Where?

Ila: That's true, that's true, this is a big problem. So many varieties of poison in this world—but not a bit to be had to kill oneself. What's to be done, Shobhon, what's to be done?

Shobhon: What if you don't kill yourself?

Ila: (After a brief silence) Yes, you're right. You're right. No, I shan't die, I shall live. I shall live. I'll show him that he means nothing to me. I consider him insignificant, I loathe him—no, I don't even loathe him. He will realise I never loved him a bit. (Suddenly stops, then speaks hoarsely) But I did love him, Shobhon, you know that.

Shobhon: Come and sit down here, have another cigarette.

Ila: (Sits down beside Shobhon, puts her hand on his) You're a nice boy, Shobhon, a very nice boy.

* * *

[One year later]

Shobhon: (Answering the phone) Hello.

Ila: (On the phone) Is that you, Shobhon?

Shobhon: Yes, it's me.

Ila: Listen Shobhon, I'm going to . . . it's Ila . . .

Shobhon: I know. Tell me.

Ila: I'm going away. I'm leaving Calcutta tomorrow, India three days later.

Shobhon: Our misfortune.

Ila: No, don't say that. I'm feeling just as horrible about leaving all of you.

Shobhon: Why are you going?

Ila: Just . . . holidaying.

Shobhon: You don't care for India any more?

Ila: It's not that; I have to go somewhere far away—that's why.

Shobhon: What! Are you planning to settle in England?

Ila: I might. It was all very sudden—I didn't even get a chance to meet everyone . . .

Shobhon: So soon after Ranajit babu's wedding . . .

Ila: Don't say that, Shobhon, don't say that.

Shobhon: I'm not saying it—everyone is.

Ila: Who is?

Shobhon: Everyone.

Ila: What kind of people are these, what kind of people. But Shobhon, that's why, that's why I have to get out of this country.

Shobhon: You're wise. It's far too hot here.

Ila: (After a pause) Um, Shobhon, let me ask you something. Have you run into him . . . Ranajit?

Shobhon: I have. I went to their house the other day—we were invited.

Ila: What did you see? Is he happy?

Shobhon: So it seemed.

Ila: (After a pause) I'm glad to hear that.

Shobhon: Really?

Ila: Yes, Shobhon, really. Let him be happy, I don't want anything more than that. Let him be happy—I'm going away. Now I do think I'm not coming back—no, I shan't come back. Perhaps we'll never meet again, Shobhon, don't forget me.

Shobhon: You and I shall meet. I'll go to England next year, as soon as I've passed the ISC examination. And I'll bring you back when I return. If you don't want to come, I'll force you to.

Ila: (Laughing) Shobhon, Shobhon, of all the people I know, you're the only one who loved me a little.

Shobhon: Do you want to know my plan? I'll have a job waiting for me here as soon I've got my engineering degree in England. Then . . . then I'll marry you.

Ila: You're getting too impertinent, Shobhon . . .

* * *

[Four more years later]

Shobhon: Hello.

Ila: Is that Shobhon?

Shobhon: Yes it is.

Ila: It's Ila.

Shobhon: Oh, Ila. So glad. So kind of you to . . .

Ila: Not at all.

Shobhon: You're the first person I thought of when I came back. How are you?

Ila: I just found out that you're back. I had phoned earlier too—you weren't home. Listen, will you come over? Just once?

Shobhon: Of course I will. And not once, but a thousand times. I would have even if you hadn't asked.

Ila: Ah, Shobhon, what a good time we had in London those first few months, do you remember?

Shobhon: I'd expected you to stay, if not forever, at least a little longer.

Ila: Do you suppose I was unwilling? But I had no choice, my mother fell ill suddenly . . . but we didn't meet the day I was leaving, I had hoped . . .

Shobhon: I tried my utmost, but something came up . . .

Ila: Never mind all that now. Do you remember what you told me on the phone the day before I left Calcutta, Shobhon?

Shobhon: I wanted to marry you, and you scolded me. (Laughing) Oh Ila, the things people say when they're children!

Ila: When are you coming over, then?

Shobhon: How about this evening?

Ila: Yes, come right away, this evening.

[A pause]

Ila: We'll meet after such a long time. Three years—no, even longer. Where was it that we met last? Wait, let me recollect—at the Chinese restaurant in Soho, wasn't it?

Shobhon: Ah, that Chinese restaurant. What a funny place. How funny the man's accent was. But still, the food was superb. Later I took Marjorie there quite often.

Ila: Took whom?

Shobhon: Marjorie.

Ila: Who's Marjorie?

Shobhon: My wife.

Ila: (Choking) What did you say?

Shobhon: My wife. I'm telling you in confidence, Ila, don't tell anyone else. I haven't let anyone know yet. The idea is, once Marjorie gets here . . .

A Scent of Tulsi

Between sleep and wakefulness lie many unknown footsteps, several unconscious moments; between sleep and wakefulness is the bridge of dreams, dreams that blend strangely with reality towards the end. On this winter morning, just such a dream was built for Mihirkumar Som through the sounds of music. There was a rise and fall of melody, like waves on an ocean of sleep—then the waves washed ashore on the conscious mind; the bridge of dreams ended at the edge of wakefulness. A succession of waves, an extraordinary congregation of sounds, scattered and dispersed every moment across the world—melody, melodious sounds. A succession of waves, the soft, muted notes of an organ caressing the air in the room. Mihir realised well after waking up that he was awake, the sound of the organ became clearer; only now did the music become entirely audible, but still, it was like a caress for Mihir, like the warmth of the part of the bed which his wife had left a short while ago. As though Kamala had

220

left the essence of her body over there. Even without opening his eyes Mihir could clearly see the hollow in her pillow, where Kamala had rested her head all night, her black hair like a signal, an invitation. He had been caressing her hair, winding several strands of it around his fingers. As soon as he recollected this, Mihir's mind was filled with the golden warmth of an unusual pleasure, as golden as grapes that had ripened in the south—its juice, its warmth, its heart the consciousness of Kamala's being, the sensation of his complete claim over Kamala. The thought flowed in Mihir's soul like the golden wine extracted from golden grapes; Kamala was his, with all her black hair, with all her warm and tender body, Kamala was his. The thought was a luminescence which rose from within him and enveloped him; bathed in this radiance, he lay there, still, a ripe golden. He did not allow the enchantment of sleep to leave; the notes of the organ floated down on his chosen state of drowsiness, on his recently abandoned dream. He listened, or rather, a part of him listened, while with the other part he sensed Kamala within himself—within himself, and around him was spread his rich awareness of Kamala, the luxury of that awareness. And peace ran deep in his heart. Immersed in Kamala, he forgot that many things remained to be unpacked, that a lot of their household effects would have been fetched from the station and arranged in different rooms. He had been plagued constantly by trouble and anxiety during the first few days in a new house in a new place—but now, in the momentary rainbow confluence between sleep and wakefulness, he became oblivious to it. The organ kept playing, a succession of sounds, the indefatigable sport of the seven notes. What was it saying, this incorporeal melody, this series of openings for music in empty space? He didn't know, he didn't want to know. He would just be silent, and this current of sound would flow over his consciousness. He would not open his eyes—no, not even for a glimpse of Kamala's ivory neck beneath her limp and careless bun of hair, nor for the soft, curved line of her back or the concentration of memories around the end of her sari, which was in disarray. Behind his closed eyes Mihir could feel the sunlight filling the room. The after-effects of sleep had escaped by now, but still he wouldn't get out of bed.

Suddenly the organ stopped. It was like a light going out—or rather, like a harsh, prosaic, essential light being turned on in the mysterious and intimate darkness of the theatre. After the play on the stage had ended, a curtain with advertisements fell slowly. Mihir opened his eyes from the half darkness of his dream to the glare of the bright day. And at once they met Kamala's, for she had turned to look at her husband at that precise moment, to find out whether he had woken up.

'Awake at last?'

Mihir smiled into his wife's eyes without a word. And as he gazed at Kamala, love for her drowned Mihir's heart in a torrent, a blind force that he thought would destroy him.

'Come on, get up,' said Kamala softly. 'Do you know what time it is? You'll be in such a rush to get to work you won't have time to eat.'

Holding his arm out from beneath his quilt, Mihir said, 'Come here.'

Kamala rose from her seat in front of the organ and came up to her husband. Drawing her close, Mihir kissed her deeply. Raking her smooth shoulders with his nails, he said, 'Stay here, stay.'

Leaning against him quietly, Kamala was silent for a while; then she said, 'Let me go, I have to put the kettle on.'

The day began—full of the anxieties, annoyances and disquiet of the working day; the dream was left behind, the ghostly music in Mihir's sleep vanished. Recalling his legal office, Mihir experienced a minor bout of nausea—the smell of documents and dust, the groups of sickly, gowned lawyers, hopping along as though about to take wing like green birds, and the noise, the ceaseless noise. Like a gigantic swarm of insects gnawing away at his brain. And the exhaustion on his way home, as though he was walking through poisonous fumes—not sure whether he was still himself. Some of this fatigue was born in Mihir at once, on this fresh-out-of-sleep, winter-sun-washed morning.

Getting out of bed, he stood at the east window. Outside he saw a new city, the peace and sloth of a regional town spread out across the sky. A dense row of trees was visible in the distance; a horse-drawn carriage passed along the road, ringing its bell; a little

Muslim boy ran behind an iron hoop. Those who walked past were in no hurry; the boy seemed strangely quick amidst this general sluggishness. It wasn't as bad as he had feared. At least, in this morning light, under the deep blue sky, it didn't seem as bad.

But his opinion changed when he didn't get the newspaper with his morning tea. He was not yet used to the fact that the newspaper arrived in the afternoon here. The newspaper in the afternoon! Who ever had heard of such a thing? Mihir made an extremely unfavourable comment about his new workplace.

'What does it matter?' said Kamala. 'Don't read the paper till the next morning.'

Mihir raged in his head. 'How can civilised people live in a place like this? I knew all along. I said the day I was told of the transfer that . . .'

'What can you do? The government won't listen to your objections.'

'And you said, "It'll be nice, let's go. Dhaka is a nice place." Nice!'

'But I quite like it. I really do.'

'There's no accounting for tastes.' Mihir sipped his tea as though they had had a serious difference of opinion. Kamala smiled mentally at his expression. How strange her husband's obstinacy was, his inability to tolerate the slightest conflict in viewpoints, his hope that everyone would think the way he did about everything. To please him she said, 'I was here as a child, after all, isn't it nice to be back to one's old haunts after a long time?'

'Hmm,' said Mihir absently.

Kamala had always wanted to come to Dhaka again, at least once. And she had known her wish would be fulfilled. And that was just what had happened, she told herself as she walked along the sleepy afternoon road, that was just what had happened. In her sari of Murshidabad silk and her colourful umbrella, she was a picture on the quiet afternoon streets of the regional town; the handful of people who passed paused to take a good look at her. But none of this caught her eye, she only reflected how odd it was that she was back here. She was back, she was back; just like the sky drinking in the sunlight with all its blueness, Kamala absorbed this thought with every tiny molecule in every fibre of her mind. Not for a moment did she consider where she was going or why. But it was as though she had already made a plan to meet someone; she had left home soon after her husband had gone to office. It wouldn't matter in the slightest, she would be back long before her husband. A noisy old Ford passed, throwing up so much dust that everything turned dark. You had to see it to believe that the turning of four wheels could generate so much dust. But it did not spoil things for Kamala; this dust and its smells were familiar to her, she regarded these part of her return. It was an acknowledgement of her claim over this place. When she abandoned the road to take a shortcut through the field, she considered herself extraordinarily happy, truthfully speaking, almost like the time she was in school. Suddenly she felt, truthfully speaking, that she had forgotten what happiness was. She was alive, that was about all, in comfort, in affluence; according to her husband, according to everyone else, according even to herself now and then, she had been living happily. But she had come to the conclusion that there was actually no such thing as happiness or misery; there was either conflict with or adjustment to the environment, either hiding from oneself or revealing oneself. Happiness and misery, she told herself often, were superstitions she had acquired in her schooldays. But she had fallen under their spell again today. She began to feel as though there was something distinct from herself, something that she had sought for a long time, but never found, never even identified when it was close by. She crossed the undulating fields with light footsteps, her movement natural; as bright as a clouded feather between an empty field and the unending sky, her body moved effortlessly.

Her destination was suddenly at hand. At first glance she did not recognise the locality. There used to be an enormous banyan tree at the edge of the neighbourhood, but the spot was desolate now. She felt a jolt in her heart, but this was inevitable. Progress could not be halted. Just see how the area had been overrun by houses now. A middle-class suburb—from where letters on women's rights were written to weekly magazines, where little girls put up dance drama performances on the occasions of Saraswati Puja and New Year, where boys actually read H.G. Wells. A gathering of retired deputy magistrates; flawlessly genteel, excessively polished, supremely immaculate. It was hardly surprising that they wouldn't let a banyan tree survive there, a tree which had spread its roots in the deep darkness under the earth for long, immeasurable years, spreading out beneath the sky, the shimmering life blooming in its countless leaves.

Now, reflected Kamala, the cry of vulture chicks at midnight would no longer send shivers down her spine here, there would no longer be the old dense darkness outside the window, the fields would no longer be waterlogged in the rains. The iron fist of urban improvement had fallen on the neighbourhood, the vulture family had had to move house, iron poles had sprung up every few yards, bearing pairs of electric wires. There was nothing to be surprised at; such changes were expected. Still, walking along the paved road between rows of house with colourful curtains in the windows, Kamala could not help recollecting the time when getting home on a monsoon day meant stopping the carriage on the main road and wading through water and mud with great difficulty—when home was one of the few houses on the vast, vacant expanse. Dust rose from the unpaved road in April, the entire path turned saffron with piles of dry leaves shed by the banyan tree. Wherever there was a pool of rainwater, groups of green-yellow frogs with swollen bodies displayed even more swollen vocal cavities, croaking in exultation; innumerable burrs stuck to the clothes when walking through the field; on August mornings, nature in the grip of monsoon reached out its

blue palm through gaps in the clouds for alms of light.
And at night . . . such desolation, such darkness! How
enormous the indistinct apparition of the dreadful,
mysterious banyan tree was. Once all this had been
forest land; reckless schoolboys who came here to play
made sure to return home before darkness fell. Since
that time—much, much earlier, in fact—the banyan
had reigned over this place; a world strangely alive
with its birds and insects and boughs and vines. With
its giant network of branches spread out towards the
sky, drinking the sun and rain, it had despatched the
energy from the sun into the millions of fibres hidden in
the darkness of its body; it had expressed the renewal
of the rain in a wealth of fresh, green leaves. This entire
life, the indefatigable, unending play of this life, had
ended suddenly one day. Perhaps a violent cry had risen
when this jungle god fell. Kamala seemed to hear the
lamentation within herself—a scream of death renting
the sky. But it was fruitless to complain, pointless to
mourn this; this was irresistible. The population was
increasing, more space was needed. Man had come
with his tools of civilisation. The tree taking up so
much space had turned out to be redundant. The force
that had set up taps for water and electric poles by the
road had also been used to uproot the tree. Who was
going to stop it? Kamala herself could not survive a
minute without it. No, protesting would be in vain.

   The neighbourhood was absolutely quiet. The front
doors were closed, post-prandial bourgeoise siestas
hung in the air. Most of these houses had not existed

in Kamala's time—the area had changed entirely. And yet nothing appeared new to her, in fact, her eyes did not even register any of the additions and changes. The picture constantly in her mind was from that earlier time, when the roads in winter were covered with a white dust. She seemed to be carrying some memory, some keepsake, from that period that had lain in her head, which her soul had recognised here. Although she was in a time-ordained present, she seemed overcome by a sensation of the past; wrapped in this feeling, she walked along. Suddenly one particular house caught her eye—it was old. She used to know the people in this house a little. How strange it would be if she were to enter. The widowed old lady would not recognise her at first, but when she did—there would be the same rigid, middle-class courtesy, ironclad civility, and so much attention that it would be clear to her that the sooner she left, the better. Kamal knew all this very well—she behaved the same way when anyone called on her at home. Her neighbours had already become aware of their presence; one of them had visited her yesterday, she had apologised profusely for the lack of furniture—and was surprised afterwards, wondering why she had. For, as a matter of fact, the room could already be said to be overstuffed. What else was she doing, after all, but informing the neighbour indirectly that they possessed a great many more things? Never mind, there could never be any real hope of rising above the environment. Besides, one had to behave as expected. 'Dhaka is infested by mosquitoes,' the visitor had said. 'So I see,' she had responded. 'You can keep them away if you sleep beneath a mosquito net.' 'But they often manage to get in through the holes,' she had replied. Amazingly, she had not burst into laughter. Nor had it seemed particularly funny. She could not afford to laugh at such things, she had to behave the way one was expected to behave.

A small garden in front of one of the houses was aflame with a multitude of marigolds. In one corner an enormous sunflower had bloomed. But although she slowed down, she did not stop; she continued walking. In the distance she could see the familiar house with brick walls and a thatched roof; from a distance it looked unchanged—it had never been particularly clean and sparkling. As Kamala approached the house, her footsteps slowed down automatically, the lightness that had been fused into her body was lost. She had made the journey up to this moment on her own volition; now a certain desire propelled her forward, a desire not quite her own. She paused near the wall of the compound. Many of the bricks had fallen off. Amidst affluent middle-class families, this dilapidated house was an anomaly, an arrogance. It was a wonder that it had been allowed to survive all this time. The wooden door set into the wall was wide open. She looked in; the yard was swamped by weeds, a red cow and several goats wandering among them. In one corner, in the shade of the house, a dog was snoozing, its head tucked into its outstretched legs. Kamala looked at the scene, kept looking. It wasn't as though she was thinking of anything in particular; her mind was blank for the moment. She walked in slowly through the door. Startled by her footsteps, the dog opened its eyes, threw a sidelong glance at her, rose to its feet, shook itself, walked a few feet away and lay down again. The cow, uninterested, tore and munched the grass noisily with her teeth, the tuft at the end of her tail swaying lazily. The veranda was filled with goats' excretion and other forms of garbage; a sharp stench suddenly seemed to assault Kamala's brain. Clearly no one had lived in this house a long time, it had long been abandoned. The locks on both the doors leading into the house were intact, no thief had as yet considered the house worthy of his nocturnal profession. Kamala walked around the house; there used to be a guava tree at the back—it was largely dead now, with only a few leaves sprouting here and there. She paused at the bed of tulsi near the front door, next to the wall. The place had become a veritable jungle of tulsi, the boughs ripening to a red colour. During the monsoon a creeper would climb up this plant, its deep blue flowers blossoming—like her eyes. She had never been able to decide whether her eyes really were blue. She would have been happy had there been a few flowers in bloom now. Bending, she tore off a tulsi leaf and kneaded it between her fingers, its scent wafting up to her nostrils. This, this was all she would take away from here; this was what she had come for.

Back on the road, she saw a man with a loaded cycle approaching. He looked familiar. Kamala signalled to him as he was passing. Dismounting deferentially, he stood with holding his head at an uncertain angle.

'Is that your shop?'

'Yes,' answered the man, attempting to adopt the accent of West Bengal as best as he could. Kamala was right, he was indeed the neighbourhood grocer she used to know. But nothing in his expression suggested that he had seen Kamala before.

'Listen, this house . . . doesn't anyone live here any more?'

'This house has long been empty.'

'Where have they gone—the people who lived here? A young man and his mother . . .'

'Yes, she was a wonderful lady—she used to buy everything she needed at my shop.' The grocer was gaining in confidence, the small eyes beneath his flat brow brightening. 'I had just started my shop when they built their house here. Ever since then she . . .'

'Yes, of course. Do you know when they left?'

'Well . . .' Furrows appeared on the grocer's flat brow. 'That was a long time ago.'

'How long?'

'About two years,' answered the grocer after some thought. 'Or longer.'

'Do you know where they went?'

'I don't.'

Kamala was silent.

The grocer continued, 'I met her the day before they left. She said . . .'

'Yes, of course. They never came back?'

'No. I had asked her; she said, "We probably won't return ever again."'

'Hmm. And the house?'

'It's been empty ever since. Such a wonderful location, and look at the state it's in. People hereabouts keep talking about it. If a new house came up here . . .'

'All right.'

Stopping midway, the grocer made another uncertain gesture with his head and was about to mount his cycle again when Kamala looked back. 'Listen . . .'

'Yes?'

'Here you are.' Kamala took a rupee out of her handbag.

The man looked in surprise at the money and then at Kamala. 'Perhaps you're . . .' But Kamala almost forced the money into his hand and began to walk off in the opposite direction, although, had anyone asked her, she would not have been able to explain why she gave him the money.

The scent of tulsi travelled with her, the leaf she had kneaded between her fingers. Once, she spread her fingers out in front of her eyes—there were yellow stains on the thumb and index finger. A stain on two of her fingers—that was all. She knew it would turn out this way. She knew, and still she had walked all this way. During the journey, she had not thought of anything, she had not been able to. But the tulsi seemed to be awakening her gradually from her trance, the trance she had been sunk in all this time. Finally she seemed to become genuinely aware of her surroundings; she felt the distant, disconnected contrast of this middle-class neighbourhood, and the sharp emptiness of the abandoned house, in her heart. Sharp, as though her heart had turned bitter and hard. Just for a glimpse of him. Kamala bit her lower lip firmly to prevent tears from appearing in her eyes; her steps grew quick, even quicker, without her own knowledge. Just for a glimpse of him. But time was indefatigable, time kept flowing, scattering the dust in its wake and turning into dust all that wasn't dust already. But not just yet, Kamala almost said aloud, not just yet. Before the dust was scattered, just a single glimpse with her own eyes. The wish grew in Kamala like an illness, like an invisible wound on her flesh. She felt one warm teardrop on her cheek. She reached into her bag for a handkerchief, but suddenly her eyes misted over, the bright winter sky turned colourless. She walked on, not pausing for a moment, wiping the corner of her eyes and her cheek carefully with her handkerchief.

Kamala had no idea how she went home, which road she took. When she entered, she discovered her husband lying on his back on the bed, smoking a cigar and reading an English novel with a jacket made out of a newspaper. Raising his eyes from the book, Mihir looked at Kamala for some time. This was one of his habits—staring at Kamala for a few moments before telling her something. She felt as though his eyes were tonguing her body. Mihir needn't have been at home at this moment to stare at her this way, need he? 'Back so soon?' she couldn't help asking.

'Yes, a hearing was adjourned suddenly—so I could leave early. Thank goodness. How nice it is just to lie back.' Wriggling with comfort, Mihir stretched. 'Where did you go?'

'Out for a walk.'

'You look very tired.'

'It's so dusty outside.'

Going into the next room and changing her clothes, Kamala came back after a while. 'It's three o'clock. Do you want your tea right away?'

'Not a bad idea.' A little later Mihir said, 'Come, let's watch a film today.'

'Not today.'

'Why not? It would be nice to—an unexpected holiday . . .'

'I don't lack for holidays.'

'It's really horrible,'—an affectionate, almost pitying look appeared in Mihir's eyes— 'the way you have to pass your afternoons alone, isn't it?'

'Not particularly, that's what the magazines are for.'

'Let's go to the cinema today. There's a Janet Gaynor film on at Monica Theatre opposite our office. It's been a long time since I've seen one of those, I'd like to go today.'

'Very well, why don't you go?'

'You come too.'

'I don't want to.'

'Impossible. I won't enjoy it if you don't go.'

'And I won't enjoy it if I do.'

'You will if you come along, take my word.' As though it was all settled, Mihir said, 'Make the tea then, will you?'

Kamala did. Pouring her husband his tea, she took some for herself as well. Mihir was in a splendid mood. He smiled continuously, displaying his teeth generously, as if tickled by something extremely funny. Kamala was distracted, as though she wasn't really here.

'Oh no,' Mihir paused suddenly as he was about to bite into a piece of cake. 'I forgot to get the things fetched from the station.'

There was no evidence that Kamala had heard. 'Even the drawing room is still in a mess—but it's not as though no one's calling on us just because we've moved in recently. No, we really have to make the time and organise the house. What do you think? You could have got some of it done this afternoon, you know, with the servant's help.' Mihir took another bite of cake.

'Tell me, what do you think of putting the large mirror in the other room instead of the bedroom? I realised my antimacassars are getting old, they need to be replaced. I wish I'd remembered while we were still in Calcutta. Will we get decent cretonne fabric here? What is it, why don't you speak?'

'Am I not allowed to be quiet?'

'But this is important, very important. Listen, if we put the large mirror in the other room . . .'

'Let's talk about all this tomorrow. Not today.'

Finally Mihir seemed to notice something different in his wife's voice. 'What's the matter?'

'Nothing.'

'Nothing? Why are you so quiet then? Are you upset about something?'

'What if I am? Can't a person be upset?'

'I see no reason to be,' Mihir observed, a trifle acidly. He was looking grim. His intolerance was childish. Everything around him had to be just the way he wanted them; he couldn't bear the slightest deviation. This was an unrelenting blindness, an inherent single-mindedness, which would never accept anything that did not reflect his own thoughts. Leave alone accepting, he would not even acknowledge it, pretending—possibly even believing—that they did not exist. 'I am an extremist,' he liked to state, 'I either hate or I love.' To tell the truth, though, his speciality lay in hatred. He ended up hating almost all of the people he met, he discovered something to dislike in practically each of them, and this slight dislike coalesced into loathing in his extremist mind. He expressed in this sharp, clear terms to his best friend of the moment, or, in the absence of anyone else, to Kamala. 'I hate him' or, 'That loathsome man' or, 'He's simply detestable.' The stringer his adjectives, the brighter his smile with the bared teeth. There was no doubt that Mihir was an extremist. And love . . . yes, love. Which meant Kamala. He loved Kamala—loved her violently, loudly, and announced it frequently. When he called on someone with his wife, he made it very clear that he loved his wife. He established this by any means possible, in order to display it to everyone, to charm everyone. A sacred, beautiful, love. His glory, the jewel of his life.

The latter half of the tea was completed in silence. The servant took the cup away, and Mihit leaned back in his chair and lit his cigar. 'Then you won't go for the film?'

'Why don't you go?' said Kamala.

'But without you . . .'

'Oh, never mind.'

'What do you mean, never mind?'

Kamala levelled a steady look at her husband. A faint smile made her lips curl upwards. 'Go and watch Janet Gaynor,' she told him softly. 'I don't want to.'

'Nonsense,' declared Mihir contemptuously. 'What are you upset about?'

Suddenly a hidden fire flashed in Kamala's eyes. 'Of course not, only you have a monopoly on being upset, on unhappiness, on not talking.'

Even the suspicion that he was being mocked was like poison for Mihir. His face darkening, he said, 'All these feminine ploys disgust me.'

'That's why I'm telling you to go to the cinema, so that you don't have to be disgusted too long.'

'You do not appear to be enjoying my company any more.' Mihir bared his large white teeth in anger.

'Everyone wants to be alone sometimes.'

'So I have to spend two hours at the cinema in order that you may be alone.'

'It's up to you,' said Kamala, rising to her feet. When she went to the door, Mihir asked, 'Where do you think you're going?'

'Am I supposed to sit here all day?'

'So you've turned into an empress suddenly. What's the matter?'

'Can't you ever be quiet?'

'No. I want to know—I must know—what's wrong with you.' Pushing his chair back noisily, Mihir jumped to his feet. 'Out with it—what are you hiding from me?' He went up to Kamala and stood facing her.

Every nerve in Kamala's tightened and stiffened. 'It's best for you not to know,' she answered, as though in someone else's voice.

'Tell me, tell me at once,' Mihir all but screamed. 'I have to know.'

'I'll tell you then,' responded Kamala very calmly, her eyes meeting Mihir's. 'I used to love someone—I'd been to meet him today.' As soon as she had finished, Kamala left the room without giving Mihir a moment to respond and entered their bedroom, locking the door behind her.

Soon there was a hammering on the door. 'Kamala, please, open the door, open the door.' The banging on the door and Mihir's screams were heard all over the house. The servants exchanged glances.

'Open the door, Kamala, Kamala.'

A little later Mihir heard Kamala say, 'Just a minute.' He waited in silence.

'The door's open, come in.'

Entering, Mihir found Kamala sitting on the bed. He began very gently. 'Was it true what you just said?'

'Yes, it's true.'

'Who is he?' Mihir's voice was agonised.

Kamala was silent.

'Who is he? Where does he live?'

'If I tell you,' said Kamala, 'if I tell you, what will you do?'

'I know what I have to do. Just tell me.' Mihir grabbed Kamala's wrist. 'Tell me at once.' Mihir squeezed her wrist harder, even harder. Tears of pain sprang to Kamala's eyes.

Suddenly she said hoarsely, 'How can I tell you where he is. Do you think I know?'

'What do you mean?' Mihir's grip on Kamala's wrist slackened. 'You weren't telling the truth, then?'

'Not the truth?' The words were torn out of Kamala's throat.

'Then tell me—tell me who he is. Where is he?'

Freeing her arm with a jerk, Kamala declared, 'You fool, you fool. He's dead—he's dead, I'll never see him again.' Burying her face in her pillow, Kamala broke down in tears. To stop herself from sobbing, she inserted her fingers in her mouth; they still smelt faintly of tulsi.

Jay Jayanti

' . . . So long as you were writing, you were thinking of me, you were mine. Can anything be as wonderful as a letter? So personal, confidential, constant. There's nobody else besides the one I'm writing to, nothing else, whether it is for half an hour or ten minutes or even two. A letter is a woman on a tryst, a veiled lover, mysterious but guileless—the moment I draw the veil aside, she submits herself entirely. How often do secrets and whispers come to us in our lives—but whenever a letter comes, it is always in secret. When it speaks, it is always in our ears. A letter is as intimate as a kiss; but a kiss, even the longest kiss, does end; the same kiss does not offer itself twice—the letter remains, it can be reread, regained, it is never lost, never finished . . .'

Sumitro stopped. His rolling script in jet black ink on the smoky paper looked like crows flying past clouds. He had so many things to say that he could fill one page after another; the envelope would swell like a woman nine months pregnant. Pregnant. Carrying another self. Himself, the essence of himself—that was what he was squeezing out on to this paper, and sending in an envelope to . . . whom? To Tandra? But Tandra hadn't written him a letter, and even if she did, she wouldn't write anything that could get a reply such as this. Where was the time for Tandra to write letters? She was always surrounded by people, her days and nights were filled with celebrations, her hours and minutes were replete with the boundless froth of life. If she did have to write a letter, she would write it—not in Bangla, but in English; that too, not in what Sumitro considered English, but in a sharp, tart, terse, cutting tone. What would Sumitro have written in reply? Nothing. He did not know this language—nor those who spoke, woke, and broke it. But had she written, had Tandra written him the letter she should have, this is how he would have replied.

Sumitro read what he had written once more and then slipped it into an envelope and put it away in the dark cavern of the large drawer of the desk. He wasn't done with it; could this letter ever be done? Another day—no, not this letter again, another one . . .

Rising from his chair, he went to the window. The long April afternoon lay like a sheet of aluminium. He was supposed to visit her this evening . . . should he? He would see her again. They had met only a few times. He wanted to see her, he liked seeing her. There was the body, there was vision, hearing, touch, smell— it was because of them that living was so enjoyable. But they were the enemies too.

As he moved away from the window, his reflection appeared in the large mirror opposite. A slim young man in a loose kurta, subdued complexion, dishevelled hair. The image of a poet. But he WAS a poet. Rather a good one. Not a trendy poet, nor one representing his generation—but a pure poet. Like Blake in the eighteenth century, followed by Tennyson and then Yeats. He had published two volumes, of course—he needn't have—no one read them, no one mentioned his name. But so what?

The image in the mirror crossed the floor slowly, coming up to him. The room on the other side of the mirror was magical; in it the dust was beautiful, the dilapidation was beautiful, the impossible chaos on his desk was beautiful too. This magic was eternal—only a piece of glass kept slavish life, the salve of time, change, death, at bay.

Sumitro greeted himself with a smile. This was how he would meet her, the welcome meant for him would cross the floor of the drawing room to stand at the door. 'Oh, you're here!' As though she was very pleased. But they talked that way with everyone. 'How are you?' 'You? How are you?' The eyes in the mirror were a trifle melancholy, the smile a little wan. Why did she have to speak such an affected Bangla?

Parting the curtains of the magic room, Mahesh entered with tea on a tray. Sumitro retreated quickly. What must Mahesh have thought? That the master was checking in the mirror how handsome he was. No matter how much I look in the mirror, I will never know how I appear to others. Never.

Sitting near the tea things, he opened a new anthology of English poetry. What's wrong with you, England? Will no more poets be born? 'We are the last romantics', Yeats had sighed. Was it a sigh though, or a proud, inspired declaration? Was it really all over? Or would they be born again, would poets come again, would poetry be written again? He had wanted to ask Tandra whether there were any signs of this. She had returned from England just a few months ago after completing her apprenticeship with the BBC. But he hadn't heard her tell any stories yet besides those about the war. The arrangements to cope with bombs, the dearth of decent food, how dark the nights were. Did she not know where she had been, to whose land, to the land of Shakespeare and Blake and Shelley, the land whose words had conquered the world. There was Ireland, the age-old enemy, and yet its name still blew in the wind thanks to Yeats's intensity and George Bernard Shaw's eloquence. And India—how bitter our fate, how deep our misery because of it—but still, England, Sumitro raised his cup to his lips, how would I have lived without you?

He would bring it up today. Wouldn't someone with a face like hers even behind the mask of cosmetics, with a glance so natural despite all the poses she had learnt, understand what he was saying? If she wasn't meant to understand, why had he come to like this girl, to like her so much that ever since they had been introduced, he had only thought of her, only been with her?

What colour would her sari be today? The colour of the night, the colour of the March sky after the crescent moon had set. And a blouse the colour of clouds, the soft puffy white clouds occupying the spot where the moon had been a little while ago. Would she wear a pearl necklace? Muted, sedate, sorrowful pearls—wrapping themselves around her neck, they would drop to the mounds of her breasts. He had never seen her in them—but then how many times had he seen her anyway? He would buy a pearl necklace for her, they would look perfect beneath her black hair, around her luminous throat, against the cloud-coloured border of her night-coloured sari. Because he would take the necklace for her today, he had flouted the tradition of poets and not kept the company of poverty; his father had built bridges over rivers, channelled the river into canals, blasted mountains to lay railway tracks, so that he could rescue an imprisoned princess this evening.

. . . When he arrived he found that Tandra's sari was parrot green in colour, and her blouse parrot yellow, while blood red corals clung to her neck. He was astounded. This wasn't the woman he had expected, the woman he thought he was visiting. Scarlet lips, sparkling teeth, their gift a flashing smile. But this was not how it was supposed to be; she was to have smiled sadly, its effect visible in her black eyes, the intensity of the night in her dark hair. Sumitro felt uncomfortable, as though he wasn't supposed to have been here, as though he had made a mistake.

There were several others present. Some young men from the radio station; three or four of Tandra's parent's friends; an American soldier; a literary sort of travelling Englishman. An uninhibited party, uninhibited behaviour; people sat where they liked, ate—or not—what they wanted; talking in groups of two or three. They changed their seats many times . . . But Sumitro remained in the first chair he had taken, stock-still. Several people came up to him to start a conversation, he didn't hit it off with any of them. Suddenly Tandra appeared and sat down on the carpet near his feet. Sumitro stood up.

'Why did you get up?'

'Please take a seat.'

'Oh no, I'm going to sit right here.' Tandra leaned back against the sofa. 'Sit down, please.'

'I'd prefer to stand.'

With a smile Tandra asked, 'Will it disturb you if I sit here?'

'Yes, it will,' answered Sumitro.

'Why?' Tandra raised her eyes.

'I'm not used to sitting with a lady at my feet.'

Tandra laughed in English when she heard this. Stopping abruptly, she said, 'Then I'd better sit on the sofa, and you can sit down there instead. I hope you're used to sitting at a lady's feet.'

'Nor that.'

'What to do, then?' Tandra seemed worried about the seating arrangement.

'Then, Tandra Debi, allow me to take my leave.'

'So soon?'

'I feel I've been here a long time—a long, long time.'

Tandra rose to her feet, setting off a wave of red coral. She was tall, her head reaching up to Sumitro's ears. Standing close to him, she said, 'But you were sitting quietly all this while.'

'I'll talk when the time is right.'

Tandra lowered her eyes for a moment. 'When will you come again?' she asked softly.

'I will.'

'When? Tell me.'

'You tell me.'

'Come tomorrow . . .' It wasn't clear whether it was a question, a request, or an order.

Come tomorrow. Come tomorrow. The night breeze sang in his ear, the breeze on the road, raising a wave of leaves. Sumitra sat in an open-roof taxi with his head thrown back, the trees above his head waved as they passed, a swarm of stars raced in the sky. He wanted to go back to her at once—but he also seemed to savour the fact that she wasn't near. The agony, the sheer agony of wanting someone close. Wanting her all the time, wanting her with everything, but what could a person trapped in a body give, how much could she give?

While taking the fare out of his pocket, his hand found something soft. He had remembered at last. He had taken along a jasmine bud encased in a leaf—the first jasmine of the year, but he had forgotten to give it to her. How could he give her a pearl necklace, he barely knew her, and there was no occasion either. A flower would not have offended her; the people of the world measured the worth of a gift in money, after all. Taking it out of his pocket when he was back home he looked at it, a summer jasmine, patient and resilient, it had not faded even after all these hours in a black hole—it cast a sharp sweet breath on Sumitro's face as soon as it emerged. 'No, let me send you to her.' Opening his drawer, Sumitro put the flower in the thick ash-coloured envelope, next to the heart of his unfinished letter.

* * *

'Hello.'
    'Is that Sumitro?'
    'I am Sumitro. Is that Tandra?'
    'I am Tandra. Why didn't you come yesterday?'
    Silence.
    'Why didn't you? Did you forget?'
    'No.'
    'Well, then?'
    Sumitro did not know what to say. He had been writing poetry, the idea of a conversation had not appealed to him. He had chosen not to visit her—for a meeting was far too constricted an experience, lacking in freedom. But how could he tell her this?
    'Hello? Why don't you speak?'
    'I'll go another day.'
    'You don't sound enthusiastic at all.'

'What are you doing?' Very softly.

'What did you say?'

'What are you doing now?'

'What am I doing? I'm about to go out. I have to go to office.'

'Office? Whatever for?'

'How strange? Don't you know I work at the radio station?'

'That's what I'm asking—why do you?'

'What do you mean, why?'

'Do you need to earn a living?'

'Is that the only reason to work?'

'If work means a job, yes.'

'I quite like it. The time passes easily.'

'Don't you know a better way to pass the time?'

'Why don't you tell me one or two?'

'What's wrong with just being beautiful without doing anything?'

'What? Be beautiful without doing anything! Oh my . . .'

Sumitro put the phone down before Tandra had finished laughing. He could see her racing down the stairs, dressed in slacks and a shirt unbuttoned till her breasts. And he had imagined her sitting on the veranda on the south after her bath, dressed in a white handspun sari, gazing at the rows of trees on Loudon Street. Tandra had taken abode in his days, in his nights, in his heartbeats, in his metred rhymes—how could he bear to see her leave her home? The poem he was writing now said nothing about love, but it was Tandra too;

these black letters drew the very path which would lead him to her company, to intimacy, endlessly. Meanwhile Tandra had telephoned suddenly to inform him of the limits of flesh and blood. The lover's union was interrupted. Tandra herself was Tandra's enemy.

* * *

'Why so quiet?'

'No reason.'

'Your prowess for silence is amazing.'

'Really?'

'Maybe there were people all this time, but now . . .'

'There still are.' Sumitro looked at the door. Following his eyes, Tandra said, 'What is it, Nilotpal?'

'I think I left my handkerchief behind.' Nilotpal advanced into the room, dressed from tip to toe in western garb. They had met in London, returning on the same ship; it had taken so long to sail around the tip of Africa that they had had to become friends.

Rummaging between the cushions did not reveal the handkerchief. 'Did you have something in it?' asked Sumitro softly.

'Something? In the handkerchief?' Nilotpal would not have been as astonished had he been told his tie had not been knotted perfectly.

'You did.'

'I did? You know?' Nilotpal was vastly amused to hear the pale, listless poet say this. 'Can you tell me what it was?'

'Your heart.'

Tandra clapped, laughing. 'Really? Really, Nilotpal?'

'Why not, that would be wonderful,' Nilotpal also answered lightly. 'Whatever is lost here comes back doubled.'

'Should I get you two of my father's handkerchiefs?' asked Tandra at once.

Nilotpal's restless eyes settled on Tandra for a moment. Then he said with an alluring smile, 'Don't trouble yourself. I'm off.' He strode out, his head held high.

'Such a lively young man,' said Sumitro.

'Young man? Is he younger than you?'

'That's how it feels. With most people.'

'The truth is you don't like anyone.'

'Yes,' said Sumitro, speaking slowly. 'I have to be careful about this; when I like, I like far too deeply.'

* * *

'Deeply, I like deeply. I'm not used to loving human beings; I love the grass, the sky, the sunshine, pictures, music, poetry. The way I love a poem is the way I want to love you, Tandra. You don't know this, which is why you thwart me again and again, you have no choice but to thwart me. Can you come out of your physical frame, can you be a poem, Tandra?'

Sumitro wrote haltingly, with careful thought, progressing slowly. Tirelessly scraping the wide expanse of paper with the sharp nib of his pen was his work, his life, this was his existence. Everything that existence means is slavery to an invisible, inviolable force; we are compelled to eat, compelled to purge the rejected portions of our food from the insides of our bodies; compelled to be born, to give birth, to die. Barbaric, chaotic events are our lord; time is our chain. Even when we love being alive, our lives disintegrate bit by bit, moment by moment. And when we don't like being alive, but still there is no release, no respite for even a second—how terrible, how unbearable, the burden is. The very life that we clasp to our bosom with all our might destroys it. It is because we are alive that we cannot live forever.

Only when I write am I released. Here I am independent; I am the lord in this indefatigable coitus between paper and pen. Everyone follows my will here; everything is subservient to rhythm here, a disciple of beauty, because I so wish it.

'You too,' wrote Sumitro, taking up his pen again, 'I want you here too, Tandra. The physical form in which you are bound is temporary; the you who is diffused within me is the one who's constant. That is why, Tandra, my meeting you any more is pointless. Not just pointless, but also painful for me. You have turned into poetry in my hands—do you think I will allow you to be marred? No, Tandra—I will never meet you again.'

Completing the letter, Sumitro inserted it in an envelope and put it next to the others in the darkness of the drawer. This was the twelfth letter.

* * *

'Why do you send for me again and again?'

'Are you angry because I do?'

'I don't like it. What do you want, what do you want from me?'

'Do you think it's easy to tell you?'

'Look, Tandra, you're making a mistake . . .'

'No, don't say that. I haven't made a mistake. I'm not a child; I've seen a great deal, been in the company of a great many people. Sumitro.'

'Don't say my name that way.'

'Why not?'

'I'm forbidding you.'

'Who are you to forbid me?'

'It seems it's finally time to tell you.'

'Tell me.'

'Can you bear it?'

'You think I am afraid?'

'Can you give me what I want?'

'Can't I?'

'What can you give me, tell me.'

'What *can't* I give you? Everything, everything . . .'

'Do you think that will quench my thirst? I want you in every moment of day and night, in every beat of my heart—do you know what such wanting is?'

'I'd have been relieved if I hadn't known.'

'No, you don't know, you don't . . .'

Entering the room silently, Tandra stood by his side. 'Very worried?'

Sumitro was startled, a little too startled. He stared in silence at Tandra, as though he couldn't believe his eyes.

'What were you thinking of?' asked Tandra, taking a seat.

'Nothing.'

'Who is it?'

Sumitro smiled faintly.

'Who is the person whom you were thinking of with such rapt attention?'

'Nobody.' Sumitro looked grim.

'That's not true . . . but then why should you tell me the truth anyway.'

Without a word, Sumitro raised his eyes towards her. Shifting in her seat, Tandra chuckled suddenly. 'What?'

'Sometimes I feel you aren't you, but someone else.'

'I'm not that someone else,' Tandra answered, still smiling. 'If I were, would you have come to me in my house and been so startled to see me?'

'How is it that your drawing room is empty today?'

'Hardly empty,' came the answer, a little late. She continued almost instantly, 'You refused to join our steamer party the other day.'

Sumitro was silent.

'The other night too, when we went to Barrackpore in the moonlight, you ran away. Why do you behave this way?'

'Really, why am I so strange?'

'You'd have enjoyed it. The moonlight looks lovely during blackouts.'

'Can anything be as lovely as we think it is?'

'Why live if you think that way?'

'That's true.' A little later, looking out the window, Sumitro said, 'It's overcast. There'll be a storm.'

The plaintive murmuring of the trees on the road reached the second-floor drawing room. Tandra hummed, 'Although you've disappointed me twice over, I'm asking again. Will you go to the Czech celebrations next Saturday?'

'I don't care for all this, Tandra Debi.'

'But have you considered the fact that I don't care for anything unless you come along?'

Sumitro turned to stone.

Tandra continued, 'Isn't there anything you like? Nothing? No one? How long will you remain silent— speak, say something.'

Sumitro rose to his feet abruptly, so abruptly that his hair swept down to his forehead, shaking.

Tandra stood up at once too, coming close to him, very close, face to face. Looking into his eyes, she said, 'Sumitro.'

The expanse of Sumitro's lips trembled.

'Tell me now that you don't care.'

Sumitro was stilled as he looked into the black eyes. Moving away, he said, 'I'll go now.'

'No . . . no . . .'

But Tandra could not stop him; Sumitro went down the stairs. There was a storm on the road, flying gravel, fat drops of rain. Tandra was slight when she was near him, but the moment he came away, she was everywhere—spread across the clouds, wrapped around the wind, falling as the rain. Tears of joy sprang into Sumitro's eyes.

* * *

'I have taken up home inside a body; these feeble sense organs have determined the supply of all that I am entitled to. Even tearing my heart apart will not increase my allocation. And so, the more strongly we want, the more sharply we fail. The glutton cannot eat all day, the lascivious lose their libido from time to time. But there also exists another world, a different world. Its messengers are our senses, its memories are objects. It is memory that we confuse for the truth, the messenger whom we place on the throne; so it is impossible to get anything that won't be lost the instant we get it. Isn't it better to lose something in order to get it than to lose it because we have got it? I shan't tie you down with reality, Tandra . . .'

'Hello.'

'It's you!'

'You! So late at night?'

'Can't sleep. How lucky you're awake too.'

'Why can't you sleep?'

'Why? Are you actually asking why?'

'What did you do this evening, Tandra Debi?'

'Still Debi?'

'Habit. Or perhaps the lack of habit.'

'I feel as though all my life I have . . . did you get drenched in the rain?'

'A little. I enjoyed it. What did you do this evening?'

'I was home. It felt as though . . .'

'No, don't tell me.'

'Didn't you want to come back?'

'But even after going back I would have to go back.'

Tandra was silent for a few seconds.

'Tandra . . .'

'How clear your voice is. How lovely.'

* * *

'What is it? What's wrong with you?'

'Nothing.'

'Nothing! You're so . . .!'

'I love the fact that you telephone me every night.'

'Do you think I wouldn't if you visited me?'

After a silence Sumitro said, 'I never see you when I visit you.'

'It will be as you want it, Sumitro. No one else will be here . . .'

'No, that's not what I'm saying.'

'Then what are you saying, what? You haven't been here three days—do you want me to die?'

'Tandra, you . . .'

'Shut up! . . . What, are you really going to shut up? Can you hear me?'

'Tell me.'

'Something's happened meanwhile.'

'Happened?'

'I'll tell you tomorrow. When will you come?'

'Let me see . . . What? You're not going to talk now? Are you angry?'

'I need you most of all in the world today, Sumitro, and you . . .'

'Don't worry. Don't worry. Go to sleep.'

'. . . My eyes cannot see you as deeply as I'd like to. My ears aren't strong enough to hear you as closely as I'd like to. I will never get as much as of your touch as I want to, even if I were to smash through all the limitations of my body. Then why, then why . . .'

Then why—what? Language is so meagre, feeble, reflected Sumitro, raising his eyes from the notepaper. When he lowered them again, the paper seemed to have acquired a green glow, while a line of light twinkled on the silk-black body of his pen. Looking over his shoulder, he discovered Tandra. Tall, dressed in a sari the colour of tender leaves with a red border, standing in his silent room, ringing a bell of colours.

'Don't you recognise me?'

'In the middle of the day, with such a strong sun!' Putting a book on his letter, Sumitro stood up.

'I couldn't wait any more . . . you won't go, so . . .' Tandra looked around the room. 'May I have a glass of water?'

'Sit down, please.' Flashing a glance at the divan against the wall, Sumitro fetched a glass of water.

Tandra looked at the bright water in the glass tumbler, and then at Sumitro. Sipping her water, she said softly, 'How cold the water is. How cold the room is. How cold you are.'

With a smile, Sumitro said, 'You're cold too. Green lily petals on a white stalk, white petals on a red . . .' Pausing, he continued in the same tone, 'You must have had a lot of trouble getting here. It's so hot in the afternoon.'

Tandra sighed. 'Are you going to keep standing?'

'Why not? Let me watch.'

Lowering her eyes to the glass of water, Tandra said, 'Your house is absolutely silent. Isn't anyone home?'

'I am.'

'And?'

'Just me.'

'Completely alone?'

'Really! How did I survive all these days without seeing you?' Sumitro sat down next to her.

Tandra shifted further from him and looked at him. Then she said:

'Listen now to what I came to tell you.'

'Does Nilotpal want to marry you?' Sumitro asked with a smile.

'How did you know?'

'You don't have to be an astrologer to know this.'

'Even when you know . . . even though you've realised . . .' Tandra could not finish.

'Nothing unusual there, it's quite natural. I'm surprised that ten others don't want to as well.'

'How strange you are! How easily you say this!'

'If every married man does not sigh on seeing you—oh, why didn't I meet her earlier—what good is it, Tandra?'

'I don't like such humour.' Tandra looked grave. 'I think of myself as only one specific person's wife these days.'

Sumitro's eyes closed for a moment. When he looked again, it was with an ancient despondence in them. Without noticing, Tandra continued on her own, 'Still Nilotpal is adamant. He has appointed my father his barrister. Not that that matters, nothing anyone in the world can say matters, but you . . . you mustn't delay any more, Sumitro.'

A smile appeared in Sumitro's melancholy eyes like light on the water. 'No, I shan't delay,' he said, lowering his head and running his hand through his hair. Tandra looked thirstily at his long, unkempt hair. A little later she said, 'What were you writing?'

'I don't remember now.'

'I disturbed you. I'm glad; I'll disturb you more.'

'It'll do no harm. No one reads what I write. Even the letters I write stay with me.'

'Oh all right, I accept that you write brilliantly, but is what you write as wonderful as you are?'

Raising his eyes, Sumitro looked at her in silence. 'What?' Without saying 'what' any more, Tandra leaned forward, touching Sumitro's hair lightly with one hand. As though in a dream, he saw a face, lips red with desire, the darkness of memories in the eyes, a face like a dream, breasts like heaven, arms like the shaded paths of heaven. The music of the constellations flowed in his blood, in his young body, he could not tear his eyes away. He kept looking, her black eyes closed, her lips parted, the junction of the neck and the breasts pulsed constantly, and a wave rose in the sari the colour of tender leaves . . . Can you achieve so much, life, do you have so much to offer? But how much was all this? Only a little time—a few moments, a few days, a few years. Just one life! Was there no alternative to the body? No language besides touch? Could there never be worship without the idol? The body was the route, the body was also the impediment. The invitation was also the shroud. Her company was her barrier, her physical form was her concealment. If such a great wanting had been awakened, why should it be met with such deprivation? No, never. I will never accept defeat.

'Your bag's fallen,' Sumitro said suddenly, reaching towards it.

Tandra stood in silence for one long moment. Then, opening her bag and applying a little make-up, she rose to her feet slowly. Hoarsely, she said, 'I'll go now. Come over this evening.'

Seeing her off, Sumitro came back upstairs, calling, 'Mahesh! Mahesh!' Startled out of his siesta, Mahesh entered, rubbing his eyes.

'Pack my things.'

'Sir?'

'Pack the suitcase and bedding. I'm leaving.'

'Sir?'

'We're leaving today. For the hills.'

'Today?'

'Today. By the evening train.'

* **

While Tandra was exhausted after trying to telephone Sumitro repeatedly, the Dehradun Express sped through the night with him on it. The night lamp was burning in the compartment, and Sumitro was seated by the window. A thousand stars were travelling with him, but there were still more; a waning moon rose diagonally in the sky; its light making the ocean of darkness froth. A pain, a suppressed, mute, heartbreaking pain—he simply could not forget. Even as he had crossed Howrah Bridge, entered the platform, got on the train, he had told himself, no, I cannot do this, let me go back. When the train really did begin to move, when it left the station, twice or thrice he had wanted to jump out. Where was he going—into what darkness, what emptiness? I cannot live without you. I cannot live a moment without you, I shall get off at Bardhaman—of course I shall—but the train simply wouldn't get to Bardhaman.

Bardhaman passed. Asansol. Raniganj. Bengal was left behind. The night deepened, the train quickened; who was that racing in the darkness outside along with the train, her flying up to the stars? Tandra, it was Tandra. What was she thinking? What? Whom was this breathless passion of the wheels meant for? Which wind did it want to overtake with this wildness? The more he travelled, the more the wind rose—no end to it, no end to it. You are this wind, this night, this star-studded sky. I am taking you along with me, in my heart, Tandra, I can never lose you again. Resting his head against the window, he was overcome by the touchless thrill of inexhaustible night; peace descended on him in his sleep, a smile appeared on his lips. Tandra stood in front of him, lighting up the darkness behind his closed eyes—just the way he had seen her that afternoon—the same sari the colour of tender leaves, moist eyes, heaving breasts—but silent, without impatience, deflected from inevitability, beyond existence. Sumitro gazed at her, melting in happiness, melding into Tandra, collapsing in sleep on his bunk. She's mine at last, at last. Charlatan reality, you have not been able to deceive me.

The Shadow

I was inordinately delighted the day I passed my Intermediate examinations and enrolled at Dhaka University. Oh, what a huge building. From one end of the corridor the other end looked deserted. A succession of rooms, a splendid office, a bustling library, easy-chairs in the common room, card tables, ping-pong, magazines from all over the world—shouting, chatting, smoking, everything was allowed, no one objected. I cannot describe how much I liked it. I felt that I had finally grown up, finally become a gentleman. Such an enormous affair—where there were deans, provosts, stewards, and so much more; where you had to walk half a mile at the end of the day to reach your tutorial classrooms; where you were fined if you didn't exercise in the field afterwards; where no one cared about your attendance in class; where you didn't have to take annual examinations; where a play or a lecture or a concert or something else was held every day—and now even I had a role to play in this educational institution which covered half of Ramna; this was no small matter. The professors were extremely personable, dressed well, spoke in a unique style; even the one who taught Sanskrit used impeccable English—when they scattered in different directions at the ringing of the bell, their solemn faces and imperious movements made it appear that they carried every responsibility in the world on their shoulders. My self-esteem rose at all this, making me extremely conscious of my presence on this planet. My mind turned to my appearance, and I began to lavish attention on my hair and clothes. I gave up my shirts for kurtas, ran a razor needlessly and frequently over my fresh growth of facial hair and succeeded in developing such a strong beard in a mere six months that even now I repent for my own act with tears when I shave. At that time, of course, the future was not my concern; the only objective was to shed the shell of boyhood and acquire the form of a young man as quickly as possible.

There was another reason for this, though. Girls studied at the university too. Among the various novelties, this was the greatest one for me—for practically every male student. I am talking about the time when the flood of higher education had not yet washed over girls; there were no more than five or six girls in the entire university. Someone named Aparna Dutta had enrolled along with us.

Slim and slightly built, on the dark side, she came to college in a light blue sari. It wasn't a simple matter, being the only girl acquiring an education amidst two hundred boys, especially when there were watertight systems for keeping her apart from the boys everywhere except in the classroom. I don't know how Aparna felt about it, but I used to feel sorry for her. I would hear all sorts of discussions about her among the boys, and not all of them bear repetition. The standards of civility were not uniform across all of them. Each of us had a different method for expressing the excitement that rose within ourselves in natural course; most of us were content to just talk about it—stories born of imagination about things that were absolutely unlikely to take place in their lives. A few of the bolder ones stopped at the girls' common room door on some pretext or the other and struck up conversations with Aparna. Yet others remained resolutely silent. I should add that I belonged to this last group. In class I sat on the very last bench; sometimes I would notice Aparna through the gap between numerous other heads—seated on the separate chair set aside for her, gazing at her book, her cheek resting on her hand. Her face and way of sitting, like a photograph, was imprinted in my memory—I can still recollect it. Just the one bangle on her slender wrist, the broad border of the sari wrapped around her head framing her face. I observed that Aparna kept her eyes fixed on her book all through, shyly trying to hide behind herself. Only sometimes her eyes seemed to penetrate the dense rows of black heads to alight on me. But then this was probably my imagination.

Aparna was my classmate for four years, but this was the extent of our acquaintance in all this time. I didn't even hear her voice during these four years, nor stood face to face with her. There were many others far worthier than me of receiving such rewards. Among them Ashok was the first. He was a flamboyant character, the son of a very rich father who sometimes came to college in his family car. In winter he dressed in flannel trousers and English shirts, distributed more cigarettes than he smoked himself, and was undoubtedly the most popular person in the entire university. He was handsome and had many qualities besides—he could play tennis, he could act well, he was an unbeatable cyclist, etcetera, etcetera. He won every election effortlessly—whether it was for Dramatic Secretary of the Hall or for Secretary of the University Union—with a landslide of votes. To tell the truth, there was no one who could compete with him.

This same Ashok would talk a lot about Aparna to us. He was an artful sort; he had not been content with chatting with her for a couple of minutes at the common room door—he had visited her at home, had afternoon tea with them, addressed her mother in familial terms, discussed politics with her father, made friends with her brothers and sisters; to put it simply, he had done all that was required to be done. In a year this fortunate man had established the sort of relationship that made the other boys envy him privately—and flatter him in public, in case he could lead them to the abode of the goddess too. But ignoring all of them, Ashok chose to consort with me, possibly because I was the perfect listener—baring everything in his heart to me gave him great comfort. He often made me cut classes with him; we would lie down together on the grass on lovely winter afternoons and he would tell me his unending stories about Aparna. These stories were usually tiresome, but I have to admit that, never mind anything else, I used to get pleasure out of hearing the name Aparna over and over again.

When he had finished his stories, Ashok would often say, 'Come with me to their house.'

'Are you mad?' I'd respond.

'She wants to meet you. Dr Kar is her tutor, he tells her about you quite often.'

I must state here with a spot of embarrassment that I have always been one of the better students in class. My family and expected me to become an important officer, but none of that materialised—I survive today as a mere teacher.

I did not keep Ashok's request—I didn't accompany him to Aparna's house even once. I am not asking you to believe the impossible statement that I had no desire to meet Aparna. Indeed I did want to meet her. But despite my shyness, I was very proud at heart. It would have been dishonourable to meet Aparna through Ashok's mediation. I was no less than him, after all. And besides, I was so busy with all sorts of useful and useless activities as a student during the day and with my studies at night that I did not even have sufficient leisure to think of Aparna.

The days passed in a blur, and the B.A. examinations ended. My subject was philosophy—I passed in the first class with absurdly high marks. Aparna and Ashok were both in the pass course, but in the final year of M.A., Aparna became the closer of my two classmates, for she too was reading philosophy for her Master's degree. Ashok, the modern young man, had chosen economics, but he had bridged the gap of academics to stake the claim afforded by proximity. He confessed to me in secret one day—everything had been fixed, they were only waiting for their M.A. examinations.

Among subjects to be studied, the market value of philosophy had begun declining already. There were seven of us in all in the class—six boys and one girl. There were unrestricted opportunities to meet and talk. The excuse of helping with studies was always available, and coming from me, it was not an empty promise either. But every time the thought occurred to me, someone else spoke within: 'Go up to someone and introduce yourself? Shame!'

Meanwhile Ashok kept pleading with me to visit Aparna at home She was finding Kant inscrutable, she needed my help. Smiling, I said, 'Do you think I can explain what the most erudite teachers cannot?' Another time Ashok ordered me to provide all my notes on Hegel. Oh, why hadn't I kept notes like the other students, I asked myself. But Ashok probably did not believe that I had no notes at all; he assumed that I did not want to share my secret magic incantations for the examinations with anyone else. Still, he never asked me again for anything to do with academics on Aparna's behalf.

Therefore my final year at the university passed gazing at Aparna across two benches in the tiny philosophy classroom. I thought Aparna looked at me frequently, but surely it was my imagination.

The M.A. exams ended. As the time drew near to bid farewell to the university and join the ranks of the unemployed, Ashok came home to deliver the good news. Even the date had been fixed. The *aashirbaad* ceremony of the bride was scheduled for that evening at Aparna's house, I must be present, I was told.

'I shall be,' I said at once. Suddenly I felt there was no obstacle to my going today, although I was not sure what obstacle there had been all this while.

For the first time I saw Aparna so near, heard her speak. But that evening her appearance was completely different—with chandan patterns on her forehead, she was dressed in a russet sari and was covered in ornaments. She was unrecognisable. The room I sat in was full of people, most of them strangers. I sat stiffly.

Coming up to me, Ashok whispered, 'I know you aren't enjoying yourself here. Come with me.'

He took me to a small room—Aparna's study. The sight of philosophy books everywhere gave me a lot of comfort. Making me sit in there, Ashok disappeared somewhere; he was very busy. I began leafing through a book by myself.

Startled by a soft sound, I looked up to discover Aparna standing at a distance. I jumped to my feet awkwardly, but didn't know what to say.

Aparna broke the silence. 'You're here at last.'

'My congratulations,' I said.

'Why didn't you come all these years?'

'I . . . er . . . I . . . didn't get round to coming . . .'

'Didn't Ashok tell you to come?'

'He did.'

'Didn't you believe him?'

'I didn't disbelieve him, but . . .'

'Then you weren't keen on knowing me, is that it?'

'Oh no, why shouldn't I be keen?'

With a chuckle, Aparna said, 'Never mind, what's the use of all this politeness now—there's no time any more.'

My heart skipped a beat at this last phrase. Looking into my eyes, Aparna said, 'I sent word through Ashok so many times these past four years—not once did you come.' After a brief silence, she shook her head slightly and said very softly, 'You just don't understand anything.' And at once I heard her sigh. But that too was probably my imagination.

I couldn't sleep for a long time that night, one of the possible reasons being that I had overeaten absent-mindedly. Many thoughts occurred to me as I lay in bed. Aparna's words seemed to gnaw at my brain like poisonous insects. No matter where they began, every thought eventually turned into a blind lane, from which there was no way forward. I was astonished at my realisation of my own stupidity. My eyes open in the darkness, I told myself repeatedly, she had wanted me, she had wanted me, perhaps there was still . . . no, there was no time any more, no time any more.

Aparna was married a few days later—and I went away to Calcutta in search of employment.

Ten years have passed. I have not married yet, for my meagre pay supports my parents and brothers and sisters. If I were to get married, there would be even less for them; therefore it is my duty to be indifferent about this. Ashok got into the Income Tax department, he must be an officer by now, in Rangpur or Barishal, or perhaps he is a magistrate in Chittagong. My life is quiet and disciplined; it lacks any regret, ambition or imagination. I read and teach philosophy, I have accepted the pursuit of learning as the only happiness in my life. I am quite well.

Only, late at night sometimes, I remember a young, dark-skinned face, a single bangle on a slender wrist, the border of her blue sari framing her face. Someone whispers to me in the darkness—'You left it so late, there's no time any more.'

Scan QR code to access the
Penguin Random House India website